THE
LIGHTNING
TREE

THE
LIGHTNING
TREE

CINDY LYNCH

My Three Sons Publishing

Book 3 in the *Bye For Now* Trilogy

The Labyrinth

Aunt Marilyn,

Thank you for being my muse.

You were one of a kind and will be truly missed.

Funny thing about sleep; it can conjure up wonderful, detailed memories, unthinkable sadness, and unmentionable fear, leaving one wondering if what they are experiencing is real or make believe.

PROLOGUE
Callie

Callie drives with her eyes focused intently on the truck in front of her on the freeway. *Why didn't they shut the hatch tightly?* The back of the inconspicuous truck's roll door is chattering. *Why didn't they secure the latch?* The latch isn't hooked in properly and the door bounces open a few inches each time it hits a bump in the road. *What if the door bounces open?* No sooner does the question formulate in her mind when, *whoosh,* the hatch flies open, regurgitating the contents onto the road in front of Callie. Her reflexes aren't quick enough, and she drives with a bump over each shape that exits. Bump, bump, bump, the items continue to free themselves from the truck. Large pink smooth tubes, blue rectangles the size and shape of the top of a picnic table, and another large, solid white oblong object come at her in a blur as she tries her best to stay the course. She recklessly shimmies her car out of harm's way when one final bump flings the picnic table object to the hood of her car. It bounces into the windshield and splinters into a million pieces. It hits with such force that the windshield breaks, causing Callie to release her hands from the steering wheel, shielding her face from the onslaught of the glittering glass. She lets out a bloodcurdling scream creating a pathway for the objects to enter her bloodstream. Callie coughs, trying to clear her throat of these foreign objects. Her car stops abruptly and with brutal force as it hits the guardrail. On impact, the seatbelt clings to her forward-propelling body, locking into place, keeping her from being ejected.

The car shudders, then stills. She listens to her heart pounding in her ear. Her chest hurts from the contact with the seatbelt. She coughs once, then once more. The more she coughs, the more she must. The violent force with which she is coughing makes breathing difficult. One last skeletal shake allows her to evacuate her lungs; her face crimson from the exertion. She places her hand in front of her mouth and stares down in bewilderment at the five oblong pills landing softly in her palm.

CHAPTER 1
Samantha

Samantha sits quietly in her thoughts, slowly tracing the swirling pattern of grain on the worn bench in the small pew. She folds her hands and rests them on her lap. *I could really use a cigarette right now.* She notices, for the first time, just how fragile her small hands seem. She lets out a deeper sigh, trying to release some of the weight of the situation. The shadows hollowing her eyes appear darker than they have in weeks, along with the aching in her weary body. The hospital chapel is quiet at this hour. Not a soul around. It's just Samantha and her thoughts. *Have I been a good mother? Should I have taken him to the doctor sooner?* She lists the regrets she's had throughout Tyler's young life. Another deep sigh escapes her lips as she closes her eyes and makes promises she's not sure if she can keep, "If you just let him live. Just let him grow up." *Please, please, just let him live.* "If you'll just do this for me, I'll do everything in my power to be the best mother. I'll come back to church more often. I'll be a kinder, more compassionate person … I'll stop smoking. Anything for Tyler." She feels as if this promise is the best she can make for her son, and yet, with the pressure weighing down on her, she's unsure if she can keep up her end of the bargain. Opening her eyes, she glances up to see the stained-glass window above the pulpit. The blue, red, and yellow glass sparkles from the fluorescent bulb illuminating from behind. Deep in thought, she is unaware of the chapel door opening. The figure moves to the second row, behind Samantha.

"Sam." Upon hearing the voice, a ripple of fear encases her heart. "Sam," the figure speaks more loudly, placing a hand on her shoulder. Samantha slowly turns to find Wyatt, with moistened eyes, staring back at her. "You need to come up to the room." As if in a dream, Samantha slowly stands, taking Wyatt's hand as they exit the chapel. Turning for one last quick prayer, Samantha is too afraid to speak. *Just let him live.*

"Just tell me, Wyatt. Don't make me wait until we get to the door," Sam says uncomfortably.

"He's awake."

"Ohmygod, ohmygod, ohmygod," Samantha rattles as her knees buckle. Wyatt grabs her elbow as she rights herself. "I can't have him see me like this," she says, wiping her cheeks dry.

"He's not going to care what you look like. He just wants to see his mom."

"Is Brian with him?"

"Yep, he was there, sleeping in the recliner next to the bed when Tyler opened his eyes and called out for you."

"My baby," Samantha says wistfully as she quickens the pace back to the room.

Samantha rounds the corner to Tyler's corridor, and catches a glimpse of her son in his hospital bed as a nurse exits his room. Her breath hitches. *He looks so small. My poor baby.*

"Hi there, Tyler," she says as she braces herself, opening the door.

"Mom!" Tyler says enthusiastically from his hospital bed. He sits up. Brian fluffs his pillows. "I had the best dream ever! It seemed so real, like he was standing right here. I could touch him; it was that real."

"That sounds really cool, bud. Who is this *he* you're talking about? You'll have to tell me all about it," she says, feeling relief flood her as she sees the excitement on her son's face. She sits on his bedside, places her hand on his forehead, and kisses his cheek. Relieved to feel that his fever has broken, she smiles at him and says, "I love you, buddy."

"I know, Mom. I love you, too." For a beat, they look into each other's eyes, then Tyler breaks their gaze and says, "So, Mom, I was telling Dad, Uncle T was there in my dream." Pushing himself higher in his bed, he continues, "You never told me how much we look alike. All the way down to the way he smiles. I knew who it was the minute I saw him. He's such a nice guy. I wish he was still around …" Tyler trails off, with a faraway look in his eyes.

"Me, too," Samantha agrees, looking over at Wyatt, who sits quietly on the couch.

After an animated conversation with Tyler, Samantha can see that he is growing tired.

"I think it's time for us to leave for a bit. You need to get some rest. Your body is fighting really hard to make you better. Get some sleep, and we'll be in later to check on you." Kissing his cheek, she leaves the room. Brian is in the hallway leaning against a wall. Samantha smiles at him, taking in his wrinkled shirt, four o'clock shadow and dark circles. He opens his arms wide and envelopes Samantha in a warm embrace.

"I think we just got our boy back," Brian says as he gently rubs her back.

"Thank God," she sighs, not wanting to release her rock.

The door to Tyler's room opens and Wyatt walks over to them. Samantha releases Brian and stands to his side as he comfortably rests his arm over her shoulder.

"That was quite a dream he had. He described everything in such detail that it sounded like he was really there. Wherever *there* is," Wyatt says with fascination.

"I'm just so happy he woke up," Samantha says with a quiver.

"Come on, Sam, he's a strong kid. I never had any doubt he'd ride that wave and come out stronger."

"He made it through this first obstacle ..."

"And he'll make it through whatever comes his way. Mark my words," Wyatt says matter-of-factly.

"I hope you're right. Boy, could I use a cigarette right now."

"I'm pretty sure that's not allowed in hospitals, Sis."

"I know, I know. I vowed I'd stop if Tyler made it through." Samantha says wrinkling her nose.

"Old habits die hard," Wyatt laughs. "I'll check in with you guys later. Let me know if his condition changes." Wyatt hugs both his sister and brother-in-law before leaving.

Wyatt walks back to his car, replaying the bedside conversation in his head. Tyler spoke of his dream like it truly happened. Wyatt is eager to share this information with the most non-judgmental person he knows.

CHAPTER 2
Callie

"Ari, what would you like to work on today?" Callie asks Ari, who is wearing another colorful tutu to art therapy.

"Ummm, let's use markers and paper," Ari decides while adjusting her favorite tiara atop her head.

"Sounds good," Callie says while reaching for the basket of markers and an array of colored paper. On top of the construction paper lays a tube of glitter that Callie doesn't see, and as she pulls the paper, the glitter tube tumbles to the floor. It hits the floor with such velocity that it explodes into millions of sparkling fragments. Callie watches as the last fleck of glitter lands softly on the floor.

"Uh-oh," Ari says as she eyes the descending glitter. Unfazed, she chooses her materials and gets to work with a look of determination on her face. She colors a crooked rainbow with a smiling, white, fluffy cloud floating in the sky. Callie sweeps up the remnants of the stardust, grumbling to herself as she cleans. *Stupid glitter.*

"That's awfully pretty. Tell me about this cloud," Callie says, pointing to the paper.

"Well, I love rainbows because they happen right after it rains. That smiling cloud is Max." Ari sits still looking over the paper for a moment quietly.

"Do you miss Max?"

"Yep," she says thoughtfully before moving on, an instant later. "He's much happier now, though." Ari picks up another marker and continues with her drawing, placing another smiling cloud, and another, and another. She holds up her finished artwork and blows on the paper to release one small unwelcome shining fragment.

"There," Ari says, tenderly looking at the five smiling clouds of various sizes above her rainbow—one cloud for each friend she has lost to cancer.

"It's hard to be here sometimes, isn't it?" Callie says cautiously.

"I miss my friends," she sighs. "But that's okay, I'll see them soon." Not wanting to press the subject, Callie let's Ari continue with her art as she hums pleasantly to herself.

Driving home that evening, Callie mulls over her conversation with Ari. It's amazing how resilient these kids fighting cancer can be. It's a peculiar phenomenon when these children matter-of-factly mention leaving this world. They seem to know how things are going in their bodies. Ari may not know the day or the time she'll pass, but she senses that it's close. Feeling the weight of the day, Callie trudges from the car to her apartment, collecting the mail along the way. She sets the mail on the kitchen table and walks to the bathroom to take a long shower. Some days can be so difficult working with these kids. While it's very rewarding, it pains her physically when they are hurting.

Callie's damp hair soaks the collar of her t-shirt as she peruses her mail on the oversized couch in the family room. "Gas bill, electric bill, water bill ..." she flips through each piece of mail, placing one behind the other until she stops short. "Wyatt." Recognizing the handwriting immediately, she feels a pull deep inside. She opens the letter, tossing all other mail aside.

Dear Callie,

Tyler made it through. I've been really worried. I knew this would be tough, but my God, this is one of the hardest thing I've ever had to watch my family go through. He had us really worried right before the stem cell transplant day. It was day two, according to the way the doctors keep track. He had a fever, but nothing like the fever he had after his transplant. On day four of recovery, Tyler had an extremely high fever and we thought we were going to lose him. It was touch and go for about 48 hours. When I saw him the first time after coming out of the fever, he had an amazing story to tell. I say story, but in actuality, it felt like he truly experienced this. He described being guided to a stream by a young girl with red hair and eyes that matched.

At this point, Callie sets the letter down on her lap, astonished by the revelation. There's only one person that could be. The corners of Callie's mouth slowly rise up into a smile as she picks up the letter to continue reading.

She walked him to this stream where he met his uncle. My brother Tyler was with him. Can you believe it? I have to say, when he told me, I got really excited. Something about this is so comforting, knowing that even after all these years, Tyler is still out there watching over our family. I'm a little envious of my nephew. That sounds crazy, doesn't it? I just wish I had a chance to talk to Tyler once more.

Wyatt's letter rambles on about work and family. Samantha has promised to quit smoking, and his mom and dad are a constant presence at church since hearing about their son visiting their grandson.

Please continue writing, or you can call. I would really like to see you. Maybe when Tyler is released from the hospital, you can come up for a visit? I know he'd like that. He's mentioned you a few times in the past week. I told you he liked you.

> *Bye for now,*
> *Wyatt*

That fluttering in her chest returns with a vengeance.

Callie wakes with a rush of excitement. She hops out of bed with a spring in her step and straps on her running shoes. Outside she breathes in the crisp cool air as she witnesses the sun peeking over the horizon to start a new day. She runs her usual four-mile loop, and as she runs past Maddie and Zach's house, the familiar barking begins. If Sprout is out, he will bark at Callie until she stops to give him some love. Callie walks up to the front porch where the cute black and white dog is snorting and jumping, frantically wagging his tail.

"All right, all right, Sprout. Calm down," Callie laughs as she kneels down to pick up the wriggly dog. She scratches behind his ears, eliciting a lick to her cheek. The soft footsteps padding up behind her stop when there is a loud thud against the screened door. "Ca-Ca, Ca-Ca, Ca-Ca!" Little Dylan, in his dinosaur footy pajamas, is calling for Callie as he slaps his hands against the screen.

"Dylan, you're going to make a hole in the screen if you keep banging like that," Maddie warns as she scoops up the toddler and opens the screen door.

"Good morning, Dylan." Callie says as she leans in for a kiss. The confinement of space causes Sprout to jump from Callie's arms. Maddie opens the door for the dog and Sprout scrambles inside. They watch through the door as Sprout finds his bed, circles twice and lands softly.

"How was your run?"

"Pretty good. I'm not quite done yet, but I thought Sprout would have a heart attack if I didn't stop in."

"Dylan wouldn't be too happy either."

"It's so nice to know that I still appeal to the younger men in this town."

"Dylan talks about you all the time. What a hot babe you are. How he should get your digits."

"Is that right, Dylan?" Callie asks the toddler who is playing in the dog food. Bent over, moving the dog dish away from Dylan, Callie says, "I heard from Wyatt yesterday."

"Oh yeah?"

"I think I'm going to try and get up there for a visit. You know, to see how Tyler is feeling."

"Right," Maddie says, exaggerating the word and rolling her eyes. "More like to see how Wyatt feels," Maddie mimes a cupping gesture.

"Mad," Callie laughs, "I gotta get moving. I'm gonna be late for work. See you soon, Dyl," she says, leaning in to kiss the top of Dylan's head.

Callie waves to Maddie and Dylan as she rounds the corner of their yard, continuing to her apartment a mile down the street.

CHAPTER 3
Callie

Callie's last patient is leaving through the art room electronic door when she sees Jason walk by, looking flustered.

"Jason!" Callie calls out as she rushes to catch up to him. Jason stops in his tracks and backs up. His crisp button-down shirt in periwinkle is just a shade lighter than the periwinkle sweater vest he has on. Looking sharp as ever.

"What's up, gorgeous?"

"Better watch out. You keep calling me that and Ryan is going to have to move aside," she says jokingly.

"Yeah, about Ryan. Got a minute?"

"Something wrong?" Jason's composure flies right out the window. He's fidgeting with his hands, picking at the cuticles of his well-manicured fingernails. This behavior is completely out of character for the always calm, cool, and collected Jason that Callie knows and loves. "What's going on? Did you guys have a fight? Anything I can help with?" Jason sits down at the art table, and Callie takes that as her cue to sit and listen. It seems important. "You're making me nervous. Just tell me what's going on."

"No, we didn't have a fight."

"Jesus, Jason, just spit it out. Is Ryan sick?"

"No, Callie. I think it's time that Ryan and I make it official." Letting that sink in a minute, Jason's dilated eyes nervously scan Callie's face for a sign of recognition.

"You want to marry Ryan?" Slowly the thought registers. "Oh my God! You want to marry Ryan!" She jumps up from her seat, rushes to wrap her arms around Jason. "This is so exciting! I can't believe it! This is so exciting!"

"You already said that," Jason says with a smile.

"When? How? What can I help with? This is huge. This is *so* huge! "

"I know. But now that I've made up my mind, that's all I can think about. I don't even know where to start with the planning."

"I'm not an awesome planner for these sorts of things, but seeing as I'm always a bridesmaid, let me help you out. Do you know how you want to propose? Is Ryan expecting this at all?"

"I doubt it. I've made it pretty clear over the years that I'm content just being together as a couple. No paper needed."

"Hmmm. Then you really need to do this up right. Let me put my thinking cap on, and together we'll make this epic."

Callie gives Jason a bear hug one last time before parting to get into her car. On the drive home, once again, she's feeling melancholy. *Why can't I ever be the one?*

Turning on the radio takes her mind off the day's events. She begins to hum along, realizing a moment later what it is she's listening to. She sings the lyrics "*you can never get around what you gotta go through*" softly with singer/songwriter Griffin House. Briefly stunned, she whispers, "Thanks for the reminder." The melodic tune surrounds her as she daydreams during her drive home. She imagines herself as a blushing bride, waiting at the entrance of the church, her arm entwined with her dad's as she anxiously waits for the first glimpse of her groom. In her daydream, the doors to the church are opening. Her senses are immediately assaulted by the sight and smell of an apparition affronting her. Callie's pulse quickens and she startles to full attention in the car, narrowly missing a dog that flashes in front of her. She swerves severely and pushes on the brakes. A blur of black and white vanishes around her apartment complex. She carefully pulls to a stop in her designated parking spot.

"Sprout?" calling to the dog as she walks to the back of her apartment. Sprout, upon hearing his name, quickly bounds toward Callie, jumping and barking all the way. "How'd you get here?" she questions as she scoops up the wriggly dog. He bathes her in sloppy kisses. "EwwWeee, you need a bath," she laughs as she carries the dog inside.

"Hey Mad, missing anything?" Callie says into the phone.

"My mind."

"Besides that?"

"My figure?"

"Keep guessing."

"My libido? Well, kinda. Not really. Sometimes I'm just not in the mood. Like just the other night, Zach was reaching for my …"

"Maddie, your dog. I'm talking about your dog, Sprout," Callie says, interrupting Maddie.

"Oh, that. I was wondering where he was. It's been so quiet in here with Dylan napping that I didn't think to look for Sprout. On my days off, the last thing I want to do is deal with a missing dog."

"Well, he's not missing. He's with me and he stinks."

"Geez, I know he can be a pain in the ass sometimes, but I don't think he stinks."

"Very funny. No, literally, he stinks. I think a skunk got to him. You better stock up on some tomato juice to get that stench out. I'll bring him over in a few minutes."

"Aw, come on, you won't give him a bath for your absent-minded friend?"

"Just throw him in the tub with Dylan. You'll be fine," Callie says with a chuckle.

Five minutes later, Callie is knocking on Maddie's door.

"It's open."

"That's probably how he got out in the first place," Callie says sarcastically, releasing Sprout.

"Can you keep a secret?"

"Nope, but tell me anyway."

"I was talking to Jason at work before I left, and he wants to propose to Ryan."

"It's about time he made an honest man outta him."

"He has no idea how to go about proposing—as in where to do it."

"I don't think it really matters at this point. They've been together forever."

"But Jason wants it to be perfect, and you know Ryan will want a stellar memory for his scrapbook."

"Ha, true. I've never seen any man work on scrapbooking like it's an Olympic event. He's truly one of a kind."

"I'll just have to think about it for a bit. I'm sure I'll come up with something. I mean, I've only thought about this moment for myself a million times," Callie says, a little too bitterly. "What's that?" Callie says, pointing at Maddie's hands.

"Can't you see it? It's the world's smallest violin playing at your pity party."

"I'll talk to you tomorrow," Callie says, rolling her eyes and retreating to her car.

"Come on, Cal, you gotta stop being so dramatic."

"Bye, Mad," Callie says as she closes the door behind her.

As she drives home from Maddie's, she can't shake the dark cloud looming over her head. Her routine, day after day, night after night, never changes. *It's time to make something happen in my life.* She pulls her laptop out of the computer bag, opens her browser and begins looking at flights to Vermont for the upcoming weekend. *Even if he's not there this weekend, he'll know I was there because there's no way Samantha will keep this to herself.* Butterflies erupt in her chest as she presses the "purchase now" button.

CHAPTER 4
Jimmy

Jimmy walks quietly into his young daughter's room, as he does every morning. He sits on the stuffed rocking chair in the corner of her periwinkle room and breathes deeply. The glitter paint on the wall, from the mural Callie created seven years ago, twinkles as the streetlights filter in through the window. The light casts a warm glow across Prue's sleeping face. He watches as her chest rises and falls in a peaceful, rhythmic pace. Until recently, this peacefulness was lost on her. She hasn't been able to sleep through the nightmares that have been visiting her for months. When Jimmy asks about her dreams, she only shares that there was a monster after her. She would wake shaking, with wild eyes, perspiring through her nightgown. He would then climb into bed with her, pulling her into his arms, cradling her until the shaking subsided. Tonight, thankfully, is a peaceful night. Maybe, just maybe, she's turned a corner and she's coming out the other side. *To think I nearly lost this beautiful girl.* He still can't believe how fortunate he is. In just a few hours, he'll be driving her to her new school as the district decides what to do with the skeletal remains of Sandy Hook Elementary School. If it were up to him, it would be razed. He can't stand the thought of another student walking those halls.

"Daddy?" Prue whispers from under the comforter on her bed.

"Morning, sweetheart," Jimmy greets her with a smile.

"You look so serious," Prue says anxiously.

Jimmy sits on the side of Prue's bed as she pushes herself up to a sitting position. Her tousled hair scatters about her head.

"Just thinking about what a great kid you are."

"Daaaad," she says, rolling her eyes.

"Come 'ere you," he says, as he pulls her into his arms. With a smile, she wraps her arms around his neck and gives him a little squeeze. She knows, without asking, just what it is he's thinking about and doesn't press him on the subject. She simply enjoys the morning ritual, just her and her dad.

"Okay, time to get up and at 'em. You ready for your big day?"

"Yeah," she says, with some uncertainty.

"You're gonna do great," he says, as he stands up and stretches before walking to the hallway. "I made pancakes this morning. You good with that?"

"MmmHmm."

"I'll take that as a yes. Come on down when you're ready."

Jimmy pulls up to the front of the middle school that has been adapted to house the elementary school students, and puts the car in park.

"You want me to walk in with you?" Jimmy asks hopefully.

"I see Libby, I'll just walk in with her, if that's all right?" she ventures bravely.

"Absolutely. Have a great day," he says as they hug one another and linger a heartbeat longer than usual. "Love you, Prue-bear."

"Love you, too, daddy," Prue says, as she kisses her father's cheek and releases her hug.

He drives away slowly. Watching his daughter recede into the building from the rearview mirror pulls at his heart. He has the compulsion to turn around and run to his daughter, but fights the urge. Instead, he slows to a stop and watches the doors close behind her. With a shudder, he weeps openly in the front seat of his car. Traffic behind him in the drop-off lane slowly moves past. There's no rush to move the car along. Many of the passersby have experienced the same emotional influx. It seems the community has grown accustomed to this as the school year begins.

Jimmy gathers his wits about him, wipes his eyes, and continues out of the school parking lot.

Like clockwork, the door opens at 3:30 and in runs Prue, dropping her backpack at the front door, full of stories from her day. Jennifer waits in the kitchen with a plate of freshly baked cookies. Peanut butter—Prue's favorite. Jennifer was hired four weeks prior to the new school year to spend time getting to know Prue and Jimmy. Jimmy has been upfront with Jennifer since the first interview, stating that if Prue was not comfortable with Jennifer, even if there was a hint of uncertainty after a month, he would let her go. Jimmy, being protective of his daughter, wants this to be a pleasant experience, and as it turns out, his trepidation was unwarranted.

"These are great, Jennifer," Prue says as she hops up on a chair at the kitchen counter.

"Thanks. A little birdie told me that peanut butter was your favorite," Jennifer explains with a wink.

"They are, it's just that I'd like them even more with chocolate chips."

"Duly noted. Do you have a lot of homework tonight?"

"Not so much, but I'll get it done once I finish this last cookie."

"Good idea. So you think you're going to like second grade this year?"

"I think so. Libby is in my class, which is so awesome!"

"Who's Libby?" Prue sits, looking at Jennifer dumbfounded.

"Just my best friend in the whole world," Prue snaps.

"Sorry, I didn't know that."

"Yeah, it's okay. I'm going upstairs to do homework now."

Great, I stepped in it already, Jennifer thinks, making a mental note to ask Jimmy about Libby later on.

Prue grabs her backpack and walks up the stairs to her bedroom, dropping her backpack next to her bed. She flops backwards onto her bed and closes her eyes.

Unsure what to do next, Jennifer stays in the kitchen and begins making dinner, busying herself to help pass the time. Finally she hears the garage door rumble. With a sigh of relief, she checks on the meatloaf in the oven, wipes her hands clean on a dish towel, grabs her coat and waits for Jimmy to come inside.

"Hey, Jennifer, how was the afternoon?"

"It was fine. Prue's upstairs, and I think she's upset," Jennifer says uncomfortably.

"Did something happen at school?" Jimmy asks, alarmed.

"No, I think it was me. I asked about her friend Libby, and she immediately shut down." Jennifer's glossy, shoulder length, brunette hair, pulled loosely in a ponytail, skims across both shoulders as she shakes her head.

Jimmy explains to Jennifer about Libby in detail.

"Her ankle isn't quite the same, but it's mending. The fact that Libby's name reminded Prue of that horrific day is probably why she got upset with you. It's not your fault. She's going to have to deal with her emotions on that subject. It's going to take time, for all of us, to heal."

"Okay then, I'll see you tomorrow," Jennifer smiles, trying to shake the unpleasantness of the conversation.

This seems to be the same reaction he gets every time he tries to talk about that dreadful day with people that aren't from Sandy Hook. They don't know how to handle the heaviness, the ugliness of it all, and tend to skim right over it and move on. Sometimes Jimmy wishes it were that easy for him.

"Sounds good," he says, walking Jennifer to the door, "see you tomorrow. Same time, same place," he says, in a singsong voice, trying to sound more chipper than he feels inside.

CHAPTER 5
Callie

Callie parks her car in the airport garage and walks to the awaiting security line, pulling her carry-on bag behind her. Her mom's phrase runs through her mind: *hurry up and wait.* She pulls out her phone to text Maddie while she waits.

Callie: *Should I really go through with this?*

Maddie: *Are you asking me for permission?*

Callie: *No, I'm just having second thoughts now.*

Maddie: *I'm having third and fourth thoughts that I can't put into a text because it's way too graphic. I can only imagine what he'll do to you when you get there*

Callie: *LOL. Seriously, he may not even be there.*

Maddie: *But if he is …*

Callie: *Okay, I have to put my phone away. I'll text you when I get there.*

On the plane, Callie tries to get swept away in her book, but fails miserably as she daydreams of what may transpire. The thought that he may not be there creeps in, but she dismisses it. She rests her head against the window and watches the clouds roll by beneath her. Unable to resist the weight of her eyelids, she steps into darkness. On the other side, she sees young Tyler sitting up in bed, having an animated conversation with

Samantha. Unable to hear them, she continues to watch in silence. The feeling of wellbeing and happiness spreads over her like a gentle breeze. In the next scene, Wyatt is there listening to Tyler. His face takes on a look of astonishment. He slowly turns his head to look directly at Callie. Without knowing what has been said, she can only guess it's something Wyatt wasn't expecting. Callie stands on a clear tube that seems to be connected to Tyler. An alarm is bleating. Callie turns in a panic, swinging her arm wildly, knocking over an open bottle of pills that spill to the floor. Pink, yellow, and blue baubles with the appearance of semiprecious stones, scatter at Callie's feet as a nurse rushes in trying to communicate. She points at the floor, then towards Tyler, then once more, with emphasis, towards the floor. Unable to comprehend what is being said, she stands dumbfounded. The nurse moves her with a shove. Callie's balance is compromised. She stumbles backwards, off the line, bumping her head against the wall. Another shove, another head bump. Slowly she opens her eyes, slightly disorientated.

"Ma'am, please put your seat back in the upright position for landing."

"Oh, okay," Callie mumbles, rubbing her head.

Callie walks into the hospital with anxiety. She can't feel her feet as she moves to the elevator, up to Tyler's floor. As the elevator door opens, the vast starkness of her surroundings momentarily catches her breath. *Keep moving.* Up ahead, she sees Samantha exiting a room, pulling off her respirator mask. The eye contact is immediate, and Samantha smiles.

"Wow. Aren't you a sight for sore eyes," Samantha says as she opens her arms.

"Hi, Sam, how's Tyler doing?" Callie asks after they embrace.

"He's doing exceptionally well today. Last week not so much. This is such a pleasant, unexpected, surprise," Samantha says, reaching to squeeze Callie's hand.

"It is for me, too. I really just planned this after receiving Wyatt's letter this week. Is he here?" Callie asks, looking around expectantly.

"Not at the moment." From the look on Callie's face, Sam can tell she is disappointed. "We just never know when Wyatt will show up. Hopefully, he'll come up this weekend, because Tyler has been asking for him a lot lately."

"That seems like good news. Has he been able to draw at all since he's been here?"

"He's tried off and on, but he gets frustrated because he gets so tired so quickly. He's getting there. At least he's past the point of infection. He hasn't had a fever this past week, which is encouraging. You can see him if you'd like. I'll go check if he's sleeping." She turns to leave, but Callie places a hand on her arm and stops her.

"Oh, no, don't bother him. I'll be here all weekend. Let him rest. Give me a call on my cell tomorrow when he's bright eyed and bushy tailed. I'm staying with my aunt for the weekend, and she's not too far from the hospital. I'll talk to you tomorrow." The women embrace briefly.

Later in the evening, Aunt Marilyn and Callie sit out back in Adirondack chairs by the firepit Aunt Marilyn installed last spring, behind her farmhouse. Sitting comfortably, she breaks the silence. "So Callie, Tyler is doing better?"

"I haven't seen him yet, but that's what Sam tells me," Callie says, setting her hot chocolate on the ground. "I'm going to stop in tomorrow and see him."

"Are you going to see anyone else while you're here?"

Knowing that truth is always best when talking to her aunt, she admits, "I'm hoping to see Wyatt." Avoiding eye contact, Callie reaches down for her mug, unsure what to do with her hands. Noticing the silence has gone on longer than expected, Callie looks over to her aunt who is turned away from Callie nodding her head, whispering.

"Everything all right, Aunt Marilyn?"

Turning back to Callie, she smiles. "Absolutely." Feeling the goosebumps form on her arm, Callie changes topics.

"Have you heard from your friend? Is she still in Scotland?"

"Yep. We've decided to spend the holidays together this year, just not sure on which continent."

"That sounds nice."

"I'm looking forward to it. Now, tell me. Why did you switch topics just then? "

Blushing now, Callie stammers, "I... I... I... well, I really want to see Wyatt. I just don't know what I'm doing."

"Your heart does. It wants what it wants, and let me tell you, it wants Wyatt. Don't even think for a minute that he doesn't want the same thing. You'd be fooling yourself. Believe you me, Tyler didn't even have anything to do with this. He said it's what's been on Wyatt's mind for years. So just find him and make it right," she suggests, leaning in to place a hand on Callie's knee. "Make your heart right, honey. You're too young to not be happy and too old to have regrets. I promise he's worth it."

Callie's eyes well up as she speaks. "I know. I know you're right. I really think this is the real deal, I just don't want to be hurt by him. I don't think I could handle that again."

"Oh, sweetie, you'll be hurt again. We all will be. People say and do things without realizing how much they make their loved ones hurt, but he won't hurt you the way he did years ago. He's learned his lesson. Make it right."

Callie releases the air in her lungs. "You're right. I will. Thanks, Aunt Marilyn."

"You're welcome, but you should be thanking Tyler. He may not be the one that physically made this happen, but he is the one that gave Wyatt a little nudge," she says, winking at Callie. At the mention of Wyatt's brother's name, the flames in the firepit brighten as if being stoked by some unseen force. Callie smiles.

CHAPTER 6
Callie

Not able to sleep in, feeling anxious, Callie goes for a run around Franklin. Taking a right out of the driveway, she runs down to Camp Road and makes a left. Memories of this road flood her mind. She thinks back on how much has changed. Tyler is gone, Riley and Jimmy are no longer together, Jimmy has a daughter. Life just keeps marching on. She runs past the old farmhouse where her family used to buy vegetables. Running past the gravel road that leads to Gramp's Camp, she stops to take in the scene. The once turquoise cabin has been painted white by the new owners. A large wooden deck now looks out on the lake. Two small children play with a ball in the side yard.

A horn blast from her left makes her jump. "Hey, lady. You're in the middle of the road. Move it!"

Whipping her head around, she recognizes the voice inside the beat up red pickup truck.

Laughing, Wyatt climbs out, closing the driver side door behind him, "You're not from around here. Hope I didn't scare you too much."

"Nah, I've had worse scares than that," thinking momentarily of narrowly escaping death by a semi.

"Whaddya doin' up in these parts?" he says, closing the distance between them.

"I thought I'd come up and check on your nephew." They embrace briefly, but during the encounter, she slides her hand down his back, feeling the flex in his lats.

"Great, that saves me a phone call. Wanna come down and see my folks?"

Hesitant, she weighs running down and back up the hill wondering if it's worth it. "Come on. Hop in."

Riding down to the camp seems surreal. They watch two children play on her old swing set as they drive past her grandfather's yard. The children wave to Wyatt.

"That's Susie and Rod. They're good kids, but I prefer the former owners," he says, looking at her sideways from his seat. "I wasn't expecting to see you. This is a nice surprise."

"It was a last minute decision. I had fewer kids scheduled Friday than usual, so I thought, since I was knocking off early, I should take a few days and visit my aunt and Tyler. As a bonus, I get to visit with you, too."

Wyatt, smiling, puts the truck in park and walks up the worn steps with Callie following. "Hey, Pop, we have a visitor," Wyatt hollers as he enters the camp.

"Well, my goodness. How nice to see you, Callie." Mr. Wilson gives Callie a quick hug and a kiss on the cheek. "How long are you in town for?"

"Just the weekend. I came to check in on everyone up north."

"Great! Tyler will be excited to have you visit, among other people." Mr. Wilson gives Callie a wink and a nod toward Wyatt.

"Ha, thanks. I look forward to visiting Tyler."

Clearing his throat, Wyatt gives Callie a look.

"And visiting with you, too, Wyatt." *Butterflies.*

Callie and Wyatt sit at the kitchen table fumbling with conversation. "I can't stay long, Wyatt. I gotta run back to my aunt's."

"I can give you a ride back."

"That defeats the whole purpose of putting my running shoes on today."

"Well, I plan on going over to the hospital in a few hours. Can I give you a lift over there?"

"Sure," Callie replies, feeling anxious.

"Great. I'll text you when I leave here."

As uncomfortable silence ensues, Callie takes in her surroundings, noticing that the once immaculate home is now in dire need of repair. The wallpaper in the kitchen has started to pull away at the baseboards from years of wear and tear. The wood paneling on the walls now seems outdated. Mr. Wilson's face is creased from years of worry, she notices, as he walks outside to get the newspaper from the front lawn.

"Seems like forever ago that we were sitting here, just like this." Wyatt speaks quietly.

"It does," Callie agrees, as they watch Mr. Wilson out the front window bend slowly to pick up the paper.

"He's slowed a lot over the years."

"It happens to the best of us."

"You look better than ever." Callie's eyes turn back to Wyatt. She feels a blush creep up her neck when Wyatt places his hands on the table in front of him.

"You look great, too, Wyatt," she says, placing a hand on top of his.

For a moment, they stay still, not moving, maintaining eye contact, Callie not breathing.

"Well, look who's here." Mrs. Wilson walks to hug Callie, notices the intimate moment she has interrupted, and smiles. Callie pushes her chair back and squeezes Mrs. Wilson.

"It's so great to see you, Mrs. Wilson. Unfortunately this is hello and goodbye. I was just out for a run and ran into Wyatt, but it's time for me to finish up. Wyatt, I'll see you in a few hours. Just text when you're ready."

"Got it."

Callie walks out the front door and notices Mr. Wilson in the yard watching the lake. "It's going to be a beautiful day today, Callie. I can feel it in my bones," he says, turning to make eye contact.

"I think you might be onto something, because I feel it, too."

Callie continues past the yard with the children playing and up the gravel road back to Aunt Marilyn's house—the long way.

Wyatt watches from the front window as she ascends the hill and turns right.

Not realizing his dad is standing in the yard watching him watch Callie, he is startled when his dad comes into view.

"Yep, it's going to be a beautiful day today. I can feel it in my bones," he repeats as he walks into the camp with a knowing smile on his face.

CHAPTER 7
Callie

"Mad, he's picking me up in 20 minutes. I'm freaking out a bit. Talk me off the ledge."

"Ooooh yeeeaah, Callie's gonna get her some!" Maddie hollers through the phone while another muffled voice growls in the background. "Zach, says 'gitty up, cowboy.'"

"We're going to the hospital to visit his nephew. I don't think there's going to be any funny business."

"Hey, there's a lot of possibility in that place. I can just picture it now."

"I bet you can," Callie says sarcastically.

"Nurse Callie, I need you STAT! Yes, Dr. Wilson. Right away!" Maddie says, breathy.

"This scenario has definitely played out in your head before," Callie deadpans.

"Dr. Zachary has his scrubs on right now, ready to role play."

Laughing, Callie says, "I'll let you get back to that. At least I'm not nervous anymore."

"Have fun, Schmal. You only live once."

"Nurse! I need you ASAP!" Zach says, standing close to the phone and inciting a giggle from Maddie as the line goes dead.

And just like that, the nerves that evaporated are back as she watches the old, red pickup truck roll to a stop in the driveway. Callie watches from the kitchen as he climbs out and turns to look at his reflection in the driver side window. He smooths his hair. Both Callie and Wyatt inhale and forcefully exhale simultaneously.

"Have a great night and don't be so nervous. You know how this is going to end already," Aunt Marilyn speaks confidently, without pause, as she puts the dishes away.

"I'll see you later on."

"I won't wait up," Aunt Marilyn says to the cabinets.

Callie walks through the door, nearly toppling Wyatt. He backs down a step as she exits the house.

"Ready?"

"As ready as I'll ever be," she says nervously.

At the hospital, Tyler is playing a game of checkers with his mom on the bed.

"Who's winning?" Wyatt asks.

"Hey, Uncle Erp!"

"Hey, T, how 'ya doin?" He leans down for a hug. "I brought a visitor."

"Callie!"

"Hi, Tyler." The emotional state she's in causes her vision to blur.

Unaware of the tears lingering on Callie's eyelids, Tyler talks a blue streak about the art he's been working on, excitedly describing each piece.

"So the protector of the castle survived and defeated his foe?" she questions.

"Yep. You don't have to worry about me anymore. I'm good." Tyler speaks as if he's decades older than his years.

"Check that off my list," Callie says, miming the action.

The group settles into a comfortable rhythm of conversation and games. They enjoy dinner in Tyler's room and stay until it's obvious that Tyler's body needs to rest.

"All right, big guy. Time to call it a night," Sam says to her weary son.

Yawning, Tyler says, "Thanks for making the time go by, guys. See you tomorrow?"

Callie speaks first. "Unfortunately, I have to go back home to work with kids just like you. I'll be back sometime soon. I promise." She gives him a peck on the cheek, causing his skin to flush.

"I'll be back tomorrow, T, before I head back to Rhode Island to make more money for another trip up here. Gas is getting expensive!"

"Night, sweetheart. I'm gonna walk everyone out, and then I'll be back to pack up my things. If you're tired, just close your eyes." Kissing his cheek, she's relieved to feel his cool skin on her lips.

Samantha walks Callie and Wyatt to the elevator door, hugging each tightly.

"Thanks for coming up, you guys. Callie, hope to see you soon. This was such a nice surprise for Tyler. I haven't seen him blush like that since the day I walked in on him changing into his hospital gown."

"I'm glad I could help. Take care, and if there's anything I can do for you guys, don't hesitate to ask."

"Bye, Sis."

"Bye, Erp." The sentiment makes Callie's heart melt as the siblings release from their affectionate hug.

The elevator doors open, and Brian walks out with two coffees in his hand.

"Bye, guys."

Entering the elevator, Callie and Wyatt stand close to one another quietly.

"Hungry?"

"Nah, after that dinner Brian brought in, I'm stuffed."

"Coffee?"

"Nah, I think I've had enough hospital coffee to last me a lifetime."

Wyatt exits the elevator first and holds the hospital entrance door open, trying desperately to think of a way to spend more time with her.

"A nightcap?"

Realizing he's stalling, she gives in. "Sure."

A broad smile expands across his face.

They drive to a bar called J.D.'s, not far from her aunt's house. The floor is sticky from spilled drinks, the stench of beer clings to the air as they sit at a booth in the back. The place is fairly empty except for a few bar flies. The jukebox comes to life with a popular country ballad.

"Care to dance?" Wyatt asks with outstretched hand.

"Love to." Callie takes Wyatt's hand, and he whirls her in a circle, then pulls her in. She places her head against his chest, feeling his heartbeat through his shirt. They spin around the dance floor a few more times before the end of the song. With the last lyric, Wyatt pulls Callie close, looking deeply into her eyes, and kisses her tenderly on the mouth. Fireworks explode in her head.

"I hope I'm not reading you wrong," Wyatt asks, slightly worried.

"You're reading me right," she says, planting a kiss on his lips for good measure. Warily, he guides her back to the table and they sit across from each other, looking longingly into each other's eyes. In Callie's peripheral vision, there is a presence advancing quickly.

"Wyatt Wilson, is that you? It's so great to see you!" Wyatt's eyes glance upward, toward the approaching voice.

He stands quickly. "Riley. It's been a while. How are you?" Wyatt now stands shielding Callie.

"Couldn't be better," Riley says, spilling her beer. Setting the beer on the table, she fixes her eyes on Callie. In one swift motion, Riley turns and wraps her arms around Wyatt's head like tentacles and kisses him full on the mouth. Without releasing him she says, "It's so, so great to see you." Wyatt removes her arms, wipes his mouth and steps back. Riley's dilated eyes look directly at Callie. "As for you, tell your brother to go fuck himself," Riley says, reaching for her beer. She drags it across the table, sloshing liquid along the way to her lips. "He has my baby girl and won't let me see her."

"Riley, now's not the time."

Stepping unsteadily toward Callie, Riley speaks. "He thinks he's so high and mighty," she burps.

Wyatt, protecting Callie, says, "I'm sure this is something you and Jimmy need to discuss. It has nothing to do with Callie."

Mumbling, Riley flips her middle finger at Wyatt, swallows more beer, and stumbles into a booth along the sidewall. Riley's group cackles and tries to high five her as she falls onto the bench seat, emptying more of her beer on the floor.

"She's a train wreck," Callie says, shaking her head.

"I know. You ready to take off?"

"I am now."

Wyatt holds the door of J.D.'s for Callie to exit. They travel for the next few minutes in silence.

"I'm sorry about that," Wyatt says flatly.

"It's fine. You didn't know she would be there."

"When was the last time she saw Prue?"

"Probably last Christmas." Feeling the weight of that admission, Callie closes her eyes and shakes her head, "I thought she was pulling it together, but after that little show, it's apparent she's not."

Removing one hand from the steering wheel, Wyatt clasps Callie's left hand. They continue driving hand in hand. Pulling into Aunt Marilyn's driveway, Callie asks, "would you like to come in for a minute?" Wyatt turns the car off and follows Callie into the farmhouse.

"Good evening, Wyatt." Surprised by her aunt, Callie jumps.

"Hi, Marilyn," Wyatt says, laughing at the movement.

"I'm just heading to bed. You two make yourselves comfortable," she says, as she retreats down the hall to her bedroom on the first floor. "Goodnight."

Looking over at Wyatt, Callie asks, "Coffee or wine?"

"Wine."

Callie pours two glasses and hands Wyatt a glass in the living room. Feeling frustrated from the confrontation with Riley, Callie is unable to make conversation. Wyatt reaches for her hand and pulls her down to sit next to him on the couch. Each takes a swallow from their respective glasses. Wyatt sets his glass down first and looks to Callie to see if the next move will be accepted. As if on cue, Callie sets her glass down on the coffee table. "Cal, let's not worry about Riley tonight. It's obvious she still has issues to work through. She's not your problem."

"I know. You're right. I just feel bad about Prue. Her mom's a hot mess, and it just makes me sad."

"I'm sure it does." Wyatt says, unsure whether he should proceed.

Callie takes a deep breath and releases it completely. She leans into Wyatt and kisses him, slowly at first. He pulls her into a full embrace, kissing her neck, her earlobe, her cheek, her lips. This is something Wyatt has been thinking about for a very long time. Callie pushes her niece and Riley out of her mind and gives herself completely to the moment. Wyatt gently presses her back into the couch and continues kissing her. A soft groan escapes Callie's lips. After several minutes of passionate kisses, Callie presses on Wyatt's chest to move him aside. Feeling slightly confused, Wyatt asks, "Should I go?"

"No." Callie stands and reaches for Wyatt's hand and guides him upstairs to her room.

Walking up the creaking staircase, she's not worried about the sound. Callie is pretty certain Aunt Marilyn is asleep by now. Walking past Lilian on the landing, she takes her free hand and turns the doll's head around. Walking into the bedroom, Callie leaves the light off and lets the light of the moon guide her. Closing the door behind Wyatt, Callie turns and collects Wyatt in her arms. They stand intertwined in limbs; they grapple for footing as each feverishly caresses the other. Clothing is strewn aside as Wyatt gently guides Callie to the bed. Breathlessly, they become familiar with each other's bodies again, melting the years away. The landscape may have changed, but he memorized her body years ago. Familiarizing themselves with each other's canvasses is an adventure. Pulling back momentarily, Wyatt utters, "God, you're beautiful," caressing her skin from shoulder to knee. Callie doesn't let him speak further as she pulls his body against hers.

The sun peeks through the trees, warming the room they sleep in. Callie wakes first, with a smile. She rolls to her side and kisses Wyatt softly on the cheek, thinking how happy she is at the moment. Wyatt smiles without opening his eyes, pulls her into his arms, and with an abbreviated repeat of the night before, they lie with each other.

Wyatt speaks first. "Callie, I know we've been here before. I know how I feel and always have, but I have to tell you I'm worried that you may dismiss this as a passing thing," he says with a beautiful sigh. "I just hope I'm the man you want me to be."

She rolls to her side to look at him. He seems pensive. She traces his lips with her forefinger, thinking of how to express to him that he is her one and only, that she's never stopped loving him, that if he were to ask her to spend the rest of her life with him, she would say yes. Instead she just kisses him softly. They exit the room hours after Aunt Marilyn has risen.

"Good morning. Coffee's ready."

Sheepishly, Wyatt walks through the kitchen to pour himself a cup of coffee. Shortly after, Callie enters grinning at Aunt Marilyn. She pours herself a cup, and they sit across from one another at the kitchen table, not able to take their eyes off one another. Aunt Marilyn speaks. "What a beautiful day it's going to be. I'm headed into town. Do you need anything?"

"I'm driving to the airport in a few hours so I'll say goodbye now."

Callie walks up to embrace Marilyn as Marilyn whispers in her ear, "See? Just like I told you."

"It's so great to see you, Wyatt. Don't be a stranger."

"Yes, ma'am."

Alone in the kitchen, Callie stands with her back to Wyatt as she rinses out their coffee cups. Wyatt walks up behind her and wraps his arms around her waist, kissing the side of her neck.

"What are you thinking right now?"

Callie places the cups on the drying rack and says, "You *are* the man I want you to be." Turning in his arms, placing her arms around his neck, she continues, "You've always been the man I've wanted. It just took my head a while to catch up to my heart."

CHAPTER 8
Jason

"You *have* to think of something! I made reservations on The Hill in two weeks, and I have to have a plan," Jason says, slightly annoyed.

"Come on. You have to have some ideas brewing." Callie looks at Jason as he shakes his head. "Not even one idea?"

Jason puts his well-coiffed head in his hands. Leaning on his elbows across the table from Callie, he says, "I can't think of anything special. I mean, I need to come up with something extra special. You know what Ryan's like. He'll be so disappointed if I don't do this 110%."

"True. Don't fret. We'll think of something."

"I'm fretting. I've tried to come up with something. It's all in your hands now."

"No pressure at all," Callie jokes as she mirrors his mannerisms—head in hands, elbows on table, looking directly across at Jason. "I gotta get back to it. I have a new little one coming in today. She's four years old. It breaks my heart when they come to me so young."

Jason takes one hand off his head and takes hold of one of Callie's. "What does she have?"

"Wilms tumor, stage three."

Squeezing and releasing her hand, he says, "Well, the good news is that there's a 94% survival rate with that disease."

"Good to know. Hey, put your thinking cap on. You're the one that's proposing, not me. I'll be around until four if you need a brainstorming session later on."

Jason waves to Callie as she leaves the coffee cart area. He can't put his finger on it, but notices there's something different about her today.

"Yes, she walked right up to him and gave him a sloppy, drunken kiss right in front of me. Oh, and she told me to tell you that you can go fuck yourself," Callie explains to Jimmy.

"Is that a direct quote?"

"Yep."

Jimmy releases a sigh. "It explains a lot. She hasn't called Prue in a while. Fine by me, it's just that Prue is starting to ask more questions about her, and I think pretty soon she's going to ask to visit her."

Twisting a strand of hair as she talks, Callie says, "I wouldn't recommend that any time soon."

"Yeah, I'm not that much of an idiot."

"Depends on who you ask."

"Nice." The banter between the two of them makes Jimmy smile.

"Everything good with you other than that little hiccup?"

"Great."

"Define great."

"Wyatt and I are back together, and my job is going well. How is Prue liking school?"

"She is loving it, and doing so much better now that the nightmares have stopped. She could use a visit from her aunt some time, though. Is that your phone I hear in the background?

I should go and let you get that." The landline goes quiet after two quick rings.

"Nah, that's just Maddie. We have this little signal we started a few years ago. We let the phone ring once or twice just to let the other person know we're thinking of them. I know it's weird, but it works for us. She's so busy being a mom and I'm busy with work that sometimes it's hard to get a phone conversation in. This way we know that we're still a priority, even though we don't actually speak to each other."

"That's dumb," Jimmy says after a brief lull.

"You're dumb. Just tell Prue that her aunt could use a visit. Let me check my schedule, and I'll get something on the calendar soon."

Ending the call, she checks the text messages that came through while she was on the phone.

> Wyatt: *Hey beautiful. Just checking in. You there? Are you avoiding me? Do I appear needy? LOL*

> Callie: *Ha - No, not needy at all … All good. I miss you.*

> Wyatt: *I miss you more. I'll call you tomorrow. Sleep well.*

Callie's body tingles with delight. It's a wonderful feeling after a hard day with her art therapy patients. Checking her calendar and schedule as promised, she sets a date and sends the information to her brother. A trip is now on the books. There's nothing like a visit to the east coast in the fall.

She dials another number, waiting patiently for the recipient to answer.

"Hello?"

"Okay, so I think I have a great idea."

"Yeeesss!" Jason growls. "Tell me! Or would you rather do this in person?"

"Let's meet up for dinner tonight."

"Perfect. I have something to show you."

"How are you going to explain our dinner to Ryan. He hates to be excluded."

"I know he does. I'll think of something. If not, I'll make it up to him later on."

Walking up to the restaurant, Callie can see Jason through the window, standing at the bar, deep in thought. She walks directly to him, gives him a peck on the cheek, a quick squeeze and starts right in with her plan.

"So here's the plan …" She lays it all out, and by the time she's finished speaking, Jason has tears in his eyes.

"Oh, my God. I'm speechless. That's perfect," he says as he retrieves a handkerchief from his front pocket and dabs at his eyes. By the time the hostess has seated them, he has composed himself and they enjoy a lovely dinner.

"What did you end up telling Ryan?"

"That I was meeting you for dinner because you were having boy troubles that only I could understand. I think he's a little hurt by that." Then as he pulls a box from his pocket, he says, "I think once he sees this, he'll forgive me."

Callie opens the box and gasps.

"Jason, this is exquisite." The patrons at the table beside them turn to see what all the commotion is about, one woman at the table squeals, then utters loudly, 'Oh, my gosh, he's proposing!' Before Callie can formulate the words that they have it all wrong, Jason has taken on the role of the beloved, and places the ring on her left ring finger. The ring spins loosely across her knuckle as he tries to shove it into place. He leans in with a whisper, "Just go with it."

"Honey, it seems that gastric bypass surgery made every part of you skinnier," he chuckles. "We need to make some adjustments." She fiddles with the ring in hopes that it won't fall off her finger. "So, what do you say?"

"Yes, yes, yes! I WILL marry you, Jason!" Callie announces as she tightly hugs Jason. Loosening the grip she had on the ring causes it to slide off the end of her ring finger. She watches in horror as it tumbles through the air into a ceramic bowl of guacamole.

The table of patrons erupts with applause, then quiets as shock sets in. Without a beat, Jason fishes the ring out, pops it in his mouth, rolls it around, and places back on Callie's finger as she grimaces.

"And for my next trick, I'll attempt to make the guacamole disappear."

The strangers relax and order champagne for the two tables that have morphed into one. Riddled with questions about how they met, how they fell in love, when they plan to marry, Jason scoots closer to Callie and drapes his arm over her shoulder.

"Shall I tell them, Schnookums? Or would you like to do the honors?"

Amused, Callie says, "You're much more eloquent than I am."

"All right then. I'll start at the beginning. I met the love of my life at the circus. It was that moment that the spotlight shone on the center ring that changed my life forever. There she was, a plump ragamuffin riding around the ring in tattered clothing, on a bicycle. My heart ached for this hefty child. I had yet to see her face as her gorgeous locks hid her identity." Jason takes a moment to let the story sink in. He sees these strangers leaning in, waiting with bated breath for his next word.

"She continued to cycle around the ring, removing her hands from the handlebars and began throwing rings up and down, juggling with ease, three, four, then five rings. I was in awe. After her last dramatic toss, she stopped and jumped from her bike, catching the last ring behind her back. At that moment, I realized that the hair whipping around her face was not hair from her head, but a chestnut mane of a beard." Jason caresses Callie's shocked face for added measure and lingers there for dramatic effect, his eyes twinkling with mischief. He turns to face his audience, placing his hand on his heart and says, "Truth. My hand to God." Gasps of disbelief ring out. "It took us many months to find just the right doctor to remove the facial hair, allowing this beauty to shine through. Thankfully, we trusted this doctor immensely, because for an additional fee, he said he could remove her extra 'baggage.'" To emphasize this point, he pats her belly.

"Okay. I think we've had enough sharing," Callie suggests.

Every eye is on her, and every mouth in the wide circle around them stands agape, except for one.

"Come on. You mean to tell me that she weighed a ton *and* had a bushy beard? I'm not buying it," the doubting Thomas proclaims.

"Did it hurt?" asks one onlooker. "How long did it take?" asks another, disregarding the negative comment.

"Yes, love, how long did it take to remove the barbate, my bewhiskered sprite?"

"Several painful sessions, but that's all in the past now," she says, digging her fingernails into Jason's thigh, causing him to flinch.

"That so? Prove it," chimes in the negative bystander as he folds his arms across his chest.

Callie and Jason look at each other. Callie, feeling panicked, notices a fire ignite in Jason's eye. Jason reaches up and gently caresses the blond, downy facial hair that has been Callie's nemesis since she hit puberty. In that moment, she is horrified by his actions.

"Oh, dear. It looks as though this patch is growing back." Callie continues to look on, mortified. "Remember, sweetheart, he said this was a possibility?" She stares blankly at him and nods her head. The stranger leans in to get a closer look and spills his date's red wine. He quickly retreats and drops a napkin on the tablecloth to mop up the wine. His skin glows pink as a blush creeps up his neck to color his cheeks.

"Oh. I'm sorry. I didn't see that. Wow. That's ... that's ... I'm so ... sorry."

"It happens. It's hard to believe that this beautiful face was covered by coarse dark hair, but it does happen," Jason says to the group, thrilled that he has won this man over.

"Wow, it's amazing what modern technology can do for such a predicament. And all that led to this moment here. How wonderful," muses one woman.

"So true," Jason says, reaching out and squeezing the stranger's hand. "Of this I am profoundly grateful." They keep up the charade, and when it's time to pay the bill, the server sets the bill down in front of Jason, but he doesn't have a moment to react. The once negative man, the leader of the group, hands the bill and his credit card to the server.

"It's the least I can do for you two."

Jason walks Callie to her car at the end of the evening and gives her a hug.

"And the academy award goes to Miss Callista Lamply."

"Me? The bearded lady? No, friend, I think you deserve that honor," she says with a laugh. "Explain to me why having gastric bypass surgery is more believable than having a beard? He didn't even question that part of the equation."

Jason wipes happy tears away from the corner of his eyes as his laughter quiets. "Perhaps it was your choice of outfits?" Astonished, Callie looks at her clothing.

Laughing now, Callie shakes the ring off her finger, nearly dropping it for the second time tonight and places it back into the velvet box. "I think you need to put this somewhere safe after you clean it. Now, when do you plan on doing this?"

"Two weeks. I'll do the proposing first, then we'll whoop it up that evening. You should see if Wyatt can come out to celebrate with us. It's going to be a great weekend."

"I'm supposed to talk to him tomorrow. I'll ask him then. Thanks for a great evening. He's one lucky guy."

"Nah, I'm the lucky one."

CHAPTER 9
Jason

"Tyler is doing better?" Callie asks Wyatt over the phone, adjusting the couch cushions as she waits for a reply.

"He's doing great. He's going home next week."

"What day?"

"Next Thursday. I plan on driving up there to see that he made it home safe and sound." Silence clings to the air. "Cal? You still there?"

"Yep. I was just going to ask you if you can come out next weekend to visit. Something special is about to go down."

"What's going on?"

"Jason is going to propose to Ryan next Saturday, and he wondered if I would ask you to come out to celebrate, but going to Vermont to see Tyler is much more important. We can celebrate with them another time."

"Hold on a sec. I didn't say no yet. I can make this work. Let me get all my ducks in a row and I'll call with the details." Wyatt is determined to make this work. Callie rarely asks Wyatt for anything. He sits with the phone cradled on his shoulder as he opens his calendar to check the upcoming weekend.

"Jason, relax. It's all going to go just as planned."

"Ryan hates to hike. He's going to know something's up."

"Just tell him the hike was Wyatt's idea. He'll be in this afternoon. Tell him you want to get a jacket for the hike, that it's supposed to get chilly later on."

"Yeah, chilly. Jacket. Hike. Got it."

"Jason."

"Yeah?"

"Take a deep breath. It's going to be fine."

Waiting for Wyatt's flight to land, Callie is on pins and needles. The night at Aunt Marilyn's farmhouse replays in her mind. She daydreams of the warmth of his body, the smell of his skin, the feel of his caress. Unaware of the time passing, she nearly misses him as he deplanes, walking past with the other passengers from his flight.

"Wyatt!" she hollers as she rises from her seat, just past the security checkpoint.

"Hey, stranger," he says, dropping his carry-on bag beside him, freeing his arms to allow room for Callie.

Callie takes a deep breath, taking in his scent. *This smells like home.*

"How was your flight?"

"Uneventful. The time couldn't pass quickly enough." They walk casually, holding hands to the car.

"So what's the plan?"

"I think Jason is proposing as we speak. I'm waiting for the high sign to meet up with them at the restaurant."

"I'd love to be a fly on the wall right now."

"I'm pretty sure Jason is stuttering and flustered."

"Do you think Ryan knows anything is up?"

"I'm sure he's wondering what's wrong with Jason," Callie says with a giggle.

"Jason, hiking? Really? Do you see the shoes I have on? Suede. Not great for hiking. When was the last time I asked you to do anything strenuous?"

Jason raises his eyebrows up and down.

"Don't answer that."

"Come on. It's supposed to get chilly later on. Let me buy you a coat. Your jacket is about 20 years old."

"What's wrong with my coat?" Ryan says, holding the hanger that his favorite sport coat hangs on. "It's a standard in any polished young man's closet."

"Come on. It'll be fun. You know how much you like to shop," Jason says, replacing the coat in the closet and glancing at his watch.

"Why do you keep doing that?"

"Doing what?"

"Checking your watch? Are we on a tight schedule? Do you have a hot date?"

"Wyatt's plane just landed. I wanna get this jacket and get moving so we can meet up with them in a timely fashion."

"Fine," Ryan says melodramatically as they walk to the car.

"How about this one?" Jason suggests, subtly trying to persuade Ryan to walk to another rack.

"Nah. Not a good color on me."

Jason manages to shepherd him to one particular clothing rack. "Try this one on." Knowing full well that it's too small, he hands it to Ryan. Unable to pull it up to his shoulders, he takes it off and looks at the label.

"Really? A small? I haven't been a small since junior high." Replacing it, he begins to look at the jacket hangers labeled S, M, L. Pulling the only large from the rack, he eases it onto his broad shoulders. Looking into the full-length mirror, he admires his reflection.

"You sure that's the right size?" Jason inquires.

"It said large on the hanger."

"You better make sure the label matches the hanger."

Without questioning, he takes the jacket off and looks for the tag on the inside of the jacket. Finding the tag, Ryan is stunned into silence. Through clouding eyes, Ryan looks to Jason for understanding.

"You are my one and only. You are my yesterday and tomorrow, my past and future. I would be honored if you would be my husband."

Ryan, weeping openly now, watches as Jason pulls the velvet box from his coat pocket and on bended knee asks, "Ryan, will you marry me?"

Nodding his head at first, Jason waits for a verbal acceptance. Ryan drops to his knees in front of Jason and says, "yes. Yes, Jason, I will happily marry you." He seals the heartfelt moment with a kiss.

He said yes! Attached to the text is a photo of the tag sewn into the jacket. *Will you marry me?* In the next photo is the happy couple, with Ryan's left hand extended, showing off the spectacular eternity diamond band.

Congratulations! We'll see you at Weldon Springs hiking trail in 20.

"It's a beautiful day for a hike," Callie says after hugging it out with Jason and Ryan. Ryan rolls his eyes, but even a hike can't dampen his excitement.

Jason explains, in detail, how the proposal took place. Both Ryan and Jason talk non-stop smiling at one another along the route. Whenever one speaks of the other, he gently touches the other's arm. It's an intimate gesture that tugs at Callie's heart, but seems lost on Wyatt.

"Gotta water the trees, people. I'm gonna run ahead and take care of business." Wyatt takes off down the trail as Jason, Ryan and Callie slow the pace to allow Wyatt some privacy.

"I just can't believe you two. This is so amazing. I'm so happy for you both." "Thanks, Callie," Jason says, smiling and picking up the pace. "We better pick it up. Don't want Wyatt falling off the bluff or anything."

Wyatt is waiting for them on a bench when they arrive, over-looking the Missouri River. The sun is filtered through the trees and for a moment, Callie feels as though she is transported to the Black Forest in Vermont. The smell of the fall leaves is one of Callie's favorites. She sits on the bench next to Wyatt.

"Isn't this a pretty place?" she says to Wyatt, as Ryan and Jason walk a few paces ahead to another bench.

"It really is. Kinda feels like Vermont. Even the trees are like home. Did you see that one over there?"

He points to a tree with a knot low to the ground. Seeing it brings a smile to Callie's lips. She walks toward it, and notices something familiar about the tree. There are initials carved beneath the knot, C+W. She runs her fingers over the wounded tree and notices something white peeking out. Curious, she reaches and unfolds the paper. Gasping, the paper begins to tremble as her hands are uncontrollably quaking. Wyatt sits quietly watching her reaction. It's one he's been longing for. Slowly he walks to her and speaks.

"Callie, I ..." without allowing him to finish she is almost unable to speak, "Yes." She lunges at him with the weight of her body and they collide into one another, laughing between kisses. He looks at the tree once more, releases Callie and reaches to remove a box, handing it to Callie. As she opens it he says, "this is the promise I made to you years ago." Opening the box reveals the gold band with a heart shaped ruby.

CHAPTER 10
Prue

December 14, 2013

On the anniversary of the shooting at Sandy Hook Elementary School, Jimmy is fixed to the TV, watching bits and pieces of last year's broadcast of President Obama's visit to speak to the people of Newtown at Newtown High School. Jimmy and Prue watch, preparing for the difficulty of reliving that day. Jimmy is lost in thought, thinking about that day in the Newtown High School's auditorium. The memory floods him as if it is happening all over again.

"Daddy, does this dress look all right?"

He is so preoccupied in thought that he doesn't realize she's asked a question. "Daddy?" Prue repeats.

"What is it, sweetheart?"

"I said, is this dress all right?"

"You look beautiful, sweetheart."

"Is it okay if Libby and her parents sit with us?"

"Absolutely."

They drive silently to the high school. Prue is wringing her hands, eventually sitting on them to stop her fidgeting.

"Daddy, will Mrs. Canfield be here tonight?"

"Yes, sweetie, I believe so."

"Is she going to look the same?"

Jimmy finds a parking spot. Placing the car in park, he turns to his daughter.

"Are you nervous to see her?"

"What if she doesn't look … the same?"

"You'll know it's her. She looks exactly the same. She's just using crutches. That's the only change. She has a long way to go in her recovery, but she'll know you, and want to hug you, and seeing you will give her hope," he says to his wide-eyed daughter.

"Hope?"

"Hope that our future, your future, will be full of courageous young men and women, like yourself and Libby, who will lovingly help people through times of crisis and sadness with smiles, hugs, and love."

Thoughtful for a moment, Prue looks out the window watching the townspeople enter the building. "But will it happen again?"

"I don't know the answer to that, but we can't live in fear about that possibility. We have to live our lives being the best people we can be. If we don't, then evil wins. We can't let that happen."

Prue turns to her dad with tears welling. "Okay, I'm ready."

Smiling at Prue, Jimmy pulls Prue into his arms and kisses her cheek.

"That's my beautiful, brave Prue-bear."

Prue and Jimmy find a seat inside while they wait for the President to speak to the anxious crowd. Libby and her family are seated next to them and the crowd is eerily silent.

President Obama walks to the microphone.

Thank you. (Applause.) Thank you, Governor. To all the families, first responders, to the community of Newtown, clergy, guests—Scripture tells us, "do not lose heart. Though outwardly we are wasting away … inwardly we are being renewed day by day. For our light and momentary troubles are achieving for us an eternal glory that far outweighs them all. So we fix our eyes not on what is seen, but on what is unseen, since what is seen is temporary, but what is unseen is eternal. For we know that if the earthly tent we live in is destroyed, we have a building from God, an eternal house in heaven, not built by human hands.

We gather here in memory of twenty beautiful children and six remarkable adults. They lost their lives in a school that could have been any school, in a quiet town full of good and decent people that could be any town in America.

Here in Newtown, I come to offer the love and prayers of a nation. I am very mindful that mere words cannot match the depths of your sorrow, nor can they heal your wounded hearts. I can only hope it helps for you to know that you're not alone in your grief, that our world, too, has been torn apart, that all across this land of ours, we have wept with you, we've pulled our children tight. And you must know that whatever measure of comfort we can provide, we will provide, whatever portion of sadness that we can share with you to ease this heavy load, we will gladly bear it. Newtown—you are not alone.

Prue sits holding her daddy's hand in her left and holding Libby's hand in her right as they listen to every word the President says. Throughout the speech, the crowd sits in silence for all but the occasional sniff and moan of the mourning. At the conclusion of the speech, Prue feels as if she may explode with sadness. Tears roll down her cheeks as Libby tries to comfort her. Together they listen as some of their classmates' names are announced.

Charlotte. Daniel. Olivia. Josephine. Ana. Dylan. Madeleine. Catherine. Chase. Jesse. James. Grace. Emilie. Jack. Noah. Caroline. Jessica. Benjamin. Avielle. Allison.

God has called them all home. For those of us who remain, let us find the strength to carry on, and make our country worthy of their memory.

May God bless and keep those we've lost in His heavenly place. May He grace those we still have with His holy comfort. And may He bless and watch over this community, and the United States of America. (Applause.)

Prue watches as President Obama walks to Mrs. Canfield. They embrace and speak in hushed tones. After the exchange, Jimmy walks to Mrs. Canfield with Prue. Standing behind Mrs. Canfield is her husband and her family, including Charlie.

"Charlie, how are you?" Jimmy asks, offering his college buddy a hug, noticing how he's put on quite a bit of weight.

"Hey, Jimmy. It's good to see you. How's your sister?"

"Callie? She's fine. Busy as usual. You know she's not happy unless she's juggling 50 million things at once. How's your mom?"

"She's doing pretty well, all things considered." Turning to Prue, Charlie says, "I know for a fact she would love to give a hug to this one."

Smiling, Prue watches as Charlie whispers into his mother's ear. Prue walks over to Mrs. Canfield who instantly becomes overcome with emotion. Trying to keep it together, Mrs. Canfield bends down and kneels on the floor, taking Prue into her arms. They hug tightly.

"I'm all right, Prue. I'm all right. You were such a brave, *brave* girl that day. I can't thank you enough for helping calm your classmates. I'm so very happy to see you here looking strong, healthy, and beautiful as ever. Love wins, sweetie." Charlie helps Mrs. Canfield stand. "Jimmy, you have done such an amazing job raising such a caring young lady. I'm so proud of you."

"Thank you. I'm pretty proud of her, too. I'm so happy to see that you are recovering from your injuries. We'll see you at the reception with the President in a little bit."

Jimmy had been so caught up in his memory that he hadn't noticed the televised broadcast had finished.

"Come on, Prue-bear, time for bed."

"Okay, Dad."

Unable to fall asleep, she can hear her father's voice wafting from down below.

"Cal, I hope it wasn't the wrong thing to do. Letting her watch and relive that day. She's been doing so well lately, no nightmares."

I wish he wouldn't worry about me. Prue's weary eyes eventually close and she dreams of that fateful evening. She's back in the closet trying to remain calm. *Pop, pop, pop.* In this particular dream, however, she opens the door to see Mrs. Canfield's son, Charlie, dead beside the teacher's desk.

At the sound of Prue's scream, Jimmy runs up the stairs to cradle his only child until she calms and falls back to sleep.

CHAPTER 11
Callie

"I never thought it would happen to me, Mad. Never in a million years."

"Congratulations! I'm so excited to be planning your wedding, *finally*."

"Am I dreaming?" Callie giggles with Maddie over the phone. Discussing plans for the wedding, the invite list, and the future.

"Did you tell your parents yet?"

"Of course. We went straight to their house to tell them in person. Apparently they've been hoping this would happen for a long time. Dad immediately went to the downstairs fridge and brought up a chilled bottle of champagne."

"They must be super excited. I mean, I'm sure your mom thought you were going to turn into a recluse, or worse, a cat lady."

"I'm sure I had them worried after I broke it off with Charlie."

"Do you ever hear from him?"

"Nah. The only time I hear anything is through you. Have you talked to Liz in a while?"

"Not for a few months. She did pop out another kid, though. Did you know that? They have three ankle biters now. Crazy."

"Well, I'll be surprised if we can have any. I'd love to have two, but at my age, I'd be lucky with one."

"Being in your forties isn't ancient. You're not completely dried up yet."

"We'll see."

"So he'd been planning this for a while?"

"Apparently. When I told Wyatt about Jason's proposal, he thought it might be fun to add one more proposal to the day. Somehow he got Jason's numb … wait a minute. Did you talk to Wyatt?"

"He may or may not have gotten my number from your mother, and I guess it's possible that he got Jason's number from me."

"So you knew?"

"Well, I knew something was up. He wanted to talk to Jason, which meant one of two things: he either wanted to propose to you, or he wanted to know the best way to come out of the closet."

Callie smiles into the receiver.

Months pass with many phone calls between Maddie and Callie, Callie and Wyatt, and Jason and Callie trying to confirm all the details for all parties involved with each wedding. Callie's social calendar is full for the coming year. Jason and Ryan's wedding is in June, which perfectly fits with Callie and Wyatt's wedding plans for July. Callie knows there is only one place in this world magical enough for this fateful event.

"I'm coming out in two weeks to make sure we have everything ready to go for this summer. Doing everything remotely is making me nervous."

"It'll all work out. It always does. Besides, if it doesn't, we'll still be married in the end, and that's what really counts, right?"

They continue their weekly conversations of preparation and planning. They now have the venue for the wedding and reception in place. Every thing is a go.

Visiting in Vermont a few weeks later, Callie stays with Aunt Marilyn, as usual. As they drive over to Samantha and Brian's place to visit Tyler, Wyatt seems antsy. Callie chalks it up to excitement for their upcoming nuptials.

"Hey, T. How you doing?"

"Hey, Uncle Erp," Tyler yells as he runs to his uncle. "I'm doing great!" He can see that Tyler is indeed doing well. The pink of his cheeks is back. As a matter of fact, standing next to Tyler, now almost eye to eye, he realizes that he has grown several inches since last they saw one another.

"Dude, you've grown a ton!"

"He's growing like a weed right now," Samantha says from the kitchen as she carries a tray of snacks and drinks to the table.

The evening is warm and inviting, and they briefly discuss the wedding, but mostly tonight is about Tyler.

"Thanks for dinner, Samantha. Can I help clean up?"

"No, no, you sit and catch up with Tyler. He's been looking forward to your visit," Samantha says, winking to Callie. Samantha walks back to the kitchen counter and piles the dirty dishes into the warm sudsy water beginning to fill the sink.

"I remember when I was in the hospital, I'd have visitors throughout the day and night. The best visits were from Uncle Tyler."

Wyatt and Callie glance at each other.

"He would tell me the best stories. One he told me about you guys," Tyler says, pointing to Wyatt and Callie.

"Really? What was it about?" Wyatt asks, curious.

"He said you used to carve your initials into a tree in the Black Forest."

Immediately the hair on Callie's neck stands on end.

"And he said you guys used to write letters to each other and leave them in the tree. How do you leave something *in* a tree?"

Astonished now, Wyatt stutters a response, "Uh, well, I uh, I mean, we used to leave letters for each other in the knot of one of the trees in the woods." As he speaks, his cheeks begin to turn a bright pink.

"What's a promise ring?" young Tyler asks.

"What's going on with you? You can't sit still. And if you change that radio station one more time, I'm jumping out of this truck," Callie teases Wyatt on the ride back to her aunt's house.

"Well, first off, Tyler is freaking me out. How did he know that stuff about us?"

"Isn't it possible you mentioned that tree to your nephew at some point?"

"Doubtful," Wyatt says, scratching his head. He parks in Aunt Marilyn's driveway, letting the truck idle. "And about that promise ring."

Callie looks down at the ring on her left hand. Twisting it around her finger, she says, "Wasn't that crazy? I was floored when he mentioned it." Looking up now, she sees a familiar velvet ring box.

"I'd like you to have this as an engagement ring. I'm happy you're wearing the ruby, but that was the past, when I was just a kid. I want you to have this to represent our future."

Hands shaking now, she opens the box to find a perfectly round diamond on a simple silver band with two smaller diamonds on either side. Wyatt removes the ruby and places it on her right hand, then he places the diamond ring on her ring finger.

"Wyatt, it's beautiful." Hand outstretched, she watches how the diamond captures the light, then disperses into splintered rainbows.

"Come 'ere." Wyatt reaches for her, draws her in and kisses her with urgency. They embrace as Callie trembles with excitement.

"Do you want to come in for a little bit?"

"Thanks, but I told my folks I would run by for a visit. I'll call you later?"

"Sounds good." She sits staring into Wyatt's eyes, not attempting to leave the car. "I love you so much, Wyatt Wilson. I cannot wait to be your wife."

Smiling, Wyatt offers, "Only six months to go."

Callie exits the car with her arm outstretched. Wyatt laughs softly in the car, as he watches her retreat into the farmhouse. He feels a calmness that only Callie can create.

CHAPTER 12
Jimmy

She's finally gone and done it. Jimmy ends his phone call with Callie. He feels slightly envious and uncertain if going to Vermont for Callie's wedding is a good idea at this time. The fact that Riley is still in Vermont, and not quite on the path to recovery, he fears she may come into contact with Prue. Lost in thought, it takes a moment for him to recognize the buzzing on his desk. He smiles when he picks up the phone.

"Prue-bear, how was school today?"

"Fine. Can I have Libby over?"

"Just fine?"

"Can I have Libby over, daddy?"

"Prue, what aren't you telling me about school? I can hear something is wrong in your voice."

"It's nothing."

This is like pulling teeth.

"Prue," he says authoritatively.

"Fiiiine," Prue exaggerates. "Miss James may be calling you."

"Why, what happened?"

Exhaling loudly, "Tommy said something to me today about Libby and it wasn't nice, so I socked him."

Stifling a laugh, "Did you hurt him? What did he say?"

"He's fine. His cheek got red, but Dad, he said that Libby is a faker."

"Faking what?"

"He said that she doesn't really need to limp around school; that her ankle is fine, that she never was shot."

"Oh, I see," he says thoughtfully. "I hope you socked him real good then."

Stunned momentarily before speaking, Prue says, "Oh, I did, but I feel kinda bad now."

"Here's the thing. I'm proud that you stuck up for your friend. That takes a lot of guts. Mrs. Canfield is right, you are a very brave young lady."

"Thanks, Daddy."

"You can apologize to Tommy when we go in to speak to the principal."

"The principal?" Panic rises in her voice.

"It's going to be okay. I promise. Now, call Libby and see if she can come over. I'll be home around 5:30 tonight. I think I'll call Miss James so she doesn't have to make the call. Did you check with Jennifer to make sure it's okay with her that Libby comes over?"

"Yep. She said that I had to call you first about school. I told her all about it. She said I shouldn't wait until you get home to tell you."

"She's a smart lady. Do you feel a little better now?"

Prue lets out a sigh of relief. "Yes, I do."

"Good. I'll see you later on. And Prue, you did the right thing, sweetie. We'll work all this out. Not to worry."

"Bye, Daddy."

Will this ever end? Poor Jennifer had to deal with that mess. That's not exactly what I'm paying her for. I'll have to get the full story from her when I get home.

Jimmy picks up the phone again and dials the school.

"You must have been surprised by her being so forthcoming about the incident today," Jimmy says to Jennifer with a chuckle.

"I was a little surprised. She's not usually physical with kids that she's upset with."

"Yeah, that part is new. The good news is that she's feeling remorse. She'll be able to get it all out of her system tomorrow when we go in to meet with the principal, Tommy, and his parents."

"Oh boy. She's never going to be able to sleep tonight."

"She'll be fine. I won't need you tomorrow afternoon. I'll be going straight to school at three, and then when we're done, I'll drive her home, so I'll see you Friday."

"Sounds good. Good luck tomorrow. Oh, hey, Libby wants Prue to spend the night on Friday. I left a note from her mom in the kitchen."

"Okay, thanks."

Jennifer is hesitating at the door. "So, uh, if Prue is busy Friday night, I was wondering, if you're not busy that is, if you'd like to go to a concert in the park with me?" she says, blushing wildly.

This is unexpected. "Sure, sounds like fun. Should I come pick you up? What time's the show?"

"Show starts at eight."

"Great, I'll come get you around six. We can get a bite to eat before the show," sounding much more confident than he is feeling.

"Great." She smiles as she leaves.

What am I doing? The last time Jimmy was on a date was years ago with Becca. That coffee date he had didn't really count.

He really liked her, but the age difference would never have worked out. *But Jennifer, there's something about her.* He decides this could be a good thing.

Pulling into Jennifer's apartment parking lot draws a flutter he hadn't noticed before.

"Hey, there, you look great."

"Thanks," she says, unusually quiet and shy.

"Where to? Pick your poison."

As he drives to their dining destination, Jimmy takes the lead and fills in Jennifer about the meeting he had yesterday at Prue's school.

"It went as well as could be expected. She apologized to Tommy. He handled it pretty well. We discussed what is really the root of the problem. He understood." Stopping his dissertation momentarily, he looks at Jennifer. "I'm boring you, aren't I. Sorry about that. I tend to go on and on when it comes to Prue."

"No, you're not boring me at all. So how did the meeting end?"

"We let each of them have their say. They apologized, and that was that. Oh, and she has ISS for two days. The school has a Zero Tolerance policy."

"How is she with that punishment?"

"Fine. Two days of in-school suspension is fair. I mean, she did sock the kid in the face, after all. I'm not gonna lie; it makes me very proud."

Sharing a laugh in the car seems to lighten the mood, and they easily converse for the rest of the ride, through dinner, and enjoy the concert.

"Thanks for a great night," she says, slightly tipsy from the bottle of wine they shared through the show. Fueled with liquid courage, she continues, "I didn't know how you would react when I asked you to go out with me tonight. I'm really happy you decided to come along."

"Me, too," he says, following her to her door.

"Would you like to come in?"

"I should probably go. This was a great idea, and we should definitely do it again soon." Looking at the disappointment in her eyes, he momentarily changes his mind, but common sense stops him. Taking a step closer to her, he asks, "May I kiss you?"

Without a word, she leans into him with a warm, inviting kiss.

"Good night, Jennifer. I'll see you Monday."

CHAPTER 13
Callie

Callie walks down the aisle arm in arm with a well-dressed man, Callie feels anxious about the moment ahead. Searching for that familiar cerulean blue in a sea of blues, browns, and greens she spots them, twinkling at the sight of her. With a wink, she calms. She releases the man to her right and walks the aisle back toward another guest until the last of the guests have been seated. At that moment, she takes her place in the front of the church beside the groom. Jason fidgets with his boutonniere until the blast of the horns announces the procession of the final groom. Ryan is walking arm in arm with his mother, looking sharp in his steel gray suit and black tie. Ryan kisses his mother on the cheek and hugs her tightly, then takes his place next to his groom and the service begins.

Jason looks to Callie for the rings to exchange with his husband. She unties the rings, which are attached by a string to her bouquet, and hands them to Jason. They exchange rings, speak their vows—heartfelt and sincere. The service is sealed with a kiss. Jason and Ryan walk hand in hand down the aisle, beaming, followed by Callie, three groomsmen, and three brides-maids. They stop briefly at the last pew to hug a heavyset woman who jumped in the aisle. They are having difficulty releasing her hug as she speaks loudly. "I'm so proud of my nephew! Be loud and proud! Live your life completely in your truth!" Callie notices that she has a shaul draped over her plump shoulders in the colors of the rainbow. They each kiss her cheek and peel her fingers off their arms.

The reception is about to begin when Wyatt finds Callie.

"You make a fantastic Best Gal. I can tell you take your job very seriously."

"As a matter of fact, I do. I don't want to be the one who screws anything up. Ryan would be mad at me forever."

"Well, you look radiant," he says, his eyes sweeping the length of her body. Taking her by the hand, he gives her a twirl, causing the bottom of her navy blue dress to fluidly extend, which elicits a giggle from Callie.

"You look rather dapper yourself. Just think, in a month from now, we'll be doing the same thing as Ryan and Jason." The mention of their upcoming union opens a window in her soul, allowing butterflies to tumble over one another. Wyatt engages her in one long, sweet kiss.

"I can't wait," he says intensely.

"Time to get back to work," she says regretfully, releasing Wyatt.

"I'll see you in there."

The evening continues until the moment that Callie has been dreading.

"Now let's hear from our Best Gal, Cal," Jason's dad, who is the M.C. for the evening, announces from his perch beside the happy couple's table. Feeling her knees knock as she takes a deep breath, she reaches for the microphone. Before she utters one word, her vision clouds. She takes three deep breaths; she can see everyone watching her, waiting.

"Here's where I'm supposed to be talking," she squeaks out to a rumble of laughter. There's one robust laugh that echos out above everyone's. Callie sweeps the crowd to see who it is. Unable to find the culprit, she continues.

"Okay." Callie clears her throat and dabs at the corner of her eye. "Jason asked me to write something down to say today. He said, 'don't hold back.' It took me many weeks to find just the right words for these two beautiful human beings." She takes time again to compose herself. The room falls silent. "Marriage is not about gender or color or judgment. It's about love. Love is something we should give whenever we can—to give love to ourselves and to give love to each other. It is the reason we're here today. This world is not fair. These men have experienced heartbreak and despair, yet even when things seemed too painful or dark, they didn't lose heart. They didn't lose faith in each other to help see each other through. They lifted their spirits with laughter." Callie's voice crackles with emotion. "We are here today to witness this blessed union and to cheer Ryan and Jason into this mystery of love. My wish for you is a lifetime of happiness, laughter, and even through the tears of uncertainty, may you always have each other's shoulders for comfort. I love you both so very much. Congratulations." She sets the microphone down and begins to move away from the couple, when Jason stands to reach for her hand. Walking around the table for two, he gathers Callie into his arms and kisses her cheek gently. They release and she tries, once again, to walk back to her table, but Ryan takes hold, twirls her once and they both bow to thunderous applause. Then he, too, pulls her in for a gentle kiss and hug. Again, above everyone's applause, she can hear one voice hollering loudest. "That's just beautiful. Just beautiful."

Callie walks back to take her seat next to Wyatt and notices the rotund woman in the back steadily clapping. The large woman sits with a thud causing the parishioners on either side to shift. An image of Callie taking the woman's rainbow shawl and wrapping it around the woman's head, then stuffing the ends into the woman's mouth, flits across her mind. She continues to walk toward Wyatt with a crooked smile.

"That was sensational, Cal," Wyatt says sincerely.

"If I can't even get through my friend's wedding, how am I supposed to get through ours?" she says, rolling her damp eyes.

"You'll get through it. It'll be worth the wait even if I have to wait for you to stop crying. I've waited this long, I think I can wait through a few minutes of tears. Besides, you probably won't be the only one crying."

This tender comment takes Callie by surprise.

"See!" She sits pointing to her fresh tears. "I can't even listen to you right now," she laughs through her tears.

The week leading up to Callie and Wyatt's big day is full of preparation. Callie's parents surprise the two of them with a honeymoon to Hawaii as their wedding gift. This completely blindsides the couple, as it was something they were going to put off until they each had time to save a little more.

Everything is coming together. As is only appropriate, Callie and her parents spend the last half of the week at Aunt Marilyn's. The evening of the rehearsal dinner, Jimmy drives up with Prue, and having the whole family under the same roof makes her feel complete.

After the rehearsal dinner, Callie rides back to the family house with Wyatt. This gives them a few minutes to be alone before their big day. Callie is surprised as he drives past her aunt's house. Taking a left onto that old familiar gravel road, she glances out the window, noticing the vegetable garden illuminated by the moon. She can see through her adjusting eyes that there is someone out there watering the vegetables and smiles at the thought of the woman placing ripe tomatoes on her front porch for passers-by to stop and make a selection, leaving money on the honor system, in the mason jar on the dilapidated table. *What would happen if I took all the tomatoes and didn't leave a dime?*

Making one last right, they drive down that serpentine lake road with a spectacular view of the lake stretched out in front of them. *Wonder how hurt I would get if I opened the car door right now, and jumped out?* He pulls into his family home's driveway. "Are your parents expecting us?" Callie asks, uncertain of this destination.

"Nope. Just thought we'd take a walk down memory lane." Clasping hands, they walk through the Wilsons' backyard into the Black Forest. *Butterflies.* Even though it is July, a chill runs up her spine, not of uncertainty, but of excitement. Wyatt continues through the woods until he comes to a tall, sturdy tree on the edge of a cluster of trees.

"I wish I could take a picture of this place," she says just above a whisper. Releasing Wyatt's hand, she slowly walks in a circle, taking in the spectacle. Fireflies dot the darkness, flickering between trees like light bulbs refusing to extinguish their light. She raises her head to the heavens, notices the glow of Orion's Belt high above them, turns toward the sound of the lapping waves against the shore. The shimmer of the moon casts a ripple of incandescent light taps which into all her senses. Wyatt watches her take in the scene, marveling at the way she appreciates the beauty of nature, one of the many things he loves about this woman.

"Cal," Wyatt calls to her.

Turning, he sees her ubiquitous tears lingering, not yet fallen as she turns to him.

"Come here," he says to her with the tenderness one uses to address a small child. She walks to his open arms. They stand in the splendor of the moment. "How does this tree look? Will it do?" Uncertainty becomes clarity as he removes a Swiss Army Knife from his pocket.

"Yes, that'll do just fine." She watches as he carves WW + CW into the tree. She takes the knife and adds a heart around the initials. They walk silently back to the car after taking a moment to admire their handiwork.

"Wouldn't want you to turn into a pumpkin," Wyatt says as he checks the time on his watch. "I'm not supposed to see my bride after midnight."

In Aunt Marilyn's driveway, Wyatt climbs out of the red truck and walks Callie to the door. "Five minutes to spare," he says smiling, drawing her near. Standing with her arms around his neck, she pulls him in for a lingering kiss. "I can't wait to become Mrs. Callista Wilson." As if to punctuate that remark, she kisses him passionately, releases him and opens the door.

Wyatt, flustered, smirks with a fire in his eyes, "You better get some rest tonight, because tomorrow night, you won't be sleeping at all."

"Goodnight, Wyatt," she says, stifling a giggle. Callie leans against the closed door, with her heart pounding. *I'm never going to fall asleep tonight.*

CHAPTER 14
Callie

Standing in front of the heavy, double wooden doors, Callie is filled with nervous energy. *Hurry up already.* Her arm is linked with her dad's. She notices in her periphery that there is someone lingering. Turning, she sees that it's Mrs. Canfield. Stunned, she releases her dad and walks to her. It's obvious she wants to speak to Callie. "Mrs. Canfield, thank you so much for coming. What a nice surprise."

"Callie, you look lovely," she says, kissing Callie's cheek. "You do realize you're walking down the aisle with the wrong man, don't you?" Feeling as though she's touched an electric current with a wet finger, Callie looks on, stunned. The music begins, and like that, Mrs. Canfield exits the vestibule as the doors open.

Jokingly, Callie's dad takes her by the elbow and guides her through the double doors saying, "It's not too late if you want to change your mind."

Callie's dad kisses her cheek and releases her, turning to Wyatt to shake his hand, and returns to Mrs. Lamply's side in the first pew. Wyatt takes Callie's hand and gives it a gentle squeeze, mouthing the words *you look beautiful.* With the return of the energetic fluttering in her chest, she thinks, *this is definitely the right man.*

The service begins. Callie nods her head as she listens to the minister of Franklin Methodist Church. The flickering light from the candles on the altar causes the crystals in her veil to twinkle. It's all a blur, and before she can catch her breath, it's time for her to say her vows. She recites what the minister has her repeat, and Wyatt does the same. Callie catches her mother dotting at her eyes with a tissue, then looks beyond her and sees Aunt Marilyn turning to the end of her empty pew, nodding in an imaginary conversation. She looks back at the minister as he announces to Wyatt, "You may kiss your bride." She feels her veil shift as if a slight breeze crosses her path. He leans in, and for a millisecond, before their lips meet and she closes her eyes, there is a dark shadow that develops behind Wyatt. After the kiss the shadow is gone. Wyatt and Callie turn towards the congregation, arms raised in jubilation, and swiftly walk down the aisle. The double doors are opened for them to exit. Wyatt pulls Callie to him, "God, I love you." The wedding party files in forming a receiving line beside the happy couple before she can return the sentiment.

The limo is waiting for them, and as they walk down the steps of the church, the family lines their way with sparklers lit. The enchanting image will forever be burned in Callie's mind. This wonderfully warm reception continues at the state park where the party is held. The shelter near the lake is decorated with white lights draped along the beams. The dinner is served family style at each white linen covered table. Jimmy and Prue gently touch their glasses after the first toast. Aunt Marilyn finishes and quickly refills her champagne glass after each toast, soon conversing with herself. The speeches begin, first with Wyatt's best man, Tommy, his youngest sibling, quickly moving on to Maddie's Maid of Honor speech, laced with obscenities. At this point in the evening, it's apropos and all is spoken with the heartfelt vulgarity that only Maddie can get away with. After the last laugh, the first dance draws the crowd to the dance floor. Just as the real dance party gets underway, the fireworks begin. Oohs and ahhs resound as they drift across the lake into the open windows of the cabins.

At one particular cabin sits one person not invited to the party. Riley. She steps out of her grandmother's cabin, watching the festivities take place. Feeling a twinge of jealousy, she knows Prue is there with Jimmy. She knows this because that's all anyone in this small town has talked about for months. It's the most exciting event that has taken place in this sleepy town for quite some time, and she knows that Callie wouldn't have a wedding without her brother present. A bead of condensation drips down the side of the vodka bottle set beside her. Tracing the path with her thumb, she thinks of a way to see her daughter. She places the bottle to her lips and takes a long, hard swallow.

Oblivious to the scheming inside Riley's head, the revelers on the opposing side of the lake continue to enjoy the evening with music and dance until the wee hours. The last two standing are Callie and Wyatt. Jimmy is one of the last guests to leave.

"Cal, I gotta hand it to you. You sure know how to throw a party. It took you long enough," he says with a wink and a squeeze. "You take care of my sister, you hear?" Jimmy says, tongue in cheek, to Wyatt.

"You got it. This one I'm going to take care of until we are well past old and gray."

"Prue, you make one of the prettiest bridesmaids I've ever seen," Callie says sincerely to her niece. The affection is mutual. "Where are you guys staying tonight?"

"Aunt Marilyn's."

"Perfect. Say hi to Lilian for me."

"Who's Lilian?" Prue asks.

"I'll explain on the way over," Jimmy says to Prue, then turns and mouths the words *thanks a lot.*

"All right, beautiful, our chariot awaits," Wyatt says as he places his hand onto the small of her back, sending ripples of electricity up her spine.

Climbing into the limo, thankful that she chose a simple, lightweight wedding gown—a strapless, lace, asymmetrical, sheath dress to show off her slip-on silver-heeled sandals and her figure. This style is an attempt at comfort in this July heat. She watches with fascination out the window as the light seems to shift and buckle. It's only there for an instant, then disappears. She makes a mental list of things to discuss with Aunt Marilyn.

Wyatt had removed his beige linen sport coat, revealing his suspenders hours ago. He climbs in the back of the car and immediately pulls Callie close.

"Did you have a good time?"

"The best," she says, glowing.

Placing his arm around her, she rests her head on his chest, listening to his heartbeat. "Did you notice anything strange during the service?"

"You mean stranger than Ryan's aunt making a scene?"

"Yeah, how about that?" she says, raising her head to look him in the eye, then resuming her position. "No, I mean, did you feel an energy? Something around you at the front of the church?" She's uncomfortable having this conversation and continues to avoid eye contact. "Did you *feel* anything?"

"No, not really. Nothing more than excitement. Why are you bringing this up? Did *you* feel something?"

"I thought I saw something. Aunt Marilyn was acting like … well … herself and it gave me the willies. I have a very active imagination, and I thought I saw someone or something standing beside you. Then it was gone. It was probably nothing."

"I suppose it could have been something. You never know what's going to happen when Marilyn is around."

Shaking her head, Callie speaks, "I don't want to talk about it anymore. It's my wedding day. I have more important things to think about." The image of Wyatt waiting for her at the front of the church floats through her head.

Turning toward him, not noticing the tears springing to life in her eyes, she leans in for a long, passionate kiss. Not one of urgency, but of comfort and calm. One formed decades ago, one to last a lifetime, a kiss that holds their future. The back of his hand sweeps across her cheek, resting at the base of her neck.

"Excuse me, sir," the driver says, clearing his throat, "where to?"

"Grey Gables Mansion," Wyatt says to the driver, then to Callie, "and tomorrow we leave for our honeymoon."

"After you, Mrs. Wilson," he says with a smile as Callie walks into their room at the bed and breakfast.

"That sounds so amazing, Mr. Wilson," she says with a giggle. A feeling of nervousness creeps into her belly, something she hasn't felt in years. Wyatt walks slowly toward Callie and sits at the edge of the bed, holding her hand as she stands in front of him. He places his hands on her hips and pivots her so that her back is toward him. He slowly unzips her gown and watches as it gathers at her feet. She steps over it and removes her sandals. Turning back around, she reaches up to unclasp and remove what is left between them and stands before him.

"You are so beautiful," he says in the darkness of the room. Standing now, she removes his layers until they are baring everything for each other. A new chapter, a new beginning that feels so comfortable yet with that familiarity of one another's bodies, something has changed. As if signing that legal document, becoming one, has changed them. This feels new, uncharted. The thrill of making love as a married couple for the first time is intoxicating. Their movements are fluid, like a well-oiled machine.

The muscle memory from years ago causes their bodies to move without hesitation. Eager to please, eager for more; their appetites are insatiable. They find themselves in a pile of sheets on the floor beside the bed, breathless. Wyatt lets a deep breath escape his lips as he lies on his back.

"What got into you? If this is what's in store for the rest of my life, I'm going to have to get more cardio in."

Laughing, Callie straddles his waist. "Let's start with some hip thrusters," she says in a husky voice, undulating her hips, "and some plank push-ups, and maybe downward dog." Callie says looking into Wyatt's wide-eyed expression. After shaking the shock, Wyatt grins and says, "I think I can oblige."

CHAPTER 15
Riley

Riley shuffles to the door with uneven footing. Faltering at the steps, she rights herself. She yanks the car door handle and climbs in. *I should be able to see my daughter whenever I want to. Who does he think he is?*

When she shifts the lever on the steering column into drive, the car lurches forward. Riley drives up Lake Road and takes a left, cutting the corner too short. The sound of screeching metal reverberates through the car. On a mission now, she doesn't seem to notice the mangled stop sign she's left behind. Weaving down the empty road, she barely slows her speed and cuts a wide berth toward the State Park, where the reception is coming to an end. Gliding to a stop at the entrance of the park, she realizes that there is a guard standing at the station. Turning her car around, she parks along the side of the road, hidden from the guests. Riley climbs out of the car and walks through the tree line. Hiding in the pines, she watches the last of the partygoers as they pack up to leave. There, skimming rocks with her dad, is Prue. She watches as he picks up a rock and places it into Prue's hand, explaining how to cock her wrist and release to get a good skip across the water. She releases the rock, and though it's barely visible in the dark, Prue jumps around with excitement. Jealousy is coursing through Riley's veins. *That should be me.* Jimmy's head turns quickly, and for a moment, Riley is sure she has been seen, but then notices an elderly woman walking toward Jimmy and Prue. Jimmy turns, calls to Prue, and they walk toward the parking lot. Riley turns quickly and stumbles back through the trees. A few feet from her car, she trips and is shocked by the sting of a branch, as it slaps her cheek. Scrambling to her feet, she feels moisture on her chin. Not wanting to take the time to evaluate her injury, she forges on. *I can't miss them.* She sits in the idling car, waiting. Soon Jimmy, Prue and what seems to be Aunt Marilyn drive past the guard and wave. They take a right back toward town, with Riley driving some distance behind them. Riley can tell by the direction they are travelling that Prue and Jimmy are headed back to Aunt Marilyn's farmhouse. *Good,* she thinks to herself as she finishes what's left of the bottle.

"When I get married, I'm going to have a huge wedding party, and have it outside just like Aunt Callie," Prue smiles, "and Uncle Wyatt."

Jimmy returns the smile at hearing the *uncle* attached to Wyatt.

"You have a long time to think about that, sweetheart."

"Yeah, I know, but didn't they meet when they were really young?"

"Yes, but several years older than you are." Turning to Prue as they enter the kitchen, he asks, "Why? Is there some boy you like already?" causing a blush to creep across her cheeks.

"Day-ad," she says, rolling her eyes.

"Good, let's keep it that way. It's getting late, you should go brush your teeth and hit the hay," he says, tousling her hair as he walks past.

Riley sits on the side of the garage, out of sight, waiting for an opportune time to enter the house. Having grown up in these parts, she knows how trusting the farming community is. No one locks doors in this town. As she peeks around the corner, she sees the light in the kitchen go out. She leans too far, rolls onto her side, then quickly rolls back over, out of view. Riley squints at her watch and decides to wait an additional 30 minutes before moving forward with her plan.

Riley wakes with a snort, panic rising up in her chest. *Crap, crap, crap.* Thinking she missed her opportunity, she checks her watch again and sees that she had fallen asleep for an hour. *Still time.* Wiping drool from her cheek, she creeps toward the door, crouched and staggering with a headache forming behind her left eye socket. She places her hand on the door to the kitchen, tries to open the door quietly, but the creaking of the doorframe announces her visit, and she freezes. One foot in and one foot out of the house, she waits to see if there is movement inside. Nothing. She continues inside. In the living room, she sees family portraits on the table stand by the couch, and for a moment, she feels a bit of melancholy as she begins to walk up the stairs. The weight of her foot lands on the first step with a moan. Taking another step, willing the steps to cooperate, she makes it to the landing undetected. Looking up the remaining four steps and the closed doors in the hallway she has a decision to make. *Which room?* Opening the first door as quietly as possible she immediately hears the familiar breathing pattern of her former lover. Feelings of forgotten longing bubble up to the surface. She doesn't notice the squeak on the stairs as she continues to stare at Jimmy's chest rising and falling gently, unaware of the unwanted visitor. She tentatively steps further into the room. Standing next to him, she places a hand on his beating chest. Through the crack in the door, she notices movement in the shadows in her peripheral vision and turns with a jerk. She retreats from the room and silently closes the door behind her. As she turns, she is met with resistance. Jimmy's Aunt Marilyn stands there, arms folded over her chest. This shock to the system causes bile to rise to the back of her throat.

"Riley, I'm not sure what you're up to, but this is not the time nor the place."

"Marilyn, get out of my way."

"You're drunk. Go home."

Riley shoves Marilyn backwards, causing her to stumble. She catches herself on the armrest of the child-sized rocking chair holding Lilian. The doll falls to the ground. Marilyn dives for Lilian to keep the doll's porcelain face from hitting the floor.

"Lilian!" Marilyn yells, safely retrieving the doll.

The door behind Riley opens with a thud. "What's go— what are *you* doing here?" Surveying his surroundings, Jimmy glares at Riley, now with her hand on the doorknob of Prue's room.

"I'm here to see my daughter," she says, tripping over her own feet as she opens the bedroom door.

"I don't think so," Jimmy says, crossing the hallway in two steps.

Riley's stomach roils with the consumed vodka from hours before.

Jimmy reaches for her hand and removes it roughly as the contents of her stomach land with a splat on Jimmy's bare feet.

"Perfect," he says, mostly to himself.

Aunt Marilyn watches the spectacle with Lilian in her arms, caressing the head of the doll. She places the doll gently back on the rocking chair and walks to Riley. Taking her by the elbow, Marilyn leads her down the stairs without a word.

Jimmy walks gingerly to the hall bathroom, running water over a hand towel to clean his feet and then to clean the hall. On hands and knees, he wipes the stench filled floorboards.

"Daddy?" Prue opens the door wiping her eye, still warm from her bed.

"Hi, baby. Did I wake you?"

"What was all that noise?"

"Your clumsy dad dropped his midnight snack in front of your door as he was taking a peek into his daughter's room."

"That smells disgusting," she says, wrinkling her nose.

"Go back to bed. It's really late," he says, giving her a kiss on the cheek before she turns in.

Jimmy walks down the stairs to find Aunt Marilyn and Riley sitting at the kitchen table with mugs of hot coffee. Riley looks pale under the kitchen light, and for a moment, Jimmy feels sorry for her.

"I just wanted to see my daughter," she says with pleading eyes.

"Rye, you can't just walk into the house in the middle of the night to see our daughter. What did you think you were going to do? Take her away without any consequences? You clearly haven't stopped drinking. There's no way you can care for a child if you can't even care for yourself," he says, feeling frustrated. "Get your shit together."

"Jimmy," Aunt Marilyn coos, placing a hand on his hand.

"I can't talk about this tonight. I'm exhausted. I have to take a shower, and I have to get Prue back home tomorrow. So if you'll excuse me and my puke-laden feet, I'm going back upstairs," he announces, looking down at his feet. Then with one last glance toward Riley, "I'll be contacting my lawyer tomorrow."

CHAPTER 16
Callie

"I take it from the glow on your tanned face that you had a fabulous honeymoon?" Jason asks Callie as they walk together into the hospital to start a new week at work.

"Uh, yeah. You can say that. And how's married life for you?"

"I never knew I'd love being married so much," Jason says wistfully as he looks down at the silver band around his finger. "Ryan has become more domesticated and turned into some sort of neat freak. Something I *never* thought would happen. I walk into the house, and I can't find things anymore. He's organized all our closets, which is nice, but he's even alphabetized the chip bags in our pantry. That seems a little excessive to me. He may have a problem," Jason jokes.

"Hi, my name is Ryan and I have OCD. I *have* to arrange things according to shape and size in my kitchen," Callie continues.

"The first step is recognizing you have a problem," Jason laughs as he steps aside and lets her enter the art room first.

Callie takes her seat at the art table and waits for her first patient of the day.

Hours later, Callie meets Wyatt for lunch. Just before the wedding he was transferred to a new location, which added a little more stress to the already stressful process of getting married. Now moved into their new home, things have calmed down and they are settling into a comfortable rhythm.

"Hey you. How's your day going?" Callie asks Wyatt with a kiss as they stand ready to order their lunch.

"It's a little crazy at work today. One of the managers is flying out from Rhode Island to check on progress at this location, so everyone is trying to get organized for his visit."

"Ick. That makes for a long day."

"How's your day going? How are the kids? Anyone new this week?"

"Not yet. Good news, one of our kiddos is now in remission, so that's a cause for celebration," she says as she raises a glass to Wyatt. He clinks his glass to hers.

"Do over. You have to look at me when we toast or it's bad luck."

This time Wyatt looks deep into Callie's eyes as they touch glasses. This intimate gesture of continued eye contact causes her insides to melt.

"Why, Mr. Wilson, I do believe those are your bedroom eyes."

"I like this tradition. It's a shame we're in a restaurant," he says with a husky voice.

"Then I better get back to work to make this day go by faster. I can't wait to have your eyes above me later," she says as she grabs his knee under the table and stands to leave. Waiting for him to join her, she tilts her head and looks quizzically at him.

"You go on. I think I need a minute," he says, looking down to his lap. Giggling, Callie leaves her lunch date with a peck on the cheek and, for good measure, a quick nibble on his earlobe.

The remainder of the day is uneventful: lots of paints, construction paper, and the one thing she hates to get out, glitter. Sweeping up the remnants of the stardust draws a memory of the evening decades ago when Wyatt and Callie watched the northern lights. The thought warms her chest as she continues to sweep mindlessly. Looking down, she notices construction paper caught under a cabinet that she sometimes moves from building to building. Crouching down, she pulls a childish drawing of a castle carefully from under the wheels. It reminds her of the drawing that Tyler made for her. As she stands and steps back to resume clean up, a thought pops up in her head.

I wonder how he's doing these days? I'll have to ask Wyatt about that later ton-

The fall happens so quickly that the sound of crashing supplies doesn't register immediately. Flat on her back with the wind knocked out of her, she lies looking up at the ceiling as the glitter plumes overhead and falls slowly, twinkling as it descends around her. The pain in her head is searing. Within minutes Jason is in the room calling to her. *Is he wearing a new cologne?* It's an odd thing to think about, but it's her last thought before everything goes black.

Callie's eyes flutter open slowly. She feels the dull pain still lingering. The light from the rising sun peeks over the horizon through her hospital room window, the blues and pinks feathering the sky. The warmth of Wyatt's hand in hers makes her smile. Gently, she rubs her thumb over his, causing him to stir. He has pulled a chair over to her bedside, sitting vigil throughout the night.

"Cal?" his hoarse voice speaks. His hair looks like that of Animal from the Muppets.

"Hi."

"How are you feeling?"

She takes an inventory of her body: head hurts, back hurts, and abdomen is on fire.

"Okay. How long have I been here?"

"Since Jason called an ambulance a day and a half ago. What happened?"

"I don't know. One minute I was cleaning up the art supplies ,and the next I was on the floor in pain."

"We're very fortunate Jason was still there and heard you fall."

The attending nurse enters with a knock and checks her vitals before exiting. "The doctor should be here in a few minutes."

"Are my parents here?"

"They were here the minute they heard you were in the hospital. They went home to change, but they'll be back shortly."

"Geez. I hate to worry them like this. Can you call them and tell them to not worry and get some sleep, that we'll call when we know something?"

By the look on his face, she knows it is a losing battle.

"Uh, no. You know how your mother is. She'll want to be here with you. As it is, she'll be pissed when she finds out you woke up right after she left."

The doctor enters with a chart in his hands and takes a seat on the end of the bed.

"How's our patient doing?"

"I'm a little sore where I fell."

Standing to the side of the bed now, he places his palm on the back of his hand and presses around her belly, "And what about here?" She shakes her head no. "Here?" Again, no. He moves over her abdomen and before he can ask, she yelps. He continues surveying her body as he moves to her shoulders and the back of her head. "Here?" Her response is a grimace. He picks up his chart and makes a notation. "I'd like to take you to x-ray and check things out. I'll have someone in to wheel you down shortly. In the meantime, rest," he says, patting her leg as he leaves the room.

"Hey, doc," Wyatt calls out as he follows the doctor out of the room.

"What do you think is wrong with her?"

"Her fall was really hard. Do you happen to know how it happened?"

"Not sure yet."

"Is she on birth control?"

This question throws Wyatt. "No. She figured at her age that it wasn't necessary, and if anything happened, it would be a happy blessing."

"So you were actively trying to conceive?"

"Well, we are newlyweds."

"I see. I suspect that she is pregnant."

"What? That's amazing!"

"But the pain gives me reason to pause. Let me get an ultrasound and do some more bloodwork. The fact that she was out for so long worries me, as well."

"Okay. So I shouldn't get my hopes up. Got it."

"We'll know in a few hours what's going on."

CHAPTER 17
Jimmy

"Yes, she's still drinking," Jimmy says with a sigh to his lawyer on the phone. "I don't think she's ever going to stop."

"That may be true, Jimmy, but for now you need to take steps to ensure Prue's safety. This is very serious. I can't turn a blind eye to this behavior. If Riley had gotten away with taking your daughter, there are a number of scenarios that come to mind, one of which involves you not having a daughter anymore. Riley driving drunk has the very likely possibility of her running into something, or worse, someone. I'm sorry to be so blunt here, but Riley is an unfit mother in the state she is currently in. She's in need of some serious help."

Jimmy sits listening, running his hand through his hair. "I almost lost her when she was in first grade, and that was the worst experience of my life. What can I do?"

"This isn't an easy battle. It won't be cut and dry. Can you prove that she is drinking to excess while visiting with Prue even when it's a supervised visit? Can you prove that Prue is in danger?"

"Don't you think walking into a house unannounced, trying to kidnap my daughter while under the influence is enough to stop her visitation rights?" His voice starts to rise as his vice grip on the phone produces white knuckles.

"I understand your frustration, Jimmy. We'll get this worked out. Let me see if I can get a court date with this new information, and we'll take it from there."

Jimmy ends the call by throwing the phone across the room. He's at work and needs to remain calm, but this is getting to be too much. Magazines fall from his table by the door, landing atop the cell phone. The magazines start vibrating against the wall. "*Shit.*" He scrambles across his office and removes some magazines. "Hello?"

"Jimmy, it's Mom. Your sister has fallen and she's in the hospital." After a twenty-minute phone call explaining the situation, Jimmy feels exhausted. *Things usually happen in threes. What's next?*

Days later, he hears from his lawyer that, yes, Riley will no longer have visitation rights until she completes yet another rehab stint. Once that is completed, she will be reevaluated. "That works for me. Why do I feel a *but* coming?"

"*But,* we can't locate Riley. It seems she's run off." *And there's number three.*

"Isn't that just perfect," Jimmy says sarcastically.

"I have contacted the local authority. She'll show up."

"Great. Thanks," Jimmy says flatly, hanging up the phone.

Being a Friday night, Prue walks toward him and sits by his side. "Daddy? Is something wrong with Mom again?"

Jimmy scoops Prue up and pulls her onto his lap. She sits, balled up in his arms, resting her head on his chest. "Nothing you have to worry about, Prue-bear."

"It sounds serious. I can tell by the tone of your voice."

"Were you listening to my conversation?"

"Most of it."

"She's your mom, so you should know what's going on. It's mostly adult stuff, so I'll leave that part of it out. Here's what you need to know. You won't be having visits with Mom for a while ... again."

"Is she still drinking?"

"Yes."

"Then good. When she's drinking, she acts weird and smells funny."

"I'm sorry, kiddo. This must really stink for you."

"It's okay, Dad. It's the only way I've known her to be."

Feeling sad for his daughter, he attempts to remedy the situation.

"Whaddya say we go check out a movie tonight?"

"Oh, thanks, Dad, but some of the girls are getting together to work on a science project. Is it okay if I go with them?" This stage she's in at the moment, caught between little girl and blossoming young woman, is a struggle.

"Sure, sweetie. I'll drive you over when you're ready," he says, with a twinge of melancholy.

"Thanks, Dad," she says with a hug around his neck and a kiss on the cheek.

Jimmy drops off Prue for what has turned into a sleepover. Having his night freed up, he picks up the phone.

"Hi, Cal. How're you feeling? Did the doctor tell you what's going on?"

"Hey, Jimmy. Yes, finally. It seems I hit my head pretty hard. Stupid glitter. I hate that stuff. Nothing good ever comes from it. It gets into every nook and cranny, and in case you didn't know, it makes the ground very slippery." She keeps to herself the information that broke her heart into tiny little irreparable pieces. Listening to the doctor say the words "ectopic pregnancy" nearly sent Wyatt over the edge. Seeing him so distraught and vulnerable made it that much more difficult to hear.

"I used to hate when Prue would bring art projects home with glitter on them. It would show up everywhere and eventually end up on my face," he says with a laugh. They talk for a while about Prue and the situation with Riley.

"I'm sorry to hear that. I was really hoping she would straighten out. Prue needs a positive female role model in her life."

"That's where you come in."

"Me? I'm just the aunt."

"Yes, but you get her. She thinks you walk on water. It's a match made in heaven."

"Can you blame her?" she teases.

"Somehow I knew you were going to make a joke about this, but I'm serious. Maybe you guys can spend some time together."

"Jimmy, you need to find someone to fill those shoes. Don't you think you'll ever remarry?"

"Do you think you'll ever have kids?" *Ouch.*

"Touché."

Hanging up the phone, he thinks about what she's said and dials again.

"Hello?"

"Jennifer, it's Jimmy. Whatcha doing tonight?"

Sitting in the silence of her bedroom, the image of Wyatt's face comes to mind. He struggles with the new information that he is going to be a dad—then, *poof,* he isn't. They removed the title as they removed her damaged fallopian tube. Now, with little chance of conceiving, it looks like she and Wyatt won't be parents the old-fashioned way. At her age, she knows the chance of her having a baby is slim to none.

There is a knock at the door. She wipes her face quickly and suppresses her emotions.

"Come on in."

"Hey there, beautiful. How are feeling?"

"Still have a dull headache, but feeling better, thanks."

Wyatt sits next to her on the bed and places an arm around her shoulders.

"I was thinking. We could adopt, you know. This parent thing isn't over yet."

"I know. The thought crossed my mind, but it's too soon. Can we pin this conversation for another time?"

"Sure thing. You should rest. I'll make some dinner and have it ready for you when you wake up," Wyatt says, kissing her and closing the door softly.

Callie snuggles down under her comforter and falls into a deep sleep.

CHAPTER 18
Riley

Riley wakes, head pounding, and slowly sits up with a groan. Her memory of the night before is foggy, but slowly comes back to her. *Jimmy. Marilyn. Prue. Puke.* Her face torques in discomfort. Movement in her belly feels like a grease fire that can't be extinguished. Her stomach twists as she lunges for the toilet, purging herself of what's left of its contents: vodka and Tylenol.

I just want my baby back. She thinks to herself between each violent episode. *I'm not going back to rehab. What drinking problem? That's BS. It's his fault. I drink because he stresses me out. It's his fault* she thinks one last time, spits, and watches the sputum swirl down the toilet.

Her phone vibrates with an incoming text.

> Jimmy: *I contacted my lawyer. You'll be notified tomorrow of this, but I thought I'd be the one to tell you. You are no longer allowed to see Prue until you are clean and sober and we have notification of successfully completing rehab.*

Shocker, she thinks, as she walks into a kitchen in disarray. Her throat is bone dry and in need of quenching. She opens the fridge to find fast food containers of leftovers, month-old milk and moldy bread, all hopes dashed. She pulls on the freezer door, *bingo,* and pulls out a fresh bottle of booze. *See what you make me do?* She twists the cap off, tilts her head back and thirstily drinks four large swallows. The liquid slides down her parched throat. She welcomes it like a crack in the desert soil accepting the mist of a summer shower. Feeling liquid courage coursing through her veins, she texts back.

Riley: *Son of bitch. She's my daughter! You and your slimy lawyer can't keep her from me.*

Jimmy: *Way to keep it classy, Riley. Seriously, get some help if you ever want to see her again.*

Riley throws her phone into the couch and watches in surprise as it bounces from the cushion into a frame holding a picture that Prue drew for her as a child. The glass of the picture frame splinters and falls to the floor, like a glacier carves an iceberg. Walking over to retrieve the phone, she dials her sister Megan. Before dialing, she draws from the bottle again and throws back another four swallows.

"Meg, it's me. I need to see you."

"Want me to come get you?" she asks, knowing full well Riley has been drinking again.

"Why? I'm fine to drive."

"Are you fine? You don't sound fine. I'll be over in 20."

"Shit. Why does everyone think I'm drinking all the time? Forget it. I'm going to J.D.'s if you wanna meet me. If not, screw you." Still holding the bottle in a death grip, she decides to spend the remainder of the early afternoon emptying it.

Riley stumbles through the door and down the steps to her car, preparing to exit the driveway. She sees the car door is still open, but can't for the life of her remember when she drove here last, who she drove with, or for that matter, what day of the week it is. She continues to back out of the driveway with the gravel under the tires spitting out in every direction. A horn blares behind her and she slams on the brakes. Once the car passes, she continues on her way.

The *open* sign glows in the window, welcoming all who are eager to drink their day away. Riley slides on to a bar stool and asks for a double. Drinking that down with one gulp, she orders another. The bartender looks at her sideways as she reaches for the bottle once again. Slamming the next shot, down she asks for one more.

"Sorry, sweetheart. It looks like you've had enough already."

Disgusted with that answer, Riley throws the money to cover the drinks at the woman behind the bar. "I didn't want any more anyway."

Nearly falling backwards off the stool, she teeters on the brink of collapsing to the floor, but rights herself, and waltzes over to the jukebox. Dropping some coins in the process, she eventually gets one in the slot and presses numbers randomly. She begins to dance by herself on the dance floor. The dance is more a display of defying gravity.

"You look lonely, young lady," says the man from the corner who has been watching her make a spectacle of herself.

"Yur damn right," Riley slurs, grabbing him around the waist. As they dance, the man pulls her in and traces her back with his fingers until he has a hold of her rearend.

"I think's it time to take this pardy to yur place," Riley manages.

The gentleman doesn't need to be asked twice. He takes her hand and guides her to his car under the leery eye of the bartender.

"Joe, she a friend of yours?" she calls from behind the bar to the longtime patron.

"She is now."

On the drive to Joe's house, Riley falls asleep briefly. Once in the garage, she wakes and leans in to unzip his pants.

"Hey, hey, hey. There's time for that when we get inside. Let me help you in the house."

Thinking he's going to have a wild night, he soon realizes that she isn't capable of walking on her own, let alone trying out the crazy new positions he's been conjuring up on the ride home. Half carrying, half dragging Riley inside, he plops her down on the oversized beanbag chair he has in the living room. The moment she lands with a thud, Riley is lights out. Trying to wake her is futile. Frustrated, he decides to let her sleep it off. *I'm not taking advantage of a passed out chick; I'm not that desperate.* He pulls the afghan off the couch and covers her limp body. Checking to make sure she's still breathing, he turns toward his bathroom, unzipping his pants as he walks, ready to take care of business on his own.

Joe wakes to his alarm blaring on the nightstand. He gets up and goes through his morning routine before remembering that he had a guest last night. Not hearing any noise from the other room, he assumes she's still sleeping at this early hour. He walks quietly into the still-dark living room where he can see the outline of the woman he brought home, just as he had left her the night before. *Kiley? Bailey? Damn it, what's her name.* "Hey, sweetheart, I have to get to work. It's time to get up. You want some coffee?" he asks as he walks past her to the kitchen to turn on the overhead light. No response.

"Hey, you up?" Nothing. A steely tingling runs up his spine. Walking with purpose now, he shakes her arm gently, "Hey, you gotta ... oh shit! Shit, shit, shit!" She's cold to the touch as her lifeless body rolls off the beanbag chair. Remnants of vomit are caked to her hair, and as she lies facedown on the floor, the remaining vomit trickles from her mouth. He runs for his cell phone, which is charging at his bedside. Pressing it to life, he dials with shaky hands.

"911, what's your emergency?"

"There's a woman, I think her name is Kiley, or Bailey, or something, she's … I think she's dead."

"What's your location, sir?"

"Can you get someone here NOW?"

"Calm down, sir. What is your location?"

Not able to think straight, he's unable to recite his own address.

"Uh, shit, 165, I mean, 156 Stratton, damn it, Sutton Avenue." He relays the information and promptly hangs up.

CHAPTER 19
Callie

Weeks removed from her fall, Callie has only the laparoscopy scars from the removal of her fallopian tube to show for it. Getting back to work is her number one goal. Few people know what she really went through, and she wants to keep it that way.

Things have gotten back to normal: back to work, running again, and meeting up with old friends.

"It's about damn time we did this," Maddie says, stopping for a drink from her water bottle. "You've been like a zombie lately."

"I know. It's been a rough month," Callie says, taking a long swallow from her water bottle.

"Which trail do we take to get out of this place? If you drag my ass down the eight mile route, I'mo kick your ass!"

"Don't worry, we're only doing five. You're fine," Callie chuckles. "You're the one who said, 'I wanna start running with you, Cal. It'll be fun to work out together.'"

"It was a moment of weakness. Besides, I don't recall saying 'it'll be fun.' I'm not that crazy. I think I'd rather cut my toe on a rusty knife, land in a vat of salt, and rub the salt into my open eyes."

"Please. Don't hold back, Mad. Tell me how you really feel," Callie says sarcastically as she leads the way down the path.

Jogging slowly, Maddie continues, "Thank you, I will continue. I'd rather jump into a vat of simple syrup, crawl out and roll on top of a mound of red ants. Or how about this one: I'd rather streak through an open ... Whatcha doin?" Maddie asks, almost running into Callie as she stops suddenly.

"I think we're going the wrong way. This isn't right."

"Come on, that's not funny."

Seemingly confused, Callie says, "This doesn't look right."

"For real? You brought me all this way and took a wrong turn? What the hell Schmal? Come on, woman, figure it out, I gotta pee."

Turning in a slow circle, she looks out into the vast expanse of trees along the hillside. "Maybe it's that way."

"That's it, I can't hold it any longer." Maddie trots off behind a fallen tree babbling the entire time. "I can't believe you got us lost. Now I'll probably end up with poison ivy on my ass. If I do, you're scratching it for me. You hear me? My ass is your problem to deal with now." Finished, she returns to Callie, who is stretching her calves.

"Do you know which way to go?"

"Of course I do," she says, sounding offended by Maddie's comment.

"Of course you do? What the fuck? That's really not funny."

"Let's go," Callie says as she jogs away from the fallen tree.

Maddie feels slightly baffled by this brief confusion, but continues to follow Callie along the path.

Callie's phone rings as she's driving home after their run. She ignores the call.

"It's your brother," Maddie says, looking at Callie's phone.

"If it's important, he'll leave a message."

After Maddie sets the phone back down in the console, it emits a melody indicating there's a new message.

"Must be important," Maddie says.

"I'll check it out when I get home. Thanks for surviving the run," Callie says cheekily.

"I barely survived. Next time there better be something in it for me."

"You get the health benefits."

"Pu-leeze. If I wanted health benefits, I'd contact my employer," Maddie says, climbing out of the car.

Sitting in her own driveway, she shuts off the car and exhales. *What does he think is so important?* She listens to the message with little interest, but the sound of his voice is different. She detects a slight panic. She presses *call back,* and on the first ring, he answers.

"What's going on, Jimmy? You sound a little freaked out."

"Riley's dead."

"What? How? When?"

Jimmy goes through the scenario with her.

"Just some random guy from a bar?"

"Seems this has been her thing for a while. Drinking to excess, going home with some loser, waking up hung over, getting a ride back to the bar just to repeat the process," he says, exhaling forcefully.

"Have you told Prue yet?"

"No, she's at a friend's house. I'll have to tell her later. Not gonna lie, I'm not looking forward to that conversation."

She sits in the kitchen with elbows on the table, hands clasped and resting under her chin as if in prayer. Wyatt walks through the door.

"Hey, good lookin', whatcha got cookin'?" he says as he plants a kiss on the top of her head.

"A lot. Sit down." Noting the tone in her voice, he sits down as she relays the information.

"Oh, man." They sit quietly across from one another taking in the severity of the situation.

"Looks like we'll be making a trip up to Vermont soon. I hate funerals."

"Riley's fine, Callista. Not to worry," Aunt Marilyn speaks in a conversational tone at the end of the funeral. "She's much happier now than ever before." She turns to her left, looks up toward the ceiling, and nods her head. "Don't worry about her. She says Jimmy is a much better parent than she is. Prue will be happier this way."

"Marilyn, can you keep it down. Her body is barely cold and you're talking like she's standing right in this room," Wyatt says, willing her to be quiet.

Marilyn points to the ceiling, "Not so much standing..."

"Really not the place for this, Marilyn," he scolds.

"You can think whatever you want. I'm just telling you what she's saying to me. Take it or leave-"

"Hey, Tyler! So great to see you!" Callie breaks into the conversation to give Tyler a hug and Samantha a kiss on the cheek. Callie walks outside the church with Samantha, Tyler, and Wyatt and they sit on a bench to catch up. They eventually move to the vestibule for a reception for family and close friends of the deceased. All of Callie's cousins show up in support of the family.

"Our family seems to be getting smaller and smaller," Callie says to no one as she looks out among the small gathering. Prue stands stoically next to her father and her Aunt Megan. They receive condolences while everyone else mills about grabbing dollar sandwiches, potato salad, chips, cookies and a soda. It feels more like a family reunion than a funeral.

CHAPTER 20
Maddie

Maddie breathes heavily after an amorous early morning session with Zach. She sits up on the floor of her bedroom, pulling the comforter around her. Zach reaches out to pull down the comforter to expose her breasts.

"I'm so glad these are all mine again. That kid, Dylan, was really killing my vibe."

Laughing, Maddie tries to pull the comforter back up, but Zach reaches out to fondle her.

"Just a few minutes more? They're glorious!"

"Fine," she says, pulling it down to her waist, turning her head to giggle.

"So I was thinking about taking a trip," she continues speaking as he stares directly at her chest, playing with her breasts as if they were malleable clay.

"Mmhmm," he utters, amused with his toy.

"I think I'm going to see if Callie can road trip with me to New York City. It's been years since we've been there. Do you think you could manage a weekend without me? Or these?" she says, shimmying her shoulders, causing her chest to move as if overfilled water balloons are tethered to her skin.

"I'm not sure I can. I'll do my best."

"Okay, fella, time's up," she says as she pulls the comforter up over her shoulders. Standing, she puts a hand out to help her lover off the floor. Zach pulls Maddie in for an embrace.

"I think that's a good idea, actually. You guys need some girl time. Dyl and I will be just fine." He takes the comforter from her shoulders and continues to make the bed as Maddie pulls on her robe.

"Speaking of Little Man, I believe he's up."

Planning a trip with two headstrong women is not an easy task. Each has their own idea of the itinerary they want to follow. Eventually, Callie and Maddie come to an agreement and the date is set.

"This is exciting! I can't tell you how long it's been since I've been on a trip. And the Big Apple, man, it's been eons since I've been there. Remember when I went there with Charlie?"

"Isn't that when he kinda made it known that he wanted you forever and ever, the end?"

"Yep, and look how that turned out," Callie says sarcastically.

"This is exactly how it should be. I knew from the minute you mentioned Wyatt's name decades ago that he was someone special. Even with his flaws. I mean, we all can't be perfect. It's exhausting!"

Laughing, Callie mentions to Maddie that Wyatt will be able to take them to the airport before work, so no need to drive separately.

"Excellent. Thanks. Now we wait. Three months is a long time, but that time of year should be fun, right?" Maddie asks.

"If you think New York on the first of March is fun, I suppose. It could be freezing, rainy, or worse, snowing."

"Okay, Debbie Downer. Just look at this as an adventure. It'll be amazing no matter what the weather."

Callie and Maddie plan to fly into Newark and take a cab to the hotel in New York City on Friday the 28th of February. Everything is set in motion until a break at work the Monday before Callie is to leave. On this particular Monday, Callie pulls out her laptop to take a peek into the lives of her acquaintances on Facebook as she eats her lunch.

If I see one more photo of her kid on here, I'm going to have to defriend her. Scrolling through each post on her feed, there's always that one friend that shares too much with the world. Continuing to scan, she gets caught up by a video about how to make meals with four ingredients when an instant message at the bottom of her screen pops up from Abby. Abby is a friend she met in college who she's kept in contact with via Facebook over the years.

> Abby: *Hi, Callie … some sad news I thought you'd want to know. Charlie Canfield passed away this past Friday. We live in the same neighborhood and our kids are in school together. I don't know how or why he died at this point. Just praying for his wife and 3 children. The wake is Thursday afternoon, and the funeral Friday.*

Callie's mind goes blank, then images of Charlie float across in cinematic style: tall, dark and handsome; Charlie, the life of the party; Charlie, everyone's best friend; Charlie. The news sends shockwaves through her core. It's a physical reaction, like an electric impulse that causes her hands to tremble and her mind to go numb.

> Callie: *OMG, Abby, I can't believe this, I'm in shock. That's so sad. Poor Liz.*

Abby: *I know! Me too! I actually cried! Charlie and I went to Sandy Hook Elementary School together before I moved away in high school. I moved back sophomore year in college, and when I met my husband, surprisingly, we bought a house a few doors down from Charlie. It's a shock. I didn't mean to ruin your day, but I know he meant a lot to you.*

Callie: *You're right, he did, thank you. He's a part of my past. I'm so sad …*

Abby: *Take care and hug your beautiful family.*

Callie: *I will. You do the same. Let me know if you hear anything. As crazy as this sounds, I'm scheduled to come to NY on Friday. I'm going to see about changing my flight to Thursday so I can go to the wake.*

Callie closes her computer and tries to regain her composure to finish out the day. She puts the news out of her mind until her drive home. As she does in most stressful situations, she calls Maddie.

"Mad. I got some sad news today. Do you remember Abby?"

"Is she the one that thought it would be a good idea to give her bangs a trim at one in the morning and ended up in the hospital with stitches in the webbing between her fingers?"

"Yes, that one. She sent me a Facebook message today telling me that Charlie is dead."

Silence

"Mad? Did you hear me?"

"How is that possible? I talked to Liz last Monday and she was pissed because he was at his annual Ranger Rendezvous in New York."

"It's true, he's dead."

"What the fuck," she says as she exhales.

"I know. It's terrible."

There is a pause in conversation as each of them is in deep thought.

"Welp, I'm gonna go. This is way too depressing. I gotta put on my happy face for Dylan's preschool Spring Sing."

"In February?"

"It's never too early to sing about spring, Cal. At least that's what the music teacher, *Miss Mary Sunshine,* said when I asked her the same question."

With a short burst of laughter, she says, "All right. Talk to you later on."

Callie presses the end call button and sits in her driveway thinking.

For several years, he was the love of my life. I left Wyatt for him. There is an internal struggle going on in her head. *I love him still, but not the romantic kind of love. I madly love Wyatt. What* am *I feeling?* Over the years, it had been a badge of honor for her to see Liz, knowing she was his second choice. Deep down, Callie took pride knowing that Charlie still loved her. A sharp rap on the window startles her.

"You coming in?" Wyatt asks as he stands at the driver side door.

"Yeah, yep. Right now."

If I had married Charlie, I would be a widow.

CHAPTER 21
Callie

Wyatt drops Callie off at the airport. He walks to the trunk to get her bag out and to give her a proper goodbye.

"Bye for now," he says as he hugs her, causing tears to spring to her eyes.

I'm doing the right thing, she says to herself, giving Wyatt a kiss goodbye.

"You need to do this. I know it'll be hard, but you can do it. I'll be around this weekend if you wanna call and give me an update. If not, a quick text?" Callie nods her head. "I know you'll have fun after the business you have to take care of is done. Love you."

"I love you, too," Callie says quietly, feeling a weight on her chest.

Callie sits on the airplane, headed to Newark airport. She has two hours to think. Thoughts of Charlie filter in. She thinks back on the time he visited unexpectedly, up at Gramp's camp. She thinks about how he sat on her bed in the middle of the night, professing his feelings to her. About the time they sat under the willow tree watching ducks swimming and spoke of a future they would have together. *If I had married Charlie, I would be a widow.* This thought keeps rattling around her brain. *Thank God Maddie is meeting me out here tomorrow night.* Maddie is her saving grace. She's the one that Callie talks through all her emotions with. It is too difficult to discuss matters of the heart with Wyatt. Not wanting him to get the wrong impression, she would have to be guarded with her comments. With Maddie, however, that falls away. She can just tell it like it is with no hurt feelings to worry about. *Jealous of a dead man? Surely not.*

Callie closes her eyes recalling a conversation from days ago.

"You know what I think? I think Charlie had a hand in getting you back to Connecticut, aside from the obvious. I think he knew you were headed back east for our trip. I think he chose this week to cash in so that you can make it to his party."

"Really? You? The biggest non-believer, skeptic, cynic, doubting Thomas? You actually think he planned this?"

"You know I don't believe in all the hocus-pocus bullshit, but for some reason, this one time, I'm gonna let it slide. I think there's something to it. Maybe he wanted you to have closure. I don't know? Something feels right about you going to see him."

"I'm scared to see Liz. She hates me, you know."

"Of course she does. I do, too. You can't go on intimidating people like that."

Shocked by this admission, Callie's hand instinctively springs out and slaps Maddie across the face. Maddie continues to talk as if not feeling a thing, "She knows what kind of power you have over Charlie. When I called her after I heard what happened, she told me the services were this weekend and asked if 'that Callie' was going to be there. I said yes," and as Callie is staring morosely, Maddie pulls tiny pink, white and blue objects from her pocket. She grabs Callie's jaw, forcing it open as if coercing a dog to take his pills. One by one, Maddie shoves the tiny objects down her throat. "But she was just joking. I think." Callie, choking, stares on paralyzed with fear.

"You need to go. You guys have a history. It's necessary for your peace of mind to be able to say goodbye. Don't worry about Liz. I'll deal with her later," Maddie finishes with the last of the pills, closing Callie's mouth. She rubs the front of Callie's throat to make the pills continue on to their final destination.

The plane lands with a hard bounce, waking her from her semi-conscious state. Callie feels lingering pain from the realistic dream. She swallows three times in succession. The pain diminishes to a dull ache by the time she picks up her rental car. Callie drives the two-hour drive to Abby's house in Newtown where she is staying for the night. Thankfully, Abby is going to go to the wake with her. Callie needs a buffer. It's late afternoon by the time Callie arrives. Abby is waiting at the door with a glass of wine.

"How did you know I'd need that?"

"Because I would need something a whole lot stiffer than this if I were in your shoes."

They sit at the kitchen table for an hour catching up before it's time to go.

"We should get going," Abby says.

"May as well. It's not going to get any easier."

When they enter the mortuary, Callie is uneasy and fidgeting.

"Come on, Cal. You can do this."

There is a large crowd gathering inside, snaking through a long line that is cordoned off. With each bend in the path, there are mementos, pictures, TVs showing home videos of both Charlie as a child and his own children. At one turn in the line, there stands a small table with a baseball glove signed by all the kids that he coached on a little league team. Callie can feel her throat starting to constrict. Next to the glove is a journal that patrons can flip through, reading entries that his mother has written through the years.

"Oh, Ab, I don't think I can do this. The closer we get to the front of the line, the closer the bile is to reaching the back of my throat. I can't tell if I'm going to puke or shit myself."

Abby takes Callie's hand and squeezes. "It's a normal reaction."

"I'm gonna find a bathroom. I'll be back."

As Callie leaves to fight the flight response she is feeling, Abby opens the journal and reads several passages. The line is moving at a snail's pace. By the time Callie returns, Abby has only moved a few feet.

"You're not going to believe this."

"What happened? Did Liz see that I'm here?" Panic rising.

"Not yet. This journal over here, I was reading through the passages when you went to the restroom. Every page was about Charlie as a kid or Bible passages. Really nothing about his kids or his family, just him."

"I believe that."

"That's not the weird part. After looking through all the pages, I was closing the book, and you know what fell out?"

"No, what?"

"A picture of you and Charlie at some museum, selfie style. No mention of you on any pages. Just the picture."

"That was from the time we went to New York City together in college," Callie says, feeling nostalgic.

The line finally moves, and Callie finds herself face to face with Liz. Liz takes a step backwards, moves her head in a motion that looks as though she is being slapped.

"Callie? Whoa, whoa," Liz repeats while continuing to step backwards. Her hands outstretched as if to say stop. In the next moment, she pulls Callie into a tight hug and whispers in Callie's ear, "I've always been jealous of you." In the next breath, she says, "Thank you for coming. Friend me on Facebook."

Callie is so caught offguard by the hug that she starts to cry. Wiping her eyes, she moves on to the rest of the family. Mr. Canfield is first. He looks like a shell of a man. His eyes are vacant and he merely shakes Callie's hand and looks for the next mourner. Mrs. Canfield is next in line.

"Oh, my gosh. Callie? You came all this way?" Callie tells her she has plans in New York this weekend, but notices that it doesn't register.

"I changed my flight when I heard what happened. I'm so sorry." Callie says while hugging Mrs. Canfield.

Mrs. Canfield places a hand on the small of Callie's back and turns Callie around to the other mourners in line speaking affectionately, "This is Callie Lamply, Charlie's college girlfriend." Callie's eyes go wide as she, herself, is in shock with this announcement. Unsure how to proceed, Callie smiles and moves on quickly to Charlie's sister. She too asks if Callie has come all this way for this. Callie explains, for the second time, about the circumstances. Finally, through the receiving line, Callie is thankful to sit. There are chairs in rows for mourners to reflect quietly. Callie sits next to other college friends that have come out tonight. The girls converge on Callie like a flock of seagulls diving for that one piece of bread.

"How was that?" one friend asks.

"Rough."

"At least Liz was cordial."

"She told me she's always been jealous of me," Callie says, still in shock at the revelation, not so much because of what was said, but the fact that Liz confided this in Callie.

Sitting and watching the crowd filter in and out of the mortuary, many mutual friends of Charlie and Callie's come and sit among her close friends. In an odd sort of way, it feels like they came out to support Callie. As if Callie was the widow.

Once the mortuary empties, eleven friends remain in the reflection seats. They each stand hugging. They decide to go to a local bar for drinks in memory of Charlie.

"He'd want it this way," one close male friend says.

As they walk to Abby's car, snow begins to fall. The street is quiet and the snow dampens the sound of their footfalls. Callie feels disconnected.

"You're awfully quiet," Abby prods.

"This all seems like a dream."

"I'm glad we're all going to get a chance to hang out, like old times, tonight. It just seems right. Charlie is totally here in spirit," Abby says cheerfully, seemingly more interested in reconnecting with friends than in what they are really here for.

The group reconvenes at a local bar around the corner from the mortuary. The place is filled with the voices of friendship. Callie and Abby take their seats at the table and talk among friends. Callie turns when she hears a male friend mention her name in his conversation.

"What's that? What'd I do?" she says.

"Oh, no, you didn't do anything. I was just telling Brad that Liz, while hugging me, said '*that* Callie is here.' She's not too happy to see you. But if it makes you feel any better, I think you should be here. We were ALL friends, and you were even more *friendly* than the rest of us."

This doesn't feel like any consolation to Callie.

"Greeeaaat," she exaggerates.

Brad laughs, placing an arm around her shoulders, squeezing gently. "It's good to see you. Even under these circumstances. Don't worry about Liz. I'm not sure she'll even remember you were here today when she wakes up tomorrow."

Everyone raises a glass to toast Charlie, just like old times. Feeling melancholy, she watches the snow falling softly outside the picture window behind their table. The amber of the street-light creates a glow on the flakes as they drift directly to the ground. It's mesmerizing. A man appears to be leaning against the streetlight outside. Surprised and intrigued, she continues watching this character with a baseball hat covering his head, the shade from the brim shadowing his face. He seems to have nowhere to go, just enjoying himself under the light, extending a hand to collect snowflakes. The stranger lifts his head to look up to the sky, allowing the streetlight to reveal his identity. Callie sits frozen. With both hands, he collects snow into a ball and tosses it at the window. Smiling, he waves, as the snowball explodes into a million glittery specs of prism. The window, awash with reflective dust, conjures up the image of the snowball fight they were in on campus those many years ago. Just before all heads turn, his body dissolves, one limb at a time, into thin air.

CHAPTER 22
Callie

"Hey, Mad," Callie says as she hugs Maddie at the airport. "I'm *so* glad you're here now."

On the drive to the hotel in New York City, the two friends catch up on the events that transpired the day before.

"No shit? She said she was jealous of you?"

"She did. I was stunned."

"Do not, I repeat, do not friend her on Facebook."

"Ha, not a chance. She's a little off her rocker, I think."

"Ya' think? She's saying all that to you as her husband's body is laid out in an open casket behind her? That's messed up."

Several hours after checking into the hotel, the girls decide to walk the city streets, looking for a place for dinner. In the process of walking block after block, their conversation keeps circling back to Charlie.

"We saw all the sites when we came here together. We walked the Brooklyn Bridge; it was such a cool date. He was so good at the element of surprise and spontaneity." Callie then goes on to share the night of the wake when her friends all went to a nearby bar. Then she shares the sighting of him on the sidewalk.

"Do you think it could have been him? I mean, maybe I was just seeing things? Daydreaming or something?"

"Knowing you, you really did see him. Again, I don't believe in this shit, but you do. I guess anything is possible. Did they ever find out why he died?"

"Not sure, but they think a heart attack."

As the two continue to walk and talk, Callie looks ahead and stops in her tracks.

"Look at that bus. Maddie, look at that. Tell me that's really there."

"Yeah, there's a bus stopped on the side of the road, which in itself is kinda weird for New York City."

On the side of the bus, written on a large black banner in white lettering: 'Did I really die?'

"That's weird, but don't get your panties in a wad over it. It's just an ad for a TV show on ABC. See the small print?"

She reads the fine print, but it doesn't lessen her wariness.

"It's some show about the supernatural. I'm surprised you haven't heard of it seeing as you're a *believer*," Maddie chastises.

Callie walks silently a few paces.

"Aw, come on, Cal. You're not mad now, are you?"

"No. It's just really strange. Let's change topics. Are you hungry?"

"Does a bear shit in the woods?"

They walk to a restaurant and sit in a quiet booth looking out on the busy street. Callie sits and looks up at the lighting fixture above their booth and notices the tiny little wings made from scrap metal. They're affixed to coils of metal reminding her of when she was young, on the 4th of July and would draw in the air with a sparkler. The design would linger in the night air for just a moment, and disappear. Yet with the attachment of bare bulbs at the end, she can't help but think they are angel wings. *Just one more wink from Charlie.* Thinking she's going to keep this to herself, she looks over the menu. The girls order and discuss what to do that evening, eat lunch and then pay the bill. When the receipt is brought to the table Maddie speaks up.

"You're not going to say anything about this light right here?" she says, pointing to the angel wings fixture.

"Nope," Callie says with a smile.

The girls spend their day shopping and walking through the city. As they walk, Callie pays attention to all the billboards and continues to notice the many signs that seem to be speaking to her.

We are connected, one sign boasts.

"Did I really die?" the TV show's ad blares from several large billboards in the city. Callie feels like Charlie is speaking directly to her from the other side.

On the way back to their hotel, Maddie decides to stop at a Taco Bell for a late afternoon snack. Callie is waiting in line, next to the condiment counter, and randomly picks up a sauce packet, noticing words on the back. She reads to herself, *I knew you'd come back for me.*

"Aren't those cute?" Maddie says, noticing Callie with a packet in her hand. "They always have the funniest sayings on them. What's that one say?"

"I knew you'd come back for me."

"Oh, geez, Cal, don't. You're going to find meaning in everything you see this weekend, aren't you?"

"Come on, Mad, you have to admit that's an odd thing to write on a sauce packet."

"It's just freaking hot sauce. It's not your ex-lover delivering a message to you from beyond the grave," Maddie says, rolling her eyes.

"If you say so," she says, believing more than ever that this is all Charlie's doing.

The weekend swiftly comes to end. The fun they have had will make lasting memories. They sit side by side giggling over pictures taken over the course of the weekend. The one picture that causes them each to howl with laughter is the one where Naked Cowboy, a New York City icon, has picked up Callie in his arms as she looks at the camera in complete horror. Callie thought she was just going to stand next to the half-naked man with the tanned and toned body wearing a cowboy hat, bikini underwear, and a guitar. Much to her surprise, when Maddie asked if she could take his picture for a tip, he swooped Callie into his arms.

"Look how he cupped your ass immediately. This definitely ain't his first rodeo."

"The shock in my eyes is hilarious!"

"Best twenty bucks I ever spent."

"So you had a great weekend?" Wyatt asks as they climb into bed.

"Yep. Exhausting, but fun."

"I'm glad to hear it. Sounds like the wake was rough."

"It was. Do you mind if we don't talk about that tonight? I really want to get some sleep, and if I start thinking about that again, my mind won't shut off."

Pulling Callie into his arms, he says, "No problem" and kisses her forehead.

Callie falls into a deep sleep quickly. Her dreams begin. She's walking down a hall with Abby. It's a familiar building from college, Copernicus Hall, the science building. As she walks toward an office down the hall, she sees Charlie walk by looking just like he did in college. Handsome, well dressed, and giving that smile that melts hearts.

"Hi, Cal."

Walking past stunned, Callie turns to Abby. "Did you see that?"

"What?"

"That was Charlie," Callie turns to look down the hall that Charlie walked down, now gone from view.

"That can't be because he's dead."

Callie and Abby walk into a counselor's office and sit across from the counselor. A feeling of overwhelming sadness falls across Callie's heart. It's a crushing weight that makes it difficult to breath.

"Callie, do you want to tell us why you are here?" the counselor asks.

"I have no idea."

"Your depression is interfering with your life. You've had thoughts of wanting to take your life?"

Shock registers. "I don't want to take my life. I want to live. I'm not depressed," yet that sadness deepens as she speaks. The weight upon her chest gets heavier with each passing moment.

I wanna live. I wanna live!

Callie, tossing in bed, wakes herself. She looks at the clock, which reads 1:11, *only happens two times a day,* Charlie used to say.

CHAPTER 23
Prue

"NO!"

"Prue-bear, wake up. Honey, you're having a bad dream." Jimmy jostles Prue gently out of her dream state. She slowly emerges from her dream with tears in her eyes and heaviness in her chest.

"You wanna tell me about it?" Jimmy speaks softly, channeling years of learned behavior from dealing with her nightmares. He sits quietly next to her in the dark with only the glow of the 1:11 on the digital clock. "Hey, look at that. That only happens two …" Prue interrupts and finishes his thought, "times a day."

Jimmy looks at his daughter, surprised.

"So what were you dreaming about?" Trying to prompt Prue.

"Your friend, Charlie. That's Mrs. Canfield's son, right?"

"Yep. He was a friend of mine in college."

"He's dead now."

"He is, yes. Way too young to pass."

"How did he die?"

"They say he died from a heart attack."

Contemplating his comment, she continues, "So this all would hurt?" circling her chest from collarbone to belly button.

"I suppose so, yes. Why so many questions?"

"Can someone die from a broken heart?"

"I've heard that people can, yes, but the doctors all said it was a heart attack."

"I feel so sad."

"Okay, it's super late, young lady. Let's get back to sleep," trying to end this conversation abruptly. "This isn't something you need to be worrying yourself with."

Jimmy pulls the comforter up under her chin and kisses her nose.

"Love you, Prue-bear."

"Love you, too, Dad."

On social media the following day, Jimmy and Callie are having a conversation in the "chat box," as their mother calls it.

Jimmy: *She's having nightmares again.*

Callie: *That stinks. Are they about Sandy Hook?*

Jimmy: *No. This time it's about Charlie.*

Callie: *What'd she say about him?*

Jimmy: *That he died of a broken heart.*

Several minutes go by with silence from Callie.

Jimmy: *Are you still on here?*

Callie: *Yeah.*

Jimmy: *What do you think about the broken heart thing?*

Callie: *I think your kid is creepy.*

Jimmy: *Come on, Cal, why would you say that when you know creepy runs in our family?*

Callie: *Mom just told me about a letter she got from Mrs. Canfield where she said that very same thing.*

Jimmy: *So now you're taking credit for Charlie's death?*

Callie: *You're gross.*

Jimmy: *He really had a thing for you.*

Callie: *I think she meant that he wasn't happy at home and his wife broke his heart, not me, you ignoramus.*

Jimmy: *Riiiight.*

Some part of Callie, deep down, did feel as if she had a hand in his broken heart. It didn't make her feel good or bad, but the thought did cross her mind a time or two. There is a soft rap on the front door. The knocking persists.

"Jesus, Cal did you forget?" Maddie hollers from out front.

Callie: *Gotta run. Mad's here.*

Callie closes her laptop and hustles to the door.

"Hey, come on in."

"You did forget, didn't you?" Maddie says with disgust.

"We're supposed to run today?"

"This running sucks. I hate it, yet here I am because you're holding me to my New Year's resolution. So don't just stand there looking at me like I have three eyeballs. Get your shoes on and let's go or I'm running home to sit on my ass and eat an entire sleeve of Fig Newtons."

Laughing, Callie puts her running shoes on. *What New Year's resolution?*

They take off through Callie's neighborhood and travel a four-mile loop that is one of Callie's long-standing runs. Halfway through the run, Maddie turns right to head back toward Callie's house when Callie turns left. Looking over her right shoulder, she calls out to Maddie.

"Where're you going? We're supposed to turn left here, not right."

"Very funny. Come on, I'm hungry, don't try and be sneaky and add a few more miles on this run. We've done this loop enough times that I know it like the bottom of Dylan's cute buns."

"Seriously, stop messing around. Take a left," Callie says and stops, crossing her arms across her chest.

"No, you stop messing around. Now not only am I hungry, I have to pee. Shit's gettin' real. Let's go."

Looking confused, Callie lets go of herself and starts walking, then slowly jogging, getting up to speed, turning right. Maddie, looking at Callie as they run, says "You really thought we had to turn left back there?"

"Yeah," Callie says with her voice trailing off.

Maddie feels uneasy. They run the remaining two miles in silence.

CHAPTER 24
Maddie

"I'm saying I think something's wrong with her head. I mean, yeah, she's always had something wrong with her head, but this time, I'm not joking around."

"You should talk to Wyatt about it. Maybe he's noticing things at home," Zach says with concern as he pushes Zoe on the swing set in the backyard.

"Yeah, I will," she says, digging in the sandbox with Dylan.

"Have you mentioned your concern to Callie? Maybe she's feeling things are off, but is afraid to say anything? Or maybe she's just forgetful and nothing is wrong?"

"It's possible, I suppose, but if you were there and you'd seen her, you'd know it's not normal. I think I'll start by asking her gently. Then if she's not giving me any info, I'll go talk to Wyatt."

After kissing Zach, Maddie leaves the house feeling heavy. Now on this *new me* kick since the New Year, Maddie is taking spin classes at the local gym. She hates it, but it is making a difference in her appearance and her overall well-being.

She grabs the bag with her spin shoes and water bottle and drives to class, in hopes of shaking this foreboding feeling.

Upon entering the room, she discovers there is a new instructor. With much trepidation, she adjusts her bike for her height and clips in. The warm-up begins, and she starts removing layers. *Holy hell, it's hot in here.* The music is upbeat and fast paced, and before she realizes it, that heaviness she was feeling has lifted. She's enjoying the music as the sweat begins to roll.

"Come on, people, warm-up's over! Let's get to it! We have hills ahead. Put some road under you," the instructor yells from his perch in the front of the room. He's tall, lean, and well-muscled. *That accent, is he South African? British? Australian? Whatever he is, he's delicious.*

"That's it, pump it harder! Position three. Have those butt cheeks graze the seat, right, left, right, left. Hover! Whooo!" The instructor continues to call out.

I'd like to hover my butt cheeks over that.

Watching the instructor move back and forth, hovering above his seat in his skin-tight bike shorts and tank top leaves nothing to the imagination. However, Maddie is doing a fine job conjuring up thoughts of her own.

Finishing the hour-long spin class leaves her breathless, sweaty and with a mighty large sensual appetite. The instructor walks around the room advising all to stretch. As he does so, he demonstrates the stretches, stopping in front of every third person. Leading the last stretch in front of Maddie, he lifts and straightens his right leg and places his right heel on the empty bike seat in front of Maddie. *That flexibility certainly would come in handy.* For the final stretch, he turns with his back to Maddie and does a front fold, touching both palms to the floor while continuing to straighten his legs. *Now that's downright impressive … and the stretch is pretty impressive, too.* Everyone in the class follows the instructor except Maddie, who is so enthralled with the instructor's powerful glutes; she just stands there, gawking.

"Hey, psst, down here."

She moves her gaze from his backside to his calves and sees the instructor's brilliant white teeth smiling up at her, between his legs. Her face glows crimson.

Feeling mortified and temporarily flustered, she just smiles in return, thankful that the only light in the room comes from the monitors on each bike. The instructor walks to the front of the class and flips the lights on. He greets everyone as they leave with a high five. As Maddie leaves the room, he swats her backside, "great effort today." Flustered once more, she keeps walking without a response. *Oh, marone!*

"You gotta come with me next time. Seriously," Maddie says to Callie through the phone. "Hold on a sec, Cal, I have a delivery guy at the door. Let me call you back in a few minutes." Maddie hangs up the phone and lets the deliveryman in the house. It takes a good thirty minutes for the delivery. There are instructions to listen to, papers to sign, and packaging to be removed. After all is said and done, she calls Callie back.

"That was some delivery. What took so long?" Callie said sounding irritated.

"Oh, Zach wanted to get a new bed. He figured that our last one was old and worn out. Just like I am."

"What kind did you get?"

"One you sleep on."

"Don't be a smart ass."

"The kind of bed that you can adjust for your comfort level. Zach can set his side to the firmness he likes and I can set mine to hard, the way I like it. This thing is like sleeping on a computer. It tracks how well you sleep at night and then, and I quote, 'the bed connects to your favorite Apps so you'll know how life affects your sleep and how sleep affects your life.' Well, guess what? I'm not getting any sleep right now with these two little monkeys in my house. No sleep and no sexy time equals one unhappy mama. I hate when we're not doing it on the regular. Makes me feel out of touch with him. Plus, if Mama's not happy, nobody is happy. It's not much fun around here lately."

"Aww, bummer. I'm sure this too shall pass. They're only young once and time will fly by, so enjoy this age while you can.

At least that's what I hear." Feeling a twinge of sadness, Callie changes the subject. "When's your next class?"

"You mean with instructor sexy?"

"Yeah, him. Do you even know his name?"

"Do I need to? It's next Wednesday morning at 8:30."

"I can't make that one. Some of us have regular working schedules."

"You're just jealous that I have flexible hours at the shop. He does have one in the evening on Thursday nights," Maddie says as she looks up the schedule on the gym website. "You wanna try that one?"

"We'll see. You know me. I'm a creature of habit. I like to do my runs in the morning and swims on the weekend. Let's touch base next week."

"Hey, Callista, before you go, there's been something on my mind." Maddie fidgets in her seat, unsure how Callie will handle this conversation.

"Uh-oh, what'd I do. You never call me by my full name."

"So the other day when we ran, you couldn't remember how to get back."

Callie quickly responds. "I knew where we were going. I just wanted to run a little longer. I knew if I said anything you'd say no, so I just pretended to not know where I was going. I was kidding. Of course I knew. Why wouldn't I know. I've run this neighborhood hundreds of times. I can't believe you fell for that," she laughs unconvincingly.

"Right. Guess I should have caught on to your little scheme. I'm such a dummy," Maddie says, rolling her eyes, not believing a word her friend is saying. "Okay then. You got me," Maddie says jokingly. "I gotta get going. We'll talk next week."

Maddie hangs up the phone, closes her laptop, and puts it back on the floor. She lies back on her bed with a deep sigh and takes the remote in her hand to peruse the buttons. She fiddles with the settings until she finds the firmness she is comfortable with. Fascinated by the technology, she finds the app for her phone. *It tracks my workouts and tells me what to adjust my bed to for a good night sleep? What is this world coming to?* Maddie texts Zach.

> Maddie: *Hey, Z, got the new bed delivered. Download the app today and we can try it out tonight to see if it keeps track of sexy time.*
>
> Zach: *Sounds great. Super busy at work. I may be late tonight. Don't wait up.*

Feeling rejected, she doesn't respond. She tosses the phone on the bed in frustration and closes her eyes. From the monitor, she can hear Zoe waking up from her nap. *I don't wanna adult right now.* She pulls herself up off the bed with an exhalation and collects her daughter from the crib.

CHAPTER 25
Maddie

Four weeks pass before Callie finally agrees to go to spin on a Thursday night. Maddie is giddy as they walk into the gym with Dylan and Zoe. Maddie drops the kids off at the babysitting room and prances out with Callie in tow.

"How can you be so excited about exercise when you hated it a month ago."

"Because I feel great! You're gonna love it. Hendrik is a fantastic instructor."

"Oh, so it's Hendrik now?"

"Or Hennie, either one."

"Hmmm."

Not to be discouraged before her class, she says to Callie, "I'll introduce you two if you want."

"Sure. I'd love to meet Hennie," she says sarcastically.

Hendrik is walking around the room giving high fives and, as the two friends walk through the door, he bellows, "Let's get to it!" closing the door and turning out the lights. Individual computer screens illuminate the room.

"Okay, how's everybody doing today? Who's ready to work?"

The crowded room is mostly silent with the exception of Maddie, who hollers back, "I am!"

"I said, who's ready to work?" This time the class erupts with a response from all.

"Put your bike on the floor and let's warm up. I know some of you are warmed up already," he says with a subtle nod, almost imperceptive to the class, toward Maddie. "But let's take a few minutes for everyone else to get up to speed."

Callie turns to look at Maddie, whose eyes are transfixed on Hennie.

"What's that supposed to mean?"

Looking straight ahead, Maddie says, "What's *what* supposed to mean?"

Callie drops it, thinking they will revisit this conversation later.

"Whoo! Let's go!" Hennie shouts enthusiastically. The workout continues for another fifty minutes and Callie finds herself enjoying moving to the music. She momentarily thinks she was seeing things at the start of class.

"Some of you look a little tired. Perhaps you went a little too hard earlier in the day? Your legs are feeling fatigue? You're, once again, sweating from head to toe? Thinking you can't finish the ride because you've had a rough day? Not on my watch! Now, get going! Let's finish this hill! Stand up and climb! Straddle that seat, hover and get those cheeks grazing that hard leather!" he says, staring directly at Maddie, not trying to hide his sultry tone.

Maddie's stare is glued to Hennie's body. Hennie unclips and begins walking around the room, encouraging all participants with a "nice job" or a "looking good." As he approaches Maddie, he passes her without a comment. She looks dejected. He continues to the back row, one row behind Maddie, and as he approaches the bike behind hers, he places a hand on her lower back, then walks to the side of her and reaches between her legs to grab the lever at knee level. She lets out a gasp and her breath hitches as he says, "You're working those legs a little too hard. Time to cool down," and pulls the level down slowly, causing the flywheel to pick up until she slows her legs. "Great job, everyone. Bring that tush to the seat and let's start cooling down." He moves away from Maddie toward the front of the room. Though everyone is cooling down, Maddie's breathing is slow to calm.

"Let's stretch off the bikes, people." He continues around the room again demonstrating various stretches. As he approaches Callie and Maddie's row, he folds forward, "Let's touch the floor. If you can only go as far as your shins, that's okay, too," he says, as he places his hands on his shins, then rises and walks to Callie. "Nice stretch. Keep those knees soft," and he keeps walking. He stands behind Maddie as she is in front fold, palms on her shins. Hendrik stands directly behind her, with his knees touching the backs of her knees, "Let's try a deeper bend." He folds his body over hers and takes her by the wrist to lower her hands to the floor. Callie is shocked by this display. He backs away and says, "That's it, ladies and gentlemen. Until next week!" People clap sporadically. "Please wipe down your bikes."

"So what'd ya think of class?"

Momentarily speechless, Callie musters, "Really?"

"What?"

"Oh, *come on*. If I didn't know you better, I'd say you've been screwing *Hennie* for a while. But I know you. I know that you're married and a mother and wouldn't jeopardize your family over this guy."

Maddie's face reddens. "You think I'd do a guy I hardly know? How shallow of a person do you think I am?" she tries to sound convincing.

"He sure put on a show for you in there. If you're not doing him, he's doing you in his mind. Probably right now." They stop walking to face each other, staring at one another until Maddie speaks. "Are we done here?" They walk up the stairs to leave, when Maddie's phone plays a melodic tune. "You go on ahead. I gotta get this. I'll talk to you tomorrow. I'm glad you came to class."

"Are you?"

The gym is quieting down during the evening hours. Maddie knows she has a two-hour window where the kids are looked after. She re-reads the text that Hendrik just sent her and feels her face flush.

Meet me by the bathroom near the stairs.

She knows the one. It's the individual bathroom that hardly gets used because it's out of sight of the treadmills and elliptical machines. And it's where they had raw, hot sex for the first time last week. Practically running, she stands near the door and sees that the *occupied* sign is on the door. As the sign turns to *vacant* Hendrik opens the door and pulls her in. He leaves the lights on as he removes her bike shorts. She stares into his honey colored eyes and grows weak in the knees as he picks her up and places her on the sink, wrapping her legs around his waist. She yanks down his bike shorts, grabs a hold of his sinewy, muscular glutes, and pulls him in. *How can he do this all the while looking at himself in the mirror?* She thinks as she continues to rhythmically bump her head against the mirror. The door-handle jiggles as Hendrik completes the task at hand. Releasing her legs, he pulls his shorts up, kisses her neck and says, "See you next week, sweet cheeks." He opens the door slowly, looking both ways before exiting as Maddie waits a minute longer. Pulling the door open she nearly collides with someone trying to enter the bathroom. "Oh, sorry. It's all yours." Maddie exits quickly and climbs the stairs two at a time to get her children from the childcare room. She feels guilt momentarily as she collects her children, but by the time she reaches the car, she finds herself counting down the days until she will see him again.

CHAPTER 26
Jimmy

At work, Jimmy is intently focused on his planner, trying to figure out a good time to get up to Vermont to spend time with family. Though Riley is gone, he still has the responsibility to Prue to have her spend some quality time with her Aunt Megan and to enjoy the lake where her mother grew up. He marks July 4th on the calendar, hoping Callie, Wyatt, Mom, Dad, and extended family can reconnect for a week or two during the holiday.

After diligently sending emails to family members, he sends a message to the new owner of Gramp's Camp to see if they would be willing to rent the camp for some time during July. His last one is an email to Jennifer. The two have been seeing each other exclusively for months now. He has strong feelings for her that could possibly be love, but wants to spend some time with her in a family atmosphere to make sure she's the right fit. Before he hits send, he rereads the message.

Hi Jen,

I'm wondering if you can get some time off this summer to take a trip up north with Prue and me? Unfortunately, that would mean hanging with my extended family. It could be fun, right? I mean, they're not all bad. Well, my sister is a nuisance, but what else is new. Here are the dates. Let me know what you think.

He continues explaining the particulars in the hope that Gramp's Camp will pan out. *If not, I wonder if Wyatt's folks would* be able to have some stay at their place? I'll make sure to mention that to Callie. As he constructs an email to send to Wyatt, the computer registers a new email. Clicking on the message, he smiles.

Hi Jimmy,

Good news! I have those days off already! I'd love to spend some time with you up in Vermont. I need some girl time with that Prue-bear of yours and your sister isn't a nuisance. With all the protest I think you, deep down, really like her, so stop pretending you don't. I've heard so much about your grandparents' cabin that I'm super excited to actually stay there! Will we stay in your old bedroom? That seems so naughty! Looking forward to it! I already have it on the calendar! See you for dinner tonight?

Jen xoxo

The thought of staying in his old room brings on a wide grin. *This is going to be a great summer trip. Hurry up and wait.*

In the course of the next week, all parties send responses to each other's emails. Gramp's Camp is available and a deposit is in place, the Wilsons will house Callie and Wyatt, while Mom, Dad, Prue, Jen and Jimmy will stay at camp. It's shaping up to be a great vacation.

"Hi, Aunt Marilyn. Guess what?" Jimmy asks over the phone knowing full well he should never ask her that question, as she always guesses correctly.

"You're coming up for a stay over July 4th week."

"Gah, how do you do that?"

"Jimmy, sweetheart, Tyler told me. Oh, hey, Riley says to let Prue drive the boat for God's sake. She's not a child anymore."

It always unnerves Jimmy hearing her name. The rest of it he's grown accustomed to.

"First, let me guess, she's talking to you now? And second, she's only 12."

"One, she'll be 13 by the time you come visit, and two, actually, she told Tyler to tell me to tell you."

"Of course she did."

"She's kinda funny about talking to me. It could just be that she's new at this. I'm sure Tyler will help her get through this transition." Then she begins to laugh.

"What's so funny?"

"Tyler just said the funniest thing. He said …" She continues talking, all the while Jimmy is thinking, *she's off her rocker.*

"Okay then. We'll see you in a few months. Looking forward to seeing everyone." Hanging up the phone, Jimmy wonders how much longer it will be before she joins Tyler and Riley.

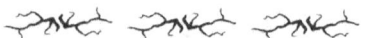

"Hey, Dad," Prue says as she throws her backpack on the floor by the front door.

"Hey, Prue-bear. How was school today?"

"Great. Libby is coming over in a little bit. Is that okay?"

"Sure thing. Hey, this summer I was thinking-"

"You want to go to Vermont?"

Stunned momentarily, "Y-yeah."

"Sounds good to me," she says kissing his cheek as she walks past him to the kitchen for a snack.

Speaking to her dad between bites of an apple, she asks, "Will I be able to see Aunt Megan?"

"Yep, and Aunt Marilyn, and Mr. and Mrs. Wilson. Nana and Papa will be coming up with us too. We get to stay in my grandparents' cabin."

"What did you used to call them?"

"Nanny and Gramp."

"Will we visit them, too?"

Confused, Jimmy says to Prue, "They've been gone a long time now."

"No, I know that," she says, rolling her eyes. "I mean will we visit the cemetery?"

"Probably. That seems to be one of the things we always do when we visit Vermont." He then went on to explain to Prue about the family cemetery and the time that Prue's Nana bought four plots: one each for Nana, Papa, Jimmy, and Callie.

"It kinda freaked Aunt Callie out." Jimmy laughs at the memory.

"I'm excited, actually, to see the place you used to spend your summers and where you met Mom. I think that'll be neat. Like reliving your past. I'll get to see it all through your eyes." Listening to his daughter speak with such enthusiasm warms Jimmy's heart. *It'll be nice to have something to look forward to. Something to share with you that holds a special place in my heart. You're growing up so fast. Breaks my heart, all the heartache you've endured in your young life.* All these thoughts roll through his mind in a split second, but the only response he can muster is, "Yeah, it'll be neat."

CHAPTER 27
Maddie

Maddie grabs her workout bag and walks to the garage. Just as she's opening the door, she hears the home phone ring once and stop. She smiles as she climbs into her car.

"Let's move it, people! Yes!" Hendrik yells into the microphone in the front of his spin class. Today he's wearing spandex navy bike shorts and a loose navy and black tank top that gives his chest full exposure.

"The bike's not gonna ride itself!" he barks. "Standing climb for three minutes, two minutes of sprints in the saddle, then a minute break. That's one loop. We're gonna do five." There's a collective groan from the group.

"If this was easy, everyone would be doing it, so stop your whining and let's go!"

Maddie is thankful to hear the cool-down music begin. Even though she's getting stronger each week, her endurance is still lacking. By the end of an hour class, the sweat has soaked through her workout clothes.

Hendrik is walking around the class, as he usually does, and as he walks toward Maddie, he says, "Meet me in about ten minutes in our usual spot." It's a statement, not a question. Maddie doesn't like the tone of his voice.

"Nah. I think I'm heading home."

Hennie stops and looks at her, confused.

"Why not?"

"You know, bathrooms aren't really my thing," she says, casually taking her spin shoes off and putting them in her bag. He moves to stand by the door to say goodbye and high five everyone. When he looks back, Maddie is the last person cleaning off her bike in the back of the room. He walks to her.

"Let's choose another location then," he says, as he wraps his arms around her midsection.

"I'll text you if something comes to mind."

Hennie moves away as they hear voices coming closer to the room.

"I'll be waiting."

Driving home, she creates scenarios in her mind trying to figure out a way to make this work. Guilt creeps in. *This isn't right. This isn't fair to Zach. He'll be crushed if he ever finds out.* Then she plays devil's advocate. *He's the one that started this. He spends way too much time at work. He's not interested in touching me. He's probably doing it with some bimbo anyway. I deserve this.*

Maddie believes this last statement and starts formulating a plan.

A week goes by without a text to Hendrik. He's starting to lose interest in class, and Maddie knows it. She realizes that if she doesn't figure out a way to make a rendezvous happen, he'll move on to another person, waiting in the wings. *Think.*

Zach is taking the kids to his parents for dinner on Friday and thinks I'm coming too. How can I get out of that dinner?

Leaving class Thursday night, she walks out, gives Hennie a high five, and smiles. On her way up the stairs to get her kids, she texts Hendrik with an address and one line, *Friday. 7 PM.*

He texts back a picture of an eggplant.

"I'll be home around six. Then we can leave to meet my folks."

Coughing with exaggeration, Maddie says, "My throat is on fire. I think I'm gonna sit this dinner out."

"*What*? Come on, Mad, it was your idea originally to have dinner today."

She can hear the irritation in his voice. That high pitched *what* is a dead give-away. The sound grates on her last nerve.

"Zach, your parents want to see you and the kids. One dinner I skip isn't going to kill you," she says, coughing again.

"Fine. Have the kids ready at six."

She watches the kids get in the car and sees disappointment on Zach's face as he backs out of the driveway. It makes her heart ache momentarily. Her phone buzzes with the notification of a text.

Sixty minutes, then another picture of an eggplant. The heartache she felt a moment before is replaced with a pounding in her chest.

She puts her phone on the kitchen counter to charge as she goes to her bedroom to shower and mentally prepare for the carnal knowledge that's about to go down.

Here is the one-word message he texts her from the driveway.

Oh, shit.

She walks to the door in her bathrobe, opens it and lets Hennie in. He's looking out of place without his gym clothes on. He's wearing worn jeans, oversized white button down oxford, and slip on loafers. *Loafers?* He smells ridiculously delicious. She takes him by the hand and leads him to the bedroom. She closes the door out of habit. Another twinge of guilt creeps in as she thinks of her children. *You don't need to do this. It can stop right here.* Pushing that thought away, she drops her robe to the floor. He pulls her by the waist and sits at the end of the bed working his magic on her from top to bottom. Maddie is finding it hard to breath. "My family is out," she speaks in fragmented sentences. "Dinner with grandparents." Taking a gulp of air, "Not much time." Hendrik lifts his head and stares at her for a moment.

"Stop talking." He stands and has her take a seat on Zach's side of the bed. She looks at the picture on the nightstand of herself and Zach on their wedding day. She reaches for the picture frame and turns it over. In the time that it takes her to turn the picture over, Hennie has magically slipped his shirt off and removed his pants. The firmness of this side of the bed seems foreign. *How can he sleep on this? It feels like concrete.* Preoccupied with her thoughts, Hennie continues until his skin is moist with perspiration. Maddie is just going through the motions. She can't stop thinking of her husband and family. Hendrik rolls off of her to her side of the bed and she lies still, feeling empty. Maddie stands and gathers her robe, noticing that the entire event took place in less than twenty minutes. Twenty minutes she can't get back. "I think you should go."

"He's not going to find out about this. I'm very discreet," Hennie says as he zips up and pulls his shirt on.

"I'm sure you are, but this can't happen again." She's overcome with the feeling of deceit. "You should really go."

He slips his loafers on and walks out of the bedroom.

"Think about it. You know how to get in touch." he says, with an arrogance that she hadn't noticed before.

She closes the front door and listens to the rev of the engine before it backs out of the driveway. Immediately she wants to shower for the second time today.

What am I doing? What am I doing? What did I do? she keeps repeating as she scrubs her body raw under a scorching shower.

Maddie opens the windows in the bedroom to remove remnants of what transpired. She turns the bedspread over to hide any evidence that may have been left behind and climbs into bed, still stunned that she was able to follow through. She turns on the TV for white noise. Maddie thinks about calling to talk to Callie but doesn't have the energy. Instead, she calls Callie's home and lets it ring once before hanging up. She just sits and stares at the tube until eight thirty, when she hears Zach and the kids enter the house. The kids come in to say goodnight, and after putting them to bed, Zach enters the room.

"You must really not be feeling well," he says with concern, "if you've been in bed since we left. Can I get you anything?"

"No."

"You're looking pale. You sure you don't need anything?"

Maddie shakes her head.

Zach leans his back against the headboard on his side of the bed and pulls her into an embrace. She leans her head on his chest with silent tears, heavy on her lids.

CHAPTER 28
Zach

"You going to spin class tonight, Mad?"

"Nah."

"Really? You've been so into it lately."

"No, Cal, I don't feel the need to exercise every day like you do," Maddie says loudly. Trying to lower her voice, though the irritation lingers.

"Okay, geez. Sorry I asked. Guess I'm going without you then."

"Good for you."

"Yeah, I kinda like the exercise. It's different than my usual routine of running or swimming."

"Mmmhmm."

"Last chance. You sure you don't wanna come with?"

"I'll pass."

"Suit yourself."

"Let's go, people! Get your bikes on the floor. Let's start with a four-minute warm-up, followed by some hills. Yeah! Let's get to it! Whoo!"

He really needs to stop hooting and hollering.

"We're climbing Mt. Washington today, so mentally prepare. It's one of the toughest hill climbs in the world." Everyone groans in anticipation.

"Seven point six miles with an average grade of 12%, some sections 18%, and the last 50 yards is the steepest grade that you *will* sprint to the finish." Callie notices some serious eye rolls. One person in the back of the room decides this isn't his night, packs it up, and leaves without a word to Hendrik.

The class starts adding road under them as they climb. Much grunting and groaning can be heard throughout the room, including Callie. Ending with a sprint is no easy task, and Callie is feeling ill from the exertion.

"You got this, people! I know it's hard. I know it's uncomfortable, but guess what? They don't cancel Mt. Washington's race if the conditions are uncomfortable! Keep going!"

Gasping for air, Callie is glad when Hendrik says to take off the road and start cooling down.

"Good job," he says as he high fives people going out the door.

As Callie approaches, Hennie asks, "Where's your little friend tonight?"

"My little friend?"

"Maddie?"

Callie looks blankly at Hendrik, unsure how to answer.

"You all right?"

"Yeah, fine. Tired."

Maddie?

"Hey, babe, have you been checking out the app that you asked me to get?" Zach says as he walks down the hall with his phone in his hand.

"What app?" Maddie questions.

"You know, the one you said to download that tracks how you're sleeping and what your sleeping patterns are like."

"Oh, yeah, that one. I did at first. I haven't been checking regularly."

"I think something's wrong with it," Zach claims as he pulls up his information.

"How so?"

"Take a look at this." He shows her his screen with the app pulled up. It displays his daily sleep patterns—when he was in a sound sleep, when he was restless, and noting when he wasn't in bed. Strangely, he notices an inconsistency which shows the previous Friday night as active between 7:10 and 7:30.

"Doesn't that seem weird to you? I was with the kids that night, and you were home. It looks like you were doing some Olympic routine on my side of the bed," he jokes.

Maddie pales as she is shocked into silence.

"I mean, the only way it would show this kind of action is if you were getting *some kind of action*." He laughs, but then looks at Maddie's face and stops.

"But that wouldn't happen because you were sick that day." His face falls as things are beginning to register. Suspicion creeps in. "Right, Mad? You were sick that day and stayed home because you weren't well enough to go with me and the kids." Anger kicks in. "Mad. Say something," he insists, as his arm falls to his side, defeated.

"I, I, I … Zach." She's unable to continue, unsure what to say.

"Oh, Jesus," he says, running his hands through his hair. "You've got to be kidding me." He starts to pace the room. "I think I'm gonna be sick." He places a hand over his stomach and runs to the bathroom. The sound of Zach gagging permeates the room.

Callie gets behind the wheel of her car, knowing it's time to go home from the gym, but for the life of her, can't remember how to get there. She absently drives around until she is out of gas and pulls into a gas station, confused. Her phone comes to life.

"Cal? Where the hell are you? Spin class ended two hours ago," Wyatt asks, raising his voice in anger.

Two hours ago?

"I don't know." Wyatt listens to a detached voice on the other end.

"Are you okay? You don't sound right. Do you recognize anything around you? Can you tell me what you see?"

"I see a Phillips 66 gas station."

Anger wanes into concern. "Can you walk in and ask the person at the counter to tell you where you are?"

Without answering, she gets out of the car and walks to the attendant behind the counter. Sounding robotic, she asks the attendant where she is. Wyatt is stunned by the attendant's response, "Springfield, Illinois."

How did she get 118 miles away?

"Callie, stay there. I'll come get you. Please don't leave, okay? Stay in the car or with the attendant. Just don't leave. I'm coming to get you. Okay? Can you do that for me?" he asks calmly as if speaking to a child.

Just above a whisper she responds with a soft, "Yes."

"Hand the phone to the attendant, okay?"

"Hello?"

"Can you please make sure she stays there? I'm her husband. There's something terribly wrong with her. I'll be there as fast as I can."

"I'll do my best."

Wyatt leaves his cell phone number with the attendant in case she leaves.

Wyatt's voice cracks as he offers a, "Thanks, man."

Already on his way, he ends the call, then immediately calls Callie's dad. Wyatt explains the situation and swings by to grab him. Together they drive to bring Callie home.

CHAPTER 29
Maddie

"Dad, why are you packing your overnight bag? Do you have a business trip?"

"Yep, Dad has to go away for a little while, Dyl." Zach picks up his son, which is getting harder to do now that he's six and a half. "Have you been eating rocks? You weigh a ton," Zach jokes, trying to lighten the mood. He tickles his son in the belly, which elicits a giggle. *Best sound in the world.*

"Hey, Pickle, will you watch over your sister while I'm gone?"

"How long are you gonna be gone?"

"I'm not sure, kiddo."

"You don't know when your trip will be over? That's weird."

"It's a little more difficult than that."

"Is it because you're mad at Mom?"

"What? Nooo. I gotta get a move on, big guy. Love you. I'll call you soon to see how everything is going," Zach says, ruffling his son's hair as he leaves the room. He stands at the front door and looks around. His bones ache from the heaviness of the moment. He picks up his daughter's discarded doll off the floor. Limp limbs, lackluster hair, eyes devoid of emotion—it's as if he's looking at a mirror image. He looks over at Sprout in the corner with his muzzle turning gray. Time marches on, whether he likes it or not. Dylan has turned into a little man. *How did he grow up so fast?* His baby girl, three already, no longer the helpless infant, wrinkles her nose as she pretends to read a board book on the floor. He hates to leave, yet knows it's best until he and Maddie can sort things out. Zach takes a deep cleansing breath, anesthetizing himself enough to leave his family behind as he reaches for the door handle.

"Wait!" Dylan shouts, running into the room. "Let me get Mom. She'll wanna say goodbye!" He leaves the room to find Maddie folding laundry and pulls her by the hand into the empty living room.

Dylan looks around the living room, "Dad? Daaaad?"

"Honey, I think he left already. It's okay. We'll talk to him soon," Maddie says as her vision blurs.

Maddie's phone buzzes to life on the kitchen counter. Thankful for the distraction, she walks over to retrieve it. It's a text from Wyatt.

> Wyatt: *Maddie, when you get a minute, can you give me a call. I have a couple questions to ask you regarding Callie. Better yet, can you come over?*

> Maddie: *Everything okay? I have the kids and Zach had to leave so I'm stuck for tonight. I can meet you tomorrow if you'd like.*

> Wyatt: *Sure. Text me tomorrow when it's good for you.*

While the kids are in school, Maddie meets Wyatt at a local coffee shop on his lunch break.

"So what's going on? You have me a little worried about our friend."

"I *am* a little worried about our friend."

"What's going on?"

"I went to the gym and spoke to the spin instructor, Manny or Denny or something."

"Hennie," Maddie whispers.

"Did you go to spin class the other night with Cal?"

It sounds like he's insinuating that he knows something.

"No, I didn't. Why?" Feeling defensive.

"Callie had some sort of memory loss after class."

"Memory loss? What? I mean, I've noticed that she's been forgetful lately, but …"

"Can you give me an example?" Wyatt interrupts.

"She forgot how to get home on our run a few weeks ago. When I asked her about it, she pretended that she was just joking around," she says, then pauses before continuing, "but I know when she's joking. She wasn't fooling me. But I can't even remember yesterday so, there's that," Maddie jokes. "What are *you* talking about?"

"She didn't make it home after class."

"What's that supposed to mean?"

"She left the gym and ended up in Springfield, Illinois, two hours away."

"Holy shit. How's she now?"

"Acting like nothing is wrong. She doesn't remember driving to Springfield. She doesn't remember her father and me picking her up. She doesn't remember the ride home. It's like it never happened. But it did," Wyatt says with concern.

"Have you taken her to see a doctor yet?"

"No. She refuses to go. She says there's nothing wrong with her."

"Driving for two hours after leaving the gym … seems like there's something wrong to me."

"You and me both. I'm gonna give her a few days to think about it. I may just give her GP a call to see if I'm just making this out to be worse than it is."

"I'll see if I can get her to go out with me soon. See if I can talk any sense into her."

"Thanks, Mad. How's your world?"

Glancing down at her watch, she nonchalantly says, "Fine. Oh, hey, I gotta get going. My shift starts in about thirty minutes." She stands and embraces Wyatt. "I'll give Cal a call tomorrow. We'll get to the bottom of this. Don't worry. It's probably something like an infection that's causing this. My grandmother had a lung infection one time, and who knows what was going through her mind, but when I went to check on her, she was stuck under her bed. It took the fire department to get her out." Maddie smiles at the memory of the young, muscular, handsome firefighters lifting the bed to retrieve her grandmother. "'Course, that part wasn't so bad."

"I bet," he says, smiling briefly before it evaporates.

"I hope you're right." He walks her out and says, "Say hi to Zach and the kids for me. We should get together sometime soon, all of us. I know Callie would like that."

"Yeah. We'll see." The mention of Zach's name twists her stomach inside out.

Maddie walks back to her car and sits in the driver's seat with her hands on the steering wheel. She rests her head against the wheel, feeling overwhelmed.

What the hell is going on? You can't leave me, too. I need you. She drives off with an ominous feeling that something terrible is on the horizon, and it may not just be with Zach.

Maddie leaves her shift at the sandwich shop to pick up the kids at extended day care. While she puts the kids in the back of the car and secures them in their seats, her phone vibrates with a new text from Zach.

Zach: *We need to talk.*

Maddie: *I'm with the kids right now.*

Zach: *This is important.*

Maddie: *I can't talk about this in front of them.*

Zach: *When you put them to bed, call me.*

Maddie: *K*

Shit. Not looking forward to the conversation, she continues her evening routine with the kids on autopilot.

"G'night, honeybunny," she sings to her daughter after she tucks her into bed, then walks to Dylan's room.

"Hey, Pickle, time to put the books away," Maddie says, leaning on the doorjamb.

"I miss Dad," Dylan says, as he places the book back on his bookshelf next to his Lego collection.

"I know, sweetheart. It's hard when he's away on business."

"When's he coming home?"

"I'm not sure yet. He's super busy," she explains, mother's guilt creeping in.

"Is he mad at you, Mom?" he asks, climbing back into bed.

Surprised at his comment, she has to think about an answer before responding.

"Because if he is, just say you're sorry. That's what you always tell me."

"I wish it were that simple, big guy. Now, let's get to sleep. Love you." Maddie says as she kisses his cheek.

If he only knew how sorry I am.

CHAPTER 30
Prue

"I want to show you something very special to me."

"Where are we?"

"If we follow this gravel path, we'll be there soon."

"Where?"

"You'll see," Aunt Marilyn says to Prue as they walk along a vaguely familiar gravel road. Prue is unsure if she's been here before or if she's just heard so many relatives talk about this place that it feels familiar. A hand carved sign hanging from a pine tree reads *Doris and Oscar*. Prue takes in her surroundings. To her right is an old split-rail wooden fence with blackberries woven and wrapped tightly around the splintered wood. The sun filters through the thick pine needles, casting shadows along the path and warms her back as she reaches a break in the trees. Ahead of them, in the midst of fallen pine needles, lies a path of well-placed rocks.

"What's that?"

"My special place. It's called a labyrinth," Aunt Marilyn says with a smile. She continues off the gravel road onto the cushioned ground and walks along the river rocks. "Several years ago I created this masterpiece as a place to clear my mind."

"Whaddaya do here?"

"Well, you walk, essentially."

"That's it?"

"No, I do a lot of thinking, too. Here, follow me," she says, reaching out for Prue's hand. Hand in hand, they walk along the very large circular path. On each side of the path, smooth river rock indicates the boundaries. "If you were way up high looking down, you would be able to see that it's like one big circular maze." They walk quietly for a moment. "As you enter the labyrinth, you begin the "letting go" process of quieting your thoughts, worries, to do lists—letting go into the experience of being present." Aunt Marilyn looks to Prue and gently wipes away tears that have spilled onto her cheeks. "It's okay to cry. It happens a lot. Oftentimes the wounds that need healing are revealed. This is a sacred place that permits the time and safety for the expression of feelings."

"That may be, but why am *I* crying?"

"Even in your young life, you have had times of deep sorrow and pain. Think back. What memory comes to mind?" she asks knowingly.

"Sandy Hook," Prue whimpers.

The two slowly approach the center of the circle indicated by a six-petal rosette created with more stones. This rosette surrounds a large Sycamore tree—the most unique tree that Prue has ever seen. It stands 175 feet tall.

"What kind of tree is that?" Prue inquires with a sniff and wipe of her nose.

"That is my Lightning Tree."

"Because it was struck by lightning? Wouldn't it be charred and black? This one is white and the bark is falling off."

"No. Not struck by lightning. Use your imagination for a moment. What do the tree limbs look like to you?"

"Bolts of lightning. I see it now," Prue says, smiling.

"In all my years, I've always felt a kinship with this tree. I sense it feels my presence when I'm around. I used to walk from my mother's cabin down here to sit by the tree and watch the lake. It was a comfort to me when I began to lose friends and family through the years. Time moves on. I started researching ways to clear my mind on the computer at the library in town and came upon the word "labyrinth." Walking the labyrinth gives insight. Or so the computer claimed. I thought, 'why not make my own labyrinth?' When my parents died, followed by my aunt and uncle—who were actually your grandparents on your dad's side, Nanny and Gramp—I needed a place to deal with the struggle of living without them. So I slowly created this beautiful labyrinth around the lightning tree. It took close to a year to create it just the way I like it. It helps with the healing and releasing of grief. I have to say, it has really helped me through some troubled times. It feels spiritual here. After all, we are spiritual beings on a human path."

"Where do we go from here?" Prue asks just above a whisper.

"There's no right or wrong way to walk. Just quiet the mind and open the heart. When you're ready to walk out, the "letting out" will take us back into our lives, empowered by spirit." Aunt Marilyn walks on slowly through the "letting out" and stands facing the lake. She looks serene. Prue stands by the tree looking up at the expanse of white branches that shoot out from the trunk like currents of static electricity. It is a beautiful tree, and she sees why her aunt is so taken by it. As she looks up into the clouds through the bolts of branches, she lets the tears flow, her sobbing rattling her rib cage. For a moment, she's back in that bathroom closet, listening to the ominous quiet of the school building as heavy footsteps approach. She closes her eyes, allowing the images to be revealed. Images she hasn't thought of for years. Feelings that she had pent up and stored away come barging through and she falls to her knees at the base of the tree. Tears for the children and teachers that were lost; tears for injured friends and administrators. It is all too much for one child to hold on to. Her tears are spent. There, for a moment under the lightning tree, she feels a presence placing a hand on her shoulder. She opens her eyes to find no one. A feeling of euphoria has replaced her former grief, like a warm blanket surrounding her. She stands, walks slowly to the "letting out," and feels a weight lifted.

"What just happened?"

Smiling, Aunt Marilyn turns to Prue and says, "That, my dear, was the divine working into your life. I have many happy spirits that visit me here. Many I'm sure you've heard of and many you'll meet along your journey. That's enough for today. You need to wake now."

Wake?

"Prue, you need to wake up. Prue-bear, it's time for school. Last day before summer vacation. Wake up, sleepyhead."

"But I want to stay by the lightning tree."

"Lightning tree?"

Rousing slowly, looking into her father's eyes, her words ring in her ears.

"Yeah, the huge white tree near the lake."

Confused, Jimmy says, "I'm not sure what tree you're talking about, but it sure sounds cool." Jimmy kisses her forehead and leaves her room. Calling from down the hall, "What sounds good for breakfast?"

"Do we have any blackberries?"

CHAPTER 31
Callie

"This isn't necessary, Wyatt. I'm truly fine. I'm not sure what all the fuss is about."

Wyatt looks at her in the passenger seat incredulously. "Because you were missing for two hours that you don't remember, and just yesterday when I started the oven I nearly burned the house down because you put the mail in there for some reason. That's why. I'm worried about you."

Mail in the oven?

"I can tell by that look in your eye you have no recollection of doing that."

"Come on, you've never put something in the wrong place? I remember when you put a jar of peanut butter in the closet in our bedroom."

"That's *so* different. I remembered doing that, *and* when I remembered what I did, I retrieved it and put it back in the pantry. Big difference."

"Fine. They're not going to find anything wrong. And when they don't, I expect an apology," she proclaims unconvincingly, staring out the windshield.

"You'll get one," he says, then under his breath, "I hope you're right."

"Okay, Callie, we're going to do a comprehensive medical evaluation today." The doctor speaks to Callie in a soft voice that strikes her as soothing.

"Let's start with some simple questions. What is your name?"

"Callista Lamply. Well, that's my maiden name. My married name is Callista Wilson. Or Callie. Or Cal," she offers, feeling nervous.

"Very good," he says with a reassuring smile. "Don't be nervous."

"What is the date today?"

The date?

"May something."

"Good. Now, what's the year?"

"2012? Is that right?" She looks to Wyatt for confirmation. He's looking back with wide-eyed dismay. Wyatt's skin tone has paled.

The doctor looks at Callie and speaks in a measured tone. "We'll go over the results when we are finished." He passes a blank sheet of paper across the desk to her. "Please take a pen or pencil in front of you and draw a face for me."

She takes the pen on the desk and draws a large round circle and stops.

Face?

She continues again with the pen and places two dots for eyes randomly on the circle. The mouth is placed at the top of the circle. The face looks very much like a Picasso painting from his abstract phase. Confused, she sets the pen down. There is an audible gasp behind her.

"Okay, thank you, Callie." The doctor looks over to Wyatt with a silencing glare. He continues his evaluation and recommends that they schedule a brain-imaging scan. "It doesn't hurt, it's just time consuming."

Wyatt and Callie walk out of the office hand in hand.

"2017? Really?"

Wyatt doesn't know how to react to this. He continues walking in silence with a reassuring squeeze of her hand.

"I'm scared, Wyatt."

The truth grabs Wyatt's heart with icy hands. He opens the car door for Callie and says quietly, "Me, too."

After the scan, waiting at home is torture. Trying to remain optimistic, they pretend that all is well with the world for the very long two-day wait. Finally, the call comes through, and once again, they find themselves in the doctor's office.

The doctor illuminates two scans, one of which is of Callie's brain. One looks plump and healthy, and the second looks as though a child had shaded in two parts with a lead pencil.

"See these areas here? This one in particular we are most concerned with. It's the Hippocampus, which involves memory, problem solving, thinking, feeling, and controls movement. I placed your scan next to a healthy brain so that you can see the affected areas."

"I don't have a healthy brain?" Callie interrupts, feeling nauseous.

"Parts of your brain are not healthy at the moment, no. But other parts are still healthy, and that's a very good thing." Turning back to the scan, he points to the other gray area and asks, "Were you ever in a serious car accident, or have you ever seriously injured your head?"

Callie and Wyatt look at each other and think for a moment. Wyatt is first to speak up. "She fell hard at work one day." *Worst day of my life, up until now.* "She slipped on glitter and fell so hard that she was out for about a day and a half."

"Ah, well that explains this spot here. That must have been some fall."

"I hate glitter," Callie utters. Wyatt gently rests his hand on her bouncing knee, a habit that is a direct result of her fall. He has noticed that she does this in uncomfortable situations. Looking at her now, she resembles a teenager waiting anxiously for the result of her driving test. He smiles and pats her knee. It stills immediately.

They continue to discuss the results and the possibility of a new type of treatment.

"This treatment is relatively new, but I feel with the type of injury that has caused this dementia, it will help reestablish cognitive abilities. You're a lucky lady."

"Dementia? I'm not even fifty yet," with that question she looks to Wyatt to confirm. "Am I?"

"Not yet, no," he says with a sad smile.

Looking back at the doctor, she asks, "You said I'm lucky. Lucky how?"

"If you waited much longer, it would have been much more difficult to reverse this cognitive impairment. I'll send a list of items that this protocol will require. Take it home, read it over, and if you have any questions, give me a call. I'll send the prescriptions, too." He looks down at the paper, "Hilltown Village, Schnucks Pharmacy?"

"Yep. Thank you."

"Yes, thank you, doctor," Wyatt says, shaking the man's hand firmly.

"Don't worry, Callie. We'll get you on the right track. There is a light at the end of the tunnel for you. I don't get to say that to many dementia patients."

"That makes me sound ancient," Callie says with a frown.

"It's just the terminology we use. Take care and we'll be in touch."

"Dementia? How old are you?" Natasha laughs on the other end of the line to try to lighten the mood. Natasha has feared this phone call ever since Callie asked for a leave of absence.

"Forty-nine going on ninety, apparently. How are the kiddos doing? I miss them so much."

"They're doing fine. They'll be so happy to hear that you're going to get better. Not everyone can say that here."

"I know."

"Oh, hey, Ari is doing great! She had clean scans the last time she went in. We're so excited for her."

"That's great news! Tell her I'm so happy for her, will you?"

"Of course. Now, you go get better so you can come back to work."

"I'll do my best. I hate taking pills, and this doc has me taking five a day. I practically gag by the time the last one is in my throat."

"It could be worse, it could be shots. That would be awful."

"True," she snickers, "that would be worse."

They end their conversation, and she looks at her calendar. Old habits die hard. She sees the red circle on the calendar in July, then walks to the bedroom where she sits on the edge of the bed.

"Hey, what are we doing in July again?"

Wyatt calls out from the closet as he gets his shoes, "We're going to Vermont with Prue, your mom and dad, Jimmy, and his girlfriend Jennifer."

"Jimmy has a girlfriend?"

"Yes, and she's really nice. Prue really likes her. Jimmy and your family are staying at Gramp's Camp, but you and I are staying with my folks because there aren't enough beds in the camp."

"Oh. Okay." She flops back on her bed. "Actually, I'm really looking forward to going up there. I haven't see Aunt Marilyn in a while, or Aunt Doris." The phone on the nightstand rings.

Wyatt pops his head out of the closet. "Uh, Cal, Aunt Doris is dead. You know that, right? She's been gone a long while. It's just Aunt Marilyn now, and she's getting up there, too."

Lifting her head off the bed, she says, "Oh, yeah. That's right. I forgot." Laying her head back down, she thinks of Aunt Marilyn. In her mind, she's still this young woman. She rolls her thumb over the ruby heart on her right hand.

Wyatt walks to the nightstand to answer the phone when, after the first ring, it stops. Callie smiles. Wyatt shakes his head and walks back to the closet.

CHAPTER 32
Maddie

Maddie drives separately to the counselor's office. She walks in and sits, waiting for Zach's arrival. The counselor walks through the door and calls Maddie and Zach's names, but Zach still hasn't arrived.

"That's okay, we can get started with you, and when he gets here, he can join us."

Maddie follows the counselor to her office and takes a seat on the striped couch near the door. The counselor pulls a chair forward to sit directly in front of her.

"So, Maddie. Tell me what brings you here."

"My stupid behavior. I think I may have done something that will end my marriage. I'm here to try to save it."

The door to the office opens and in walks Zach, looking rushed. He eyes Maddie and nods to the counselor who raises a hand to suggest taking a seat next to Maddie. He sits as far to the end of the couch as he possibly can.

"Maddie was just saying that she's here to save her marriage. Why are you here, Zach?"

"I'm not sure this is worth saving, but I'm here just in case it is."

Maddie closes her eyes tightly, as if bracing for a slap.

"I see. Okay. Thank you both for your honesty. Let's get started. Zach, can you tell me what you'd like to hear from Maddie? What is it that you need to have her tell you?"

"I need her to tell me why she destroyed our family. What is it that I'm obviously not doing for her? Am I so awful to sleep with? To live with?" Turning now to Maddie. "So awful that you had to go and screw some gym rat?" Anger and anguish fill his face. "Tell me, Maddie. Why? What did I ever do to you to make you go run off with some musclebound freak from the gym?"

"Maddie, can you respond to that?"

Maddie clears her throat and wrings her hands. "Yes. I was feeling alone. I was feeling unimportant. I was feeling insignificant, and this guy at the gym made me feel special."

Zach chortles, "Until the next 'special' woman comes along."

"Zach, please let Maddie have her say. Maddie, continue."

Zach interrupts, "No. Hang on. I want to know how many times he made her feel 'special.'"

Maddie speaks to Zach now, "Like how many times I slept with him? Like a number? You really wanna know how many times? How exactly will this help you?"

"I just wanna know. It's something I've been thinking about. I *have* to know."

Maddie looks to the therapist now, "Does this seem all right to you?"

"If Zach feels the need to have a number to be able to move on, then yes."

"Okay. Let me think," Maddie counts on her fingers in a mumbled whisper.

"Christ, you need both hands to count?" Zach says, astonished.

"You said you wanted a number."

"I thought it would be an easy number like one or two. No eight or ten."

"Let's move on now. Maddie, can you explain to Zach why you felt the need to stray during your marriage?"

"Yes. He was gone a lot. I mean *a lot* a lot. He was constantly working late hours, and, honestly, I thought you were having an affair, because by the time you came, home you were exhausted. I can't remember the last time we had sex. I got angry and figured if you were getting it somewhere else, so should I."

"I never had an affair. I have been faithful to you since day one."

This hurts Maddie. "I'm so sorry, Zach. I tried to tell you that a hundred times, but you kept ignoring me."

"I'm pissed. Can't you see that? Don't you understand what you did was wrong? Why didn't you ask me if you were so concerned about me having an affair? Why wait until now, in front of a therapist? Why wait until you slept with someone else? God, I don't get you."

The banter goes back and forth for an hour, with the therapist only redirecting a few times. *This is good,* the therapist thinks. *They are finally communicating. They just might have a chance.*

"For homework, I'd like you to both have ten questions that you would like the other person to answer. It doesn't matter how difficult it will be to answer or hear, because it will be difficult on both ends. This discussion today feels like progress. I hope you both take this new information away from our session and realize how much you have invested in the pain you each are in. Let's set up weekly sessions, same time, same day for the next two months. At the end of two months, we will reevaluate. If either of you ever feel the need for counseling separately, please don't hesitate to call. See you next week." She stands, shakes hands with both parties, and shepherds them to the door.

Maddie and Zach walk out of the building without a word. Maddie feels depleted as she sits in her car and stares in the direction of Zach's car until he exits and disappears out of sight.

Maddie takes a left, driving back to their home, alone. She feels empty, weighed down by sadness and thinks, *there has to be a way to salvage my marriage.* She is determined to fix everything. She's going to work on the vows she's broken until she puts them back together.

The light on the answering machine is blinking. *Why did we keep our landline, anyway?* Pressing the play button, she hears Callie's voice.

"Hi, Mad. I was hoping you were home, but forgot you told me that you were going to a therapy session with Zach. Shocker. Wyatt had to remind me. Hey, I wanted to tell you we got the results back on my scan." Nervously giggling, she says, "Believe it or not, there is a brain in there. Call me when you get a chance."

"Hey, Cal. What's the good news?"

"It's more like good and bad news. Remember when I slipped on glitter in my office and was knocked out for a few days?"

"How could I forget? You scared the shit out of me."

"That little fall has gotten me diagnosed with early onset dementia."

"Is that the bad or good news?"

"That's the bad news. The good news is that it's secondary dementia, and my doctors seem to think with a protocol of five different supplements, eating a certain way, exercising, and a list of other things I have to follow to a T, I should be back to my old self within a year."

"What a relief!"

"You're telling me."

"I mean, what a relief I won't have to keep repeating myself, answering the same question you ask over and over and over and over and ..."

"Okay. Okay, I get it. I'm annoying. You'll have to bear with me for a few more months, though. My brain's not going to fix itself overnight."

"Seriously, I'm happy to hear this news."

"So tell me about your session with Zach."

The girls speak for a long while on the phone, like old times, each feeling lifted by the end of their conversation.

"Get some sleep and rest that noggin of yours. Let's get you back to forcing me to run with you again."

"What about spinning?"

"Please tell me you're kidding."

Laughing out loud, "I am."

CHAPTER 33
Callie

Callie and Wyatt touch down in Burlington a day after her family arrives and drive to the Wilsons' home on Lake Carmi. Wyatt is anxious to get Callie situated and have a chance to reconnect with family. Following the rough few weeks after Callie's diagnosis, he's hoping this trip will be a huge memory boost. She's had mostly good days, but there were a few that downright scared him—one in particular. Callie had gone out for a run and confusion set in. Soon she was unable to find her way home. Rather than call for help, she sat on the street corner until a police cruiser stopped to see if they could help. The officer called Wyatt, and upon arrival, chastised him for not having looked after her. Now that she's been on her new treatment, she seems clearer and less confused.

"Callie, it's so nice to see you again," Mrs. Wilson says, greeting them both on the front steps. "And sweetheart, so happy to have you home for a spell. Why didn't you cut your hair before your visit?" she teases.

"Hi, Mom," he says, combing his hair with his fingers. Then with a hug, he says, "Where's Pop?"

"He'll be out in two shakes of a lamb's tail."

"Someone mention my name?" Mr. Wilson bellows as he enters the room.

The two men hug. "Hello there, young lady. How are you feeling?"

"Much better than a few weeks ago. I gave Wyatt quite the scare." Wyatt and Callie give each other a knowing look.

"Yes. I'm sure that was a frightening experience for both of you. I remember my grandmother had dementia and walked four miles not knowing where she was. When my dad finally got to her, she had been missing for three hours. Dementia is an awful disease. Be thankful that yours can be corrected with your new diet and exercise plan."

"It's kind of experimental because it's so new. I feel better, though. Speaking of which, I need to take my pills." Callie leaves the table and asks, "Are we staying downstairs?"

"Yes, ma'am. If there's anything you need, you let me know."

"I'll be right back." She releases his waist and walks inside. She sees her brother coming out to greet them and gives him a love tap on the shoulder as she walks past. She walks down the bi-level stairs in the Wilson home, down the hall to Wyatt's childhood room. A lone butterfly bounces in her belly at the faint memory of their youthful shenanigans down here.

Downstairs, Callie takes out her vitamin D3, fish oil, CoQ10 and her hormone replacement therapy meds. She looks down into her hand, then tosses all four pills in her mouth and takes a long swallow of water from the bathroom sink. *This sucks* she says to herself in the mirror as she leans in for another swallow of water.

Out of sight, Wyatt's parents start peppering him with questions.

"Are you sure this new regime is going to help? Aren't you worried for her safety? How long will this last? Will she have a relapse?"

"Slow down, Mom. It'll be fine. She's getting a little better each day. I'm hopeful that she'll be good as new."

"But what if she starts to slide backwards?"

"Pop, we'll cross that bridge if we come to it."

Downstairs, she pulls the suitcase open and puts her things away. In the bureau drawer, she sees a stack of envelopes tied together with ribbon. She pulls it out, removes the suitcase from the bed, and sits down. After untying the envelopes, she pulls one from the pile that dates back to 1984. *I was so young back then.* She props up two pillows against the headboard and leans into the comfort as she continues to read. Eventually, her eyelids grow heavy and she falls asleep.

When Callie doesn't come back upstairs after retrieving her pills, Wyatt gets nervous and walks to his childhood bedroom. He opens the door and sees Callie asleep with her letters on her chest and sprawled beside her on the bed. Smiling, Wyatt collects the letters and replaces them in the drawer. He retreats from the room and closes the door softly.

Callie wakes to the faint hum of a lawn mower, and for a moment wonders where she is. She walks to the window, looks out to the back yard, and just beyond, where the Black Forest stands. The memory of initials in a tree breezes through. She tries to hold onto the image, but laughter trickles in through the open living room windows above and Callie is drawn to the familiar sound. She steps through the front door to a badminton game in full swing. Prue, Jimmy and Jennifer, and Callie's parents are out on the front lawn batting the birdie back and forth. *This I remember well.*

"Come on down, Cal, we need another player on our side," her dad hollers when spotting her. It's a glorious summer day with the sun high above in the blue sky, and a cool breeze filters through. She joins in the fun and feels happier than she has in months.

"You know what happens to the losers, right?" Callie teases her opponents. Jimmy smiles at this long forgotten rule.

"What?" Prue asks.

"Just don't lose and you won't have to find out," Jimmy chimes in.

Wyatt and Mr. and Mrs. Wilson busy themselves with setting the card tables up closer to the house for dinner. Seeing the cars file in, the game is put on hold. The cousins are back, bringing with them Aunt Marilyn, who finds it more and more difficult to maneuver these days. Samantha, Brian, and Tyler drive up in one car, parking next to the cousins. Over the years, the family has become smaller in number, but the turnout is good all the same.

The family picks up where they left off when last they gathered, as if no time has passed.

"... And on this anniversary, Wyatt and Callie, I'd like to give a toast to celebrate you. I can't believe you're still together," a ripple of laughter erupts. "What I mean is, I can't believe you've been together so long. Here's to many more," Jimmy says, raising his cup. The plastic cups are a far cry from the crystal they raised at their wedding. The thought makes Callie smile.

"That looks so good on you," Wyatt says, leaning in to whisper in her ear, broadening her smile.

"I have a lot to smile about these days," Callie says, turning and wrapping her arms around Wyatt's waist. He leans in to give her a quick kiss.

"Get a room," Jimmy hollers from his perch on the Wilsons' front stairs.

Wyatt chuckles. "Before you do that, though, Samantha and I have something for you both. Something we've been working on for a year, actually."

Wyatt and Callie look at each other in bewilderment.

"Hold on a sec. I need to help Sam with the gift. Be right back," Jimmy says, as he rushes to the back of the house where Samantha is waiting. Slowly, they carry the gift with difficulty and place it in front of Wyatt and Callie.

"What is this?" Wyatt says, looking on wide-eyed. He and Callie tear the paper and reveal a slab of wood with a lacquer that shines as if liquid still stands on the surface. There are two legs of rough wood that rest on the ground where it sits.

Callie speaks in a breathy voice. "This is our tree." She speaks as if in another time and place, gently caressing the initials, visible through the liquid shellac.

"How did you? Where did you?" Wyatt mumbles dumbfounded.

"I do believe that I have rendered my brother speechless," Samantha says proudly.

"Samantha knows the contractors that have been clearing the wood for new camps. When she asked the guy if he'd ever come across a tree with initials on it, he said he had. He couldn't bring himself to grind up the tree, yet didn't know what to do with it, so he just saved it for years. It's been in his warehouse collecting dust. Samantha called me and asked if I wanted to go check it out. When we realized it was the actual tree, we decided to make something of it for you guys, and the rest is history. Happy Anniversary, you two."

The four of them embrace. Callie and Wyatt gaze meaningfully at one another feeling the warmth of their family's love. Feeling a flood of emotion, Callie whispers to Wyatt, "Hey, I'm gonna go for a quick run before dinner. You mind?"

"Right now? Everything okay?"

"Yeah, right now. Everything is great, I'm just feeling a bit overwhelmed."

Callie changes into her running clothes and walks out the back sliding glass door. Aside from taking the awful, five horse-size pills each and every day, the exercise part of the protocol she's on has been a no brainer. She's always loved to work out. The feel of her muscles working to run the gravel roads of Franklin is actually a joy. *I can't imagine forgetting this place,* she says, as she runs past the family gathering, waving.

"Where's she going now?" Callie's cousin John asks Wyatt.

"She's got to keep a regimented schedule. This new daily routine her doctor has her on has to be pretty regular. He seems to have done his research, because this protocol is really helping. She's sharp as a tack right now. I feel like when we get home she'll be well enough to get back to what she loves, working with kids at the hospital. It's been a rough few months.

"I heard about the episode she had driving two hours away. I can't imagine."

"It scared us both. She's had fewer and fewer incidents since starting this new routine. I'm so thankful we found a doctor willing to try this new type of treatment. We haven't seen any weird behavior for a few weeks now, and we're really hopeful because she seems to be back to normal. The tough part for Callie is that everything is so scheduled. She really hates taking all the pills, which have to be taken at certain times of day. The new diet has been tricky to follow, but I think she has a pretty good handle on it."

"What happens if she stops cold turkey?"

"I hope to never find out, but the doctor did say that if all the parts aren't put together, then she'll lose it all eventually."

CHAPTER 34
Maddie

The first few months of therapy seem to go as well as can be expected. Lines of communication between Maddie and Zach have opened and they are cordial to one another on the phone. It's far from perfect, but the therapist seems to feel that there is a chance for them to mend what has been broken by Maddie's infidelity.

"Welcome. Come on in and take a seat." Maddie and Zach still arrive in separate cars, but the counselor has noticed that when they come in, they sit a fraction of an inch closer to one another on the couch.

"So, did you do your homework?"

"Yep," they reply in unison.

"Great. Who wants to start?"

"I do," Maddie volunteers without hesitation.

"Okay, super. Your homework was to journal P.I.I.M.B. Physical sensation, image, inner conversation, behavior, memory. Let's hear what you've come up with so far."

"I feel nervous, like how a person would feel walking down a dark alley."

"Great! You're painting a picture with your words. And what is it that you're nervous about?"

"I'm nervous that we won't be able to move past this, that Zach will never forgive me for my stupid, stupid mistakes."

"And Zach, what have you written for us today?"

Zach reaches for his backpack and pulls out a Sponge Bob notebook.

"It's the only notebook I could find. Dylan said I could use it," he says sheepishly, opening up to his writing.

"I feel nervous like watching storm clouds roll in and I'm on a boat in a body of water, not able to get into shore soon enough. Like in the ocean."

"Great. And what do you-"

"... And the waves are crashing over the bow of the boat and I'm sinking. I can't breathe and feel like I'm going to die. Then lightning comes and zaps the middle of the boat, breaking it in half. Then a shark starts circling just waiting for me to fall overboard."

"Oh. Okay. I like how you've used nature to paint a picture. Can you tell us what you think all of this represents?"

"Sure. I feel like if I forgive her, it will happen again and I'll never survive another 'attack.'" He turns to Maddie. "I really can't do this again. I'm telling you, my heart can't take it. I want to forgive you. I really do. But what if it happens again? How can I trust you?"

"Those are some honest questions. It's very difficult to build that trust again after it's been broken. Maddie, are you willing to work on this trust issue with Zach?"

"Yes, more than you'll ever know."

"Sounds good. Here is your homework this week. I want you two to start over. Start as if you have just met and you're dating. Baby steps. Go to a park or sit by a pond. Somewhere you are on neutral ground. There doesn't have to be any physical touch. Just sit and be with one another. No expectations. See where it takes you. Let's try two 'dates' and then report back next week."

Fear clouds Zach's eyes. "How long does this date have to be?"

"As long as you're comfortable with. Like I said, no expectations. Just see where it takes you."

During the week, Zach texts Maddie to ask to meet her at Queeny Park and go for a hike. She accepts his invitation. They meet in the parking lot and walk to the trailhead. Awkward silence ensues for the first mile. Zach finds it easier to talk to Maddie walking by her side than sitting across from her at a table.

"How are the kids doing?" Zach questions.

"They seem to be doing pretty well, all things considered. They ask about you a lot. Zoe doesn't understand what's going on. As a matter of fact, she thinks it's pretty awesome that she has two bedrooms, one at my house and one at your apartment."

Climbing a hill, Zach waits to respond until he's reached the top.

"That makes me feel sad. As in watching a sad movie and the main character's mother dies."

Maddie finds this particular imagery funny and tries to stifle a laugh.

"She's a piece of work."

"Who, Zoe or the therapist?"

"The therapist. All this discussing and describing feelings, I'm sure it's the first time in your life you've had to discuss deep emotions."

"It's not the easiest thing for me to do, but I'm willing to do it if it gets us past this shitty hole we're in."

"Are you saying you're willing to try to make this work?"

Huffing and puffing up the second hill, he waits.

"Mad, as much I'm hurt and super pissed off at you, I can't stop loving you. I can't shut that part of my heart off."

Stunned by this realization, "You still love me?"

"Yes, you bitchy little whore-bag, I still love you."

They finish their hike and walk back to the parking lot to get into separate cars. "Wanna do this again in a few days?" Zach calls out.

"I do."

"Tell me, how did the date go?" the therapist asks Maddie and Zach as they take a seat with a gap of one cushion between them.

"Really well," Zach replies.

"What did you find out?"

"I found out that he still loves me," Maddie beams.

"Well, that is great news. How many dates did you take last week?"

"Two. We plan to take more this week. One with the kids."

"I'm so happy to hear you have a plan. Perhaps we should take a few weeks to let you work through this new stage. Make an appointment at the front desk for two weeks out rather than one. If you have any questions or concerns during this time, just call me. Sound good?"

They continue with their hour-long appointment and plan to meet again in two weeks. Maddie feels as light as a helium balloon. The appointments and dates continue as Maddie and Zach work through their feelings and emotions. They realize that they care deeply for one another after months of discussions, including play dates with the kids.

After one particular play date, the two decide to have dinner with the kids. Dinner ends and Maddie is saying goodbye. It's Zach's night to parent.

"Do you want to come over and tuck them into bed?"

Surprised, Maddie says, "I'd like that very much."

Maddie drives to Zach's apartment and finds it warm and inviting, albeit manly.

"Dyl, wanna read a story?" Maddie asks, holding Dylan's hand as they walk to his room. She climbs into bed with him. He hands her a book called "The Kissing Hand." As she reads how the mother raccoon kisses her babies' hands, she starts to cry.

"Mom, what's wrong? Did the book make you sad? I didn't mean to make you cry. I just think of you when Dad reads this book to me at night."

"I love you, Pickle."

"I love you, too."

Maddie kisses his hand, then kisses his cheek and leaves, turning off the light.

She walks into Zoe's room and kisses her cheek, exiting the room quietly as Zoe is fast asleep after all the fresh air they had before dinner.

Closing the door softly behind her, she walks to the living room and picks up her purse to leave. Zach stands by the door.

"Thanks for letting me do that," she says, as she wipes away the remnants of her tears.

Zach walks closer to her to hug her goodbye. The feeling of physical contact after months without any replenishes his soul.

"I can't let you go," Zach says, holding her closer.

Maddie rubs his back as they hug. "I'm not sure what the therapist would think of this. What are we supposed to do now?"

Looking into her eyes, he leans in and kisses Maddie softly. "I miss you."

"Oh, Zach," the tears begin again. "I've wanted to hear you say that for so long."

He kisses her again with a passion that he's not allowed himself to feel toward her since the discovery of another man.

"It's been so hard living without you."

"Zach, I'm so sorry. I'm so very sorry. I don't –"

He interrupts her with another long passionate kiss. He takes her hand and walks her to his room, closing the door with a soft click. Maddie is breathless in anticipation. She's been longing for this moment for months. She's dreamed of reconciliation, but never dared to bring it up.

He takes her into his arms, and they kiss again. The comfort and familiarity is back and welcomed. After taking her top over her head, she follows suit with his. Before long, they are free of all barriers. Clothes land in a heap on the floor. Zach has a ferocious appetite and Maddie is more than willing to oblige. She's so elated with this development that she takes to him like a ravenous dog to a raw piece of meat. In the moment, she wants to tell him she loves him, she's sorry, she should never have strayed, but nothing comes out. Her mind rattles on yet nothing materializes. The thoughts remain as they continue their lovemaking. She thinks it's odd that neither of them speak, but pushes that thought out of her mind and continues ravishing his body.

He pulls her up off the bed, and silently, they walk to the bathroom. Zach reaches in and turns the shower on. Puzzled, she waits. This is something out of their repertoire. The steam is condensing on the shower door, and as he opens it, the steam billows out, filling the bathroom. Zach takes her by the hand and guides her into the shower. He takes the shampoo and lathers her hair, then rinses. She watches as he gently takes the body wash in his hand and glides it over her body starting at her shoulders. She continues to stand motionless as he moves to her chest, massaging and cleansing as he works. He moves down to her hips, causing her knees to go weak. Unable to stand any longer, he holds her tight, until the sensations pass. Leaning under the warm water, he rinses her skin, pressing her forward and allowing the water to cascade down her back. She reaches out to brace herself on the soap ledge that extends from the side of the shower. The movement from behind has her gripping the ledge for stability, eventually with such force she breaks the soap ledge off the wall. Momentarily all movement ceases. She looks back at Zach, letting a giggle escape her lips. He smiles back at her before commencing in a flurry of movement. As he did for her, she washes his body clean. They embrace one another under the surging water. It feels as if they've been baptized clean of all wrongdoing.

Walking her to the door, Zach speaks first. "Maddie, I want this to work. I need this to work. I need you. I need the kids. I need this family. You're my life." He speaks so honestly, with such sincerity and vulnerability, it's difficult for her to catch her breath.

"Then this will work. No doubt. I'm all in to do the work. I'm going to make you trust me again. I need you to trust me again," she says, looking down at her shoes. He lifts her chin, and she sees the man she loves in front of her

They share a tender kiss full of hope and new beginnings.

CHAPTER 35
Callie

Down past the water pump, she turns up the hill, reminiscing about the time she and Wyatt shared a moment watching the northern lights. *That was decades ago.* The memory lightens her step as she continues to climb. She turns left and runs past the vegetable stand where she recalls Tyler and Riley having a row years ago in their youth. She remembers sitting on the side of the road with a swollen ankle, not wanting to get in the truck with Tyler. *And now they're both gone.* The thought brings on a strong breeze, whipping her ponytail off her neck. Callie takes a right and runs toward Aunt Marilyn's house. Not really having planned to come this way, she decides to let her feet guide her.

Standing at the end of Aunt Marilyn's driveway, hands on hips, she turns in a slow circle wondering why her aunt's car isn't in the garage. Turning, she stares at the traffic light and remembers the time she saw Wyatt with a girl in his front seat and how that weighed heavily on her heart. Lost in memory for a moment, her pocket vibrates with an incoming text.

Wyatt: *Don't take too long. We have dessert coming out in a minute.*

Callie: *Got it.*

Remembering now that Aunt Marilyn is with the rest of the family at the Wilsons' place, Callie gives a sigh in frustration that her memory is foggy today. *This too shall pass.*

Callie turns back the way she came and retraces her steps all the way back to the water pump, where she promptly stops. She feels an energy pulling her as if she is a paperclip being drawn to a magnet. She looks over at Wyatt who stands on the porch of the Wilsons' home and waves. He waves back, and then a look of confusion crosses his face as Callie takes off in the opposite direction. Wyatt watches as he walks to the table of desserts.

Aunt Marilyn, standing next to Prue, watches Callie, and a smile creeps across her face. She knows exactly where her niece is headed.

Callie continues on the gravel road past Riley's grandmother's place, past Aunt Marilyn's family camp, down to the end of the road. She steps over a row of smooth river rock with eyebrows raised. *What is this?* She follows the circular path to the center, keeping her eyes focused on the path ahead. Reaching the center, she stops and looks at the pedal pattern etched in stone around a large, white-barked tree. She's taken aback by the beauty of this magnificent tree, *the lightning tree.*

"That's the lightning tree," announces a voice from behind Callie. Startled, Callie turns to the voice.

"Huh?" Callie questions.

"I had a dream about this place," Prue says with confidence.

"Really? So have you seen it before?"

"Only in my dream."

"Whoa."

In silence, the two stare up at the tree, taking notice of objects hanging from the low branches. They hear the tinkling of a wind chime faintly playing in the breeze. Callie catalogues the items that hang from the lower branches: a glass heart ornament, a small picture frame with a black and white photo of a young child attached to twine, colorful beads, and an orb of glass. Prue explains to Callie the image that came to her in her dream.

"It was like being in a movie. Aunt Marilyn was by my side explaining what everything was."

"Did you ask her about it today, when she got to the Wilsons'?" Callie asks curiously.

"No. I kinda forgot about it until I saw you standing at the water pump. You looked like you were trying to decide which way to go. It was like I was having déjà vu watching you jog down that gravel road. Then I kinda decided to follow you. That's not right. I didn't decide it, my body just started following you. It was really weird."

"Yeah. I get it. My body was drawn to this place, too. I have goose bumps," Callie says, extending her arm to show Prue.

"Me, too," Prue says doing the same.

The two stand a few moments longer admiring the objects, then walk quietly from the circle together. As they walk back to the reunion, Prue picks some blackberries she knew would be there. She picks a few extra and hands them to Callie.

"These have always been my favorite," Callie mumbles as she wipes the juice from her chin.

"Mine, too," Prue says with a giggle.

"So tell me about this labyrinth we just walked through. What did you learn through your dream?"

Prue went through the details and how it made her feel as she exited.

"Why do you think it made you cry leaving the path?"

"The biggest impact on my life was the shooting at my elementary school. It had a lasting effect on me. More than I even knew."

Prue speaks with wisdom and insight decades older than her teenage self.

Callie places an arm around her niece's shoulder and gives it a little squeeze as they walk past the water pump. Looking up, she sees Wyatt with relief in his eye as he smiles to them.

"You missed dessert."

"Nah, we had some on our way back," Callie says with a wink to Prue.

"Where'd you guys go? You had me worried there for a sec," Wyatt says with a nervous smile.

"Did you think I forgot where I was?"

"Kinda," he says sheepishly.

"We had some investigating to do. I'll have to show it to you. I think you'd really like what Aunt Marilyn did down at the end of the road."

Before Wyatt can question what this means, it's time to pack up the car and head to the beach for fireworks. As in years past, the losing team (the cousins this time) has to bring the beer cooler and the rest bring snacks and sodas for the light show.

As colors burst in the sky like brilliant bombs, Callie looks around at her family, so happy to have them all in one place. She examines each face as the fireworks illuminate them. Resting her eyes on Prue, seated next to her dad and Jennifer, she thinks, *what a happy little family they are becoming.* Next to Prue sits Tyler, not so young anymore, in his teens, looking more and more like his uncle every day. Samantha sits with Brian, who oohs and ahhs—the loudest of the group—which tickles Samantha. Another burst of color, more illuminated faces. Callie's parents, in their seventies now, look younger in this light, sitting next to Wyatt. Her heart aches as she studies his relaxed face. This year has taken a toll on him. Feeling a twinge of guilt, she moves on to the other faces and continues searching. She comes to one face staring back at her. Aunt Marilyn produces a soft smile and nods before turning her gaze to the sky. Callie stands to find a spot next to her on the ground. As she sits, Aunt Marilyn taps Callie's knee.

"Hey there, Callie-flower."

"Awe. I haven't heard that since Wyatt called me that a thousand years ago."

"I trust your run was good?"

"It was, thanks. I especially liked the end of my run, but I'm pretty sure you know that already."

"Mmmhmm."

"Prue filled me in about what it all means," A look of surprise falls on Aunt Marilyn's face. "She said she had a dream about the maze or labyrinth or whatever you call it and that crazy, cool tree."

"The lightning tree," she smiles.

"Right. That. Can you tell me about the objects in the tree?"

As she tries to begin, squeals of delight rise above their conversation, making it difficult to hear.

"Let's save it for tomorrow."

Callie's response is swallowed up by bombs bursting in air as the finale gets under way.

CHAPTER 36
Aunt Marilyn

Callie wakes feeling antsy with the excitement stemming from her conversation the night before. Unable to stay in bed any longer, she quietly slips her running shoes on as she listens to the soft snores. She silently opens the back door and is welcomed by the morning fog. The appearance is dreamlike. The cool, crisp air tingles on her skin as if there's an energy field just out of reach, pulling her. She cruises her familiar run to Stewart's and back, but rather than head straight back to the Wilsons' she heads for the lightning tree. Slowing to a trot, she enters the sacred space. The pine needles and stone path glisten in the wake of the mist. The fog begins to lift, allowing shafts of light from the rising sun to peek through. The effect on the tree in the center of the labyrinth is eerie. Callie slows to a crawl as she processes the magic in front of her. The sound of the wind chime reverberates from the tree as if being awoken from a dream. The animated objects appear to be hovering among the bolts of branches. As she exits the path, she sees a figure sitting on a mat on the ground facing the lake, with hands to heart. The sun, burning through the fog, shines upon Aunt Marilyn's face. Not wanting to disturb her, Callie waits, breathing in long slow breaths, slowing her racing pulse. She turns to stand facing the tree and closes her eyes, releasing tension from her shoulders. She can sense someone behind her and slowly opens her eyes.

"What a glorious morning."

"It is," replies Callie.

"Care to walk through with me?" Aunt Marilyn offers as she loops her arm through the crook of Callie's elbow.

"Please."

"As your niece understands, this is a place to bring peace, a place of letting in and letting go. It's where you slow your mind, remove and let go of anger, fear, sadness, and let in the goodness, love and healing powers of this place. This tree with its solid trunk and roots deeply beneath us … you can feel the energy just drawing you near, can't you? Isn't that why you're here right now?"

"That's exactly what I felt running down here."

"This place helps your mind plant seeds of joy, peace, mindfulness, understanding, and love. These seeds are the qualities of your life that lay dormant in your mind until watered. But just as the good qualities lay sleeping, so do the unwholesome seeds of anger, fear, hate, and forgetfulness. Whichever seeds are watered frequently are the seeds that will grow with strong roots in your soul."

Callie's body quivers uncharacteristically with that last seed: forgetfulness.

Aunt Marilyn snaps out of her lucid soliloquy and smiles. "I'm being told to wrap it up." Her face reddens.

Callie looks around, still unsettled by Aunt Marilyn's unusual behavior.

"I have a tendency to bore my audience. Let's take a look at these objects, shall we? This one is by far my favorite, but you know that already," she says, as she touches the bottom of the black and white photo of Lilian. "This one is a heart that Liz sent me for Christmas one year before she passed. And this one, well this one is pretty special." Aunt Marilyn touches the glass orb dangling from the branch. "I was given this one to hang on the tree for young Tyler when he had his battle with cancer."

"Who gave it to you?"

"Samantha. When she was troubled and needed to release her anger and fear, I guided her to the lightning tree and she offered this up."

"But it's just a glass ball. I don't get its significance."

"It's much more than *just a ball*. This glass is filled with young Tyler's breath."

Goosebumps formed on Callie's arm immediately.

"At one of the Art From the Heart functions up here, she brought Tyler. There was a gentleman in the back room that was blowing balls of glass. If the kids chose to, they could blow into the glass bulb they were creating. They captured their breath in glass as a keepsake for parents in case, God forbid, something should happen to them."

"Holy cow."

"Thankfully, Tyler made it."

Feeling overwhelmed, Callie decides it's time to head back.

"Thanks for sharing this special place with me and my family."

"Any time you need a place to think, just remember it's here for you."

The aroma of bacon collides with Callie's senses as she enters the Wilson home, causing her stomach to rumble.

"Mornin," Mr. Wilson says as Callie enters the kitchen. "How was your run?"

"It was magical," Callie says with a faraway look in her eye.

Mr. Wilson stops to look at Callie. "That good?"

"I saw Aunt Marilyn."

"Ah. The lightning tree has that effect on people."

"How did I not know about this?"

"You have to discover it. It finds you when you need it most. I'm a believer in all things mystical, but this tree ... this tree is special."

"Have you always known it was here?"

"Nooooo, no, no. We discovered it a few years ago when we learned of Tyler's cancer and Mrs. Wilson relapsed into depression. It brought on all kinds of suppressed feelings she had from our son Tyler's death many, many years ago. The wind chime you hear in the tree is our contribution. It's a wind chime that our son gave us when he was in his teens. It just seemed right to attach it to the tree. Something about that tree helped pull my wife from her depression, and for that I am eternally grateful. I don't question the quirkiness of Marilyn anymore. She's found something here, real special. Can you feel it," he asks, raising his arm and running his opposing hand down it.

"I can."

"Hey, you," Wyatt says, reaching the top of the stairs. "You run already?"

"Yep," Callie says, leaning into his kiss.

"Something smells delish. Did you make all this, Pop?"

"I did indeed. I wanted to let your mom sleep in this morning."

They each fill their plates and sit around the farm table eating heartily.

"So. What's on the docket today?"

"Mind if I take the boat out? Thought I'd bring Cal around the lake."

"Sounds like a great day. Have fun. I need to bring the mower in for service. Your mother and I will be in town doing that and having lunch. I've invited your parents into town, as well, Callie. I hope they can join us."

"I'm sure they don't have anything planned other than Dad working on his tan. But as you know after all these years, Dad can get tan in the shade on a rainy day."

"True. I've always been impressed with his ability to brown so easily."

"I'm going over to say hello this morning, and I'll remind them about your lunch invitation."

Callie opens the heavy wooden door and is profoundly overwhelmed with the feeling of nostalgia.

"Good morning," Callie calls out.

"We're back here," Callie's mom replies from the back room.

The scent of Listerine wafts past her nose as she walks by the bathroom. *Hi Gramp.* The sound of dishes being stacked and the clack of silverware being collected almost drowns out the voices.

"Hi, Aunt Cal," Prue says from her seat.

"Hey, Prue-bear. What are you all doing up so early? Jimmy, you never get up before noon up here."

"I'm taking Jen, Prue, and Aunt Marilyn fishing today. You know, the early bird and all."

"Ah. So fish for dinner, I take it?"

"Only if he catches enough to feed us all," Jen jabs.

"Every man for himself," Jimmy parries.

"Good luck with that. Hey, Dad, don't forget lunch with the Wilsons in town."

"Callista, I may be old, but I'm not senile." The look on his face registers with Callie. He regrets the words once they've left his mouth. He puts on a brave face and pushes on. "You and your mother have reminded me about a million times. Don't worry, we'll be there."

"K. Just thought I'd remind you once more," Callie says as she exits the camp.

CHAPTER 37
Maddie

"Welcome. Come on in and take a seat," the therapist says to them, noticing they are walking hand in hand. Maddie and Zach sit, knees touching, on the couch.

"So tell me, how are things going? It looks to me like things are looking up."

"We're doing ..."

"It's going ..."

They both speak at the same time, causing the therapist to laugh out loud.

"This sounds promising. Zach, why don't you start."

"Okay, thanks. We're doing really well. Going on many dates each week."

"Can you tell me about the dates?"

"Sure. We have been going on hikes through some of the state parks in the area. Once we had a picnic. Once we brought the kids with us to dinner."

"Tell me how that went. Did the kids enjoy their time?"

"We all did," Maddie says as Zach's cheeks glow.

"I see," says the therapist, smiling. "I hope you both were able to establish boundaries and discuss the hurt and put into words how you will continue to work on your relationship before becoming involved physically again."

"We did," they say in unison.

"It's important you have a plan in place," she says, emphasizing her point.

"We have one. We're going to make this work. We have to. I can't lose him or the kids. I was stupid to think another man could make me feel like he does. The grass isn't always greener on the other side," Maddie adds matter-of-factly.

"That's great to hear. Continue to keep communication open. Don't let things fester. Take weekly dates together alone to discuss each other. I'm feeling good about this. Your progress has been remarkable. I commend you."

At the end of the session, they each hug the therapist, thank her for her service, and promise to keep in touch if there is a need for more sessions. Leaving the office, Zach clasps Maddie's hand and walks out of the building.

"I really wanted to go into detail about our 'date night,' but thought I may be bragging with the whole breaking the soap dish and all."

"I'm sure she's heard all kinds of stories."

"I doubt she's heard that one before." The two sit in the car, each smiling like the cat that ate the canary.

"We're home!" Maddie hollers from the kitchen to a silent house.

"We're down here," Ryan hollers back. During these past few weeks of date nights, they started using Ryan and Jason as sitters. According to Ryan, it is their "starter family," a way of testing the waters to see if they are indeed ready for parenthood themselves. They're keeping an open mind and will determine whether to have children or not based on Maddie and Zach's kids. *No pressure there.* Maddie has no doubt they will make great, adoring parents. The scene set before them serves as proof.

Jason is building a fort out of all the cushions on the sectional with Dylan. Ryan is setting a table for three: himself, Zoe, and Teddy Bear. Ryan has tied a pink apron around his waist and is serving tea from the plastic tea set Zoe got for Christmas. It's a sight to behold. Zach takes out his phone and snaps a few pictures.

"If those go on Facebook, I'll hunt you down. It's the wrong shade of pink for my complexion, plus you didn't get my good side," Ryan says, posing for a new photo. Zach laughs. This all makes Maddie feel lighthearted.

"Hey, Dad, come get in the fort. It's so cool. Jason did this one part where I have a little separate room to do my drawing." Zach walks over to check it out and looks in. In fact, Jason did build a separate section, and in it are pencils and drawing paper.

"Well done, Jason. If your day job doesn't pay off, you have fort building to fall back on."

They tuck the kids in and Zach is about to leave Dylan's room when he asks his dad, "Is everything better now, Dad?"

"What do you mean, Pickle?"

"I mean are you and Mom happy again? Are you staying here forever now?"

Hearing his son's questions pulls on his heart. He sits on the bed and gives Dylan a bear hug. "Yes, Dylan. I'm happy to say I am home now and will never leave you." After waiting for these magical words, Dylan releases tears.

"You don't need to be sad, Dyl. This is good news."

"I know. I'm just so happy." They squeeze one another a little bit tighter before Zach stands.

"Love you, kiddo."

"Love you, too, Dad."

Zach flips the light switch and closes the door. He leans his head against the door for a moment to collect his thoughts. He quietly walks past Zoe's room and peers in. Undetected, he stands in the hallway and watches as his beautiful wife rocks their angelic daughter to sleep. She hums a quiet tune in Zoe's ear. The soft glow of the nightlight creates a breath taking scene. A rogue tear clings to his lashes and he brushes it away. His heart is so full, he feels like he's going to burst. To think their marriage was in the balance and possibly over. Thankfully, with time and patience, they will overcome the past mistakes and move forward happily as a family.

Ryan and Jason

"Damn, those kids are cute," Ryan gushes from the seat.

"They really are. I swear I don't know where the time goes when I'm playing with them."

Hesitant to broach the subject, he tentatively forges ahead.

"So, what do you think about kids, J? You think this is something we should look into?"

"I've always wanted to be a dad," Jason says from the driver's seat, finding it hard to concentrate on the road.

Ryan claps his hands with enthusiasm, leans over and gives Jason a peck on the cheek. "I have the name of someone we can contact. I've had it tucked away just in case this topic ever came up. God, I want a family with you." Jason releases the wheel with his right hand and places it on Ryan's knee, giving it a little squeeze.

"Let's do it," Jason says, looking straight ahead. The silence in the car is deafening. "Rye, breath," he says nervously, taking his eyes off the road for seconds at a time. Ryan exhales and begins to weep openly. Between sobs, Ryan speaks broken sentences. "I thought," forcefully exhaling, "getting married," sharp inhale, "would be the topper." He lets his sentence trail off so that he can catch his breath. "I never dreamed," he takes a jagged breath, "we'd have," breathing in through his nose and out through his mouth, "a family."

"We'll call tomorrow and see what needs to be done. Okay? We'll figure it out tomorrow. Don't put the cart before the horse. One day at a time, okay? You all right?"

"Mmm," he hiccups, "Hmmm."

They continue their drive home comfortably, quiet in each other's thoughts. Each holds on to a part of the other for strength and calm, excited about the uncertain future soon to unfold with children. *Children,* Jason smiles to himself.

CHAPTER 38
Callie

Callie and Wyatt fly home after a wonderful family reunion. Still in the glow of family, Callie stares out the window at 10,000 feet, looking down at the tiny buildings and cars milling about like ants hard at work. *The lightning tree.* She rests her chin on her hand with her nose pressed against the windowpane, deep in thought.

She pulls her bag up onto her lap and depresses the call button.

"Can I help you?" The flight attendant appears out of nowhere.

"Yes, may I have a can of Sprite Zero, please?"

"Sure thing."

Settling back in her seat, she waits for the drink as she lines up her five pills on a napkin. *Yuck.* She says to herself, looking down at what keeps her present. *It's worth it, so stop complaining. Without it life would be a mess. Look at all you would lose.* Sighing, she reaches for the soda and tosses the pills to the back of her throat.

"Welcome back!" Natasha squeals and hops up from her seat at the art table as Callie walks through the electronic door. After a long absence and time off to figure out what is happening with Callie's brain, she's finally back where she belongs.

"Callie! I'm so happy you're back!" Ari announces as she hugs her tiny arms around Callie's waist.

"It's good to be back," Callie says, beaming at the small group that has gathered. Through the door walks Jason, and without a word, he strolls right up and gives her a bear hug in front of all to see.

"Did you miss me?" Callie jokes with her sweet friend.

"Maybe just a little," Jason says, releasing her. "I've had no one to get coffee with. I was a little lost while you were gone. Natasha's great and all, but she's no Callie." He winks at Natasha.

"Time to get to it. I'll see *you* for coffee in a few hours."

"Yes, ma'am." Jason kisses her cheek, then retreats from the room.

"Ari, let's sit. Fill me in. What's going on? Why are you here? I heard you were in remission?"

"I am," she says, straightening the tiara on her fuzzy head. "We're here for a routine check-up. I told my mama that you were going to be coming back today and asked if I could have some time for art. Since we're waiting for the doctor to look over my test results, she said that would be fine."

As Ari talks, Callie walks to the supply closet and opens the doors. She pulls out some construction paper and spies a Tupperware container with bold letters on the front: GLITTER. She shudders at the memory and pushes the box aside.

Hours pass blissfully for Callie. Kids come and go, art is hung on the wall to dry, she feels so alive. Her schedule is short for today. "Don't want to overdo it your first week back," Natasha had said. She cleans up her therapy room and walks out to find her friend waiting.

"Coffee?"

"Sounds great."

She and Jason walk to the coffee counter down the hall from the art room and find a bench to catch up.

"It's so good to be back," Callie muses.

"It's so great to have you back. I've missed you," Jason leans in for a side hug, and Callie breaths in his cologne. The scent lingers, wafting around her like a gentle hug.

"You always smell so damn good. I don't know how you do it. You're in a hospital, working with kids."

"Doesn't mean I have to smell like I do."

"Good point. So tell me what's up. How's Ryan? Did I hear correctly that you've been babysitting for Mad and Zach? Is that actually true?"

"Yeah, can you believe it? Who would have thought that we would actually enjoy it. Guess what?"

"Ryan's pregnant."

"Ha, now that would be a surprise. Close. We're meeting with an adoption agency later this week. Not gonna lie, I'm freaking out a little bit. There's a little girl that's coming into this world in two months and the parents don't have the means to keep her. They're interviewing prospective parents. I hope they like us."

"What's there not to like?"

"Not sure if you remember this, but we're gay, for one thing."

"Are you?"

Jason stops and stares at her dumbfounded.

"I'm kidding. Sheesh. They're going to love you."

"Ryan's been walking around all weekend saying and writing down all different ways to call a man Dad. I think he's sticking with Papa and I'll be Dad. Kinda cute, right?"

Picturing the two with a beautiful baby girl bouncing on their knees brings on the waterworks.

"Ah geez. There's my girl," Jason says with another squeeze.

Callie takes the last swallow of her coffee and throws her cup away.

"Let me know what you hear. I'll be sending out good vibes for you two."

"See you tomorrow. And Cal ..."

"Yeah?" she says, turning around.

"It really is great to have you back."

"Thanks, Jason. See you tomorrow."

"Jesus, Sprout, you're not coming along so si'down!" Sprout jumps around Maddies' feet, tripping her up as she tries to open the door to get outside.

"He hasn't been this excited to see anyone since Penelope was in heat."

"Let me just say a quick hello to him before we take off." Callie opens the door and Sprout jumps like a rabbit all around Callie's feet. She crouches down and lets the dog greet her with happy kisses. Callie laughs as the dog licks, runs in a circle, licks again, and repeats. Finally he lies on his back and allows Callie to rub his belly.

"Now you're just spoiling him," Maddie looks on with a smile.

Callie picks up the aging dog and sets him down inside the door.

"You know, that's the most exercise he's had in months. He'll probably sleep the rest of the day."

The two set off on their run. Callie notices there is a spring in Maddie's step and her pace is faster than Callie remembers.

"Okay, who have you been cheating on me with?"

Maddie looks at Callie in horror.

"Sorry. Wrong choice of words."

"I haven't been running with anyone. I've been doing it on my own. It's been my release of nervous energy."

"How are things going between you guys?"

"Great. Really great. Zach's back home. We're going to put all this shit behind us and work on our family. I'm so happy."

Callie can see it in her face and her body language. Maddie's shoulders relax while she talks.

"What about Hennie? Have you been back to the gym?"

"No. I quit my membership. I heard that Hendrick was fired. Apparently he hit on the wrong member and was slapped across the face in front of everyone. She complained to the manager. It seems they don't like the trainers fraternizing with the clients. Go figure. Who knew?" she says, feigning ignorance.

"And therapy?"

"Great. It was really tough at the start. Remember we talked about that on the phone? He wanted to know how many times I got the big sauce-siege."

"Yeah, I remember. I can't imagine having to go through that."

"It wasn't fun. You know what's fun? Making up. Now *that* is fun."

"Let me stop you right there. No need for details."

"Not even a little?" Maddie teases her friend.

"No, thanks. I have a pretty good idea how much you got."

Maddie looks ahead at the intersection and doesn't turn. She waits for Callie to take the lead.

"Is this a test?" Callie asks, looking at Maddie, then takes a right.

"For the record, my memory is fine now," Callie says, feeling frustrated. "I feel like everyone is walking on eggshells around me."

"Sorry. I just wanted to make sure."

"You can stop *making sure*, okay?"

They continue running back to Maddie's house in silence. Callie picks up the pace and within minutes is in a full sprint. Maddie tries to keep up. The two are shoulder-to-shoulder, breathing heavily. Callie continues to press forward, eventually leaving Maddie several paces behind. Slowing to a walk around Maddie's mailbox, Callie clasps her hands around her head, breathing heavily.

"Okay, I deserved that," Maddie says, panting.

"Yes, you did."

"I'm getting too old for this shit." Still panting, unable to slow her breath, Maddie bends at the waist, hands on her knees, taking deep breaths.

"Me, too," Callie says, laughing, "I may have pulled a hammy."

"That must have been quite a sight for the neighbors to see—two middle-aged women racing on the street. In my mind, I looked like a graceful stallion, but in reality, I'm pretty sure it was more like watching a jackass."

"Ha. Now I'm going to limp my old lady legs home and get into a hot bath. I hope I can walk tomorrow."

"I hope I can straddle my husband later."

Callie groans, "Maaaad," as she limps away.

CHAPTER 39
Jason and Ryan

After months of stalking the adoption agency website, multiple phone calls, emails, and waiting on pins and needles, the call finally comes through.

"The couple has accepted the adoption proposal."

"Oh my God. Is this real? Oh my God."

"Congratulations, you have a baby girl on the way. It's time to prepare the house. We'll have an agent come by to help with ..."

The woman on the other end of the line keeps talking and giving instructions. Jason tries his best to keep up, writing all pertinent information on a notepad. Ryan will want to know all the particulars when he gets home.

"Okay. I guess that's all for now. We'll be in contact to schedule the home visit before the baby arrives."

"Thank you." Jason hangs up the phone feeling numb. He sits in shock for a while, unable to comprehend what just happened. He is still sitting on the couch when Ryan returns from running errands.

"This asshole just cut me off," Ryan says, placing his bags on the table in front of Jason. "I gave him the double bouquet," he says, raising both middle fingers. Then he takes notice of Jason's silence, "What's going on with you?"

"Sit down."

"Oh, no. What happened? Did something happen to Dylan or Zoe? God, not the kids. Please tell me nothing happened to them."

"Nothing happened to them."

"Is it Callie? Did she drive off? Is she lost again? Please tell me it isn't Callie," Ryan pleads, picking at his cuticles—a nervous habit Jason noticed years ago. Jason reaches for Ryan's hands and pulls him to the couch.

"Say something. You're killing me over here."

"Papa, we have a baby girl moving in soon."

Stunned, Ryan emits a "Wha?" then looks away. "Wait, what? What the ... a baby?"

"I just got off the phone with the adoption agency. We're getting our baby girl."

Ryan immediately wells up and becomes a puddle of goo, squeaking out, "We are?" in an uncharacteristically high-pitched voice.

"We are," Jason confirms.

Ryan collapses into Jason, the relief palpable. Within seconds, he jumps to his feet, his mind reeling.

"We need to go shopping. I'm not ready! We don't have a crib. We don't have baby clothes. We need a humidifier. I've researched online, and they say humidifiers are very important for infants."

Laughing, Jason says, "Slow down. We have a few weeks before the due date. I'm told that if we want, we can be in the delivery room when the mom delivers. She said we're welcome."

"That's amazing. *This* is amazing. *You're* amazing!"

"No, you are," Jason plays along.

Maddie and Callie each receive a phone call with the good news and immediately call each other to plan a baby shower for the new parents. It's scheduled for the following week.

"I'll get the wind up penises. I think I still have them in a box somewhere."

"Mad, this isn't a bachelorette party. No wind up penises required."

"That sounds lame."

"They're having a baby. We need to play games with a baby theme."

"Bor-ing."

Laughing, Callie and Maddie come up with ideas and make lists of all the supplies they'll need.

"So we're all set? You'll get the napkins, paper plates, and balloons? I'll get the cake and make the board to place bets on the weight and length?"

"What about-"

"And before you ask if you can get some penis balloons, the answer is no."

"Ah, maaaan. You're a party pooper."

Callie's house is decorated with appropriate pink balloons, paper plates and napkins along with a beautiful cake, decorated with pictures of Ryan and Jason as kids, and an ultrasound photo of their baby girl.

The guests arrive with armloads of gifts for the new parents. Ryan and Jason beam with arms around each other. The party is underway and the betting board is filling in—five dollars a square, with the cash going to the person closest to the correct length and weight. Through the laughter and conversation, Callie hears Ryan and Jason telling Wyatt that the name of the baby is a secret.

"You can tell everyone you're going to call her Callista. No need to keep it a secret anymore," she teases.

"Right, as the middle name maybe. Feel free to call her Madelyn Callista," Maddie suggests.

"It's neither of those names, but thank you for the suggestions," Jason jokes.

Just as he finishes his sentence, he reaches in his pocket and looks at his phone. *Missed call.*

"I'll be back in a sec," he says to Ryan and exits the room. Standing in the front office, he dials the number. The conversation is brief. He hangs up and runs back to the party in a panic.

"We have to leave. Ryan, her water broke, and we're to meet them at the hospital."

"But she's a week early?" Ryan says, blanching.

Callie looks at Wyatt. Wyatt looks at Zach. Zach looks at Maddie. They all holler, "GO!"

Callie hustles them to the door. "Text me what's going on. I want to know all the details."

Ryan and Jason leave hastily in their car.

The partygoers remain. No need to leave: the cake needs to be eaten and the booze needs to be consumed. The celebration continues without the guests of honor. Everyone is having a good time. Callie continues to look at her phone every few seconds, not wanting to miss any communication from Jason or Ryan. The wait continues until 10:30.

Jason: *The eagle has landed.*

Callie: *I sure hope it's not an eagle.*

Jason: *Mother and 6 lbs 8 oz / 21 inch long baby are resting and Ryan and I are blissing out. Will text later.*

Callie: *Congratulations Daddy! Congratulations Papa!*

Jason: *Thanks Cal <3*

"Did you ask him what size the baby is?"

"6 lbs 8 oz and 21 inches long."

A *whoop* erupts from the kitchen as the winner comes forward to collect the winnings.

Callie finds this evening bittersweet. The yearning for a baby has dulled over the years, but still gnaws at her insides.

The partygoers funnel out of the home while Maddie and Callie clean up and Zach and Wyatt "clean" the bar.

Finally snuggling into her bed, she swallows her handful of pills, takes a long swallow from her water glass, and sets it down on the nightstand. A photo pops up on the screen as Callie is plugging in her phone to charge. Jason and Ryan's new baby is bundled in a pink and blue hospital issued blanket with a pink bow around her tiny little head. Under the photo is a message from Jason.

Jason: *Meet your godchild, Alice Elizabeth.*

Stunned for a moment, she texts back.

Callie: *Godchild? Am I the godmother?*

Jason: *Will you be?*

Not able to see the screen through her tears, she wipes her eyes on the hem of her nightshirt

Callie: *I can't think of anything I want more.*

CHAPTER 40
Callie

Callie is in heaven with her new role as godmother. She embraces Alice like a daughter. Jason and Ryan incorporate her in their lives as much as possible: birthdays, holidays, babysitting gigs. Callie can't get enough. Celebrating Alice's impending second birthday, Callie asks if she can create a mural in the birthday girl's bedroom.

"She seems to be big into princesses right now, I'll do a mystical kingdom much like the one I did for Prue when she was little."

"That sounds awesome. Are you sure you have time for this?"

"I'll make time."

"Don't peek yet," Callie warns Jason and Ryan, who is carrying the birthday girl.

"Okay, now open your eyes," Callie says, then holds her breath.

There's a deep intake of breath and a gasp. There on the wall of soft blue is a faraway castle on a hill with a flag bearing the letter A, wavering in the wind. Far below the castle there stand two Kings, one in royal red with a crown of gold atop his head. The other is dressed in royal purple with a silver crown atop his head. Between the two kings stands a beautiful princess in a pink flowing gown with a sparkling tiara atop her chestnut hair. She clasps each king's hand while they gaze down in adoration at their beautiful princess.

"Callie. I'm speechless."

"Pin-sess," Alice squeals, wiggling to get out of her Papa's arms.

"Do you like it?"

"Look at the happy dance our little princess is doing. I'd say she loves it."

"It's really beautiful, Cal. Thank you so much."

"I'm so glad," she exhales.

Pieces of Callie are hidden within the mural. If you look at it closely enough, you'll see Callie sitting in the window of a cottage on the property. Several dragonflies float about in the castle, and behind the cottage stands a massive tree with branches that resemble bolts of lightning. Jason stands closer, inspecting the art.

"Is that what I think it is?" he says, tracing the branches of the tree.

"The lightning tree, yes. That's the tree I told you about up in Vermont."

"That's so cool," Jason coos.

"You're very talented," Ryan states.

Shrugging her shoulders, Callie says, "When you make art for a living, it starts to overflow into other parts of your life."

Alice flops on her bed and rolls off partially pulling the bedspread off, before exiting to find her princess play clothes down the hall.

Jason and Ryan watch quizzically as Callie pulls at the sides of the cover.

"You gotta make sure the bedspread is on the right way," she says as she straightens the bedspread out.

"Why?" Ryan questions.

"Because the bedspread on a bed is like the frosting on a cake."

Alice runs back in with her pink princess gown on inside out and backwards. Jason helps the wiggling little girl out and back into her gown, laughing as she settles down with her teddy bears in front of the mural.

"Could she be any cuter? I mean, seriously. Could she?" Ryan oozes.

"No, she really couldn't."

Getting into bed that night, she realizes she hasn't taken her pills, but she's too tired to get out of bed. *I'll just take them in the morning,* Callie thinks as she drifts off to sleep. She wakes in a cold sweat, paralyzed with fear. Slowly, she opens one lid at a time with trepidation that someone or something will be staring back at her. To her relief, no one is there, no one but Wyatt happily slumbering next to her. *How does he do that?*

Since the diagnosis of early onset dementia, her sleeping pattern has been disrupted. She's not sure if it's due to her medications or uncertainty about what the future holds. Once she started on the melatonin, she began sleeping better, but lately she's been self-diagnosing, taking only the medication she deems necessary. *I may have to start taking that pill again. I need my sleep.* She sits up in bed, thinking hard to reclaim the nightmare she just had. She finds the task next to impossible. Finally able to settle down, she returns to her pillow and closes her eyes. Slowly, as she begins to drift off, the nightmare unfolds again, as if a premonition.

Callie walks slowly around the maze of stone in the cool
evening with only the stars giving her light. She travels in circles
until she reaches the six-petal inlay. She gazes up through curved,
stark white branches into the evening sky and feels a presence.
Her white flowing gown billows as the breeze slips through her
legs. Feeling uneasy, she walks closer to the tree, following the
sound of the wind chime that once belonged to Wyatt's brother.
The mesmerizing melody lingers in the air. She walks barefoot
around the tree, tracing the alabaster bark as she goes. It's rough
and cool to the touch. Someone is with her just out of sight, in
the shadow of the pine trees across the maze from the lightning
tree. She feels him there, but he has yet to materialize. *Hello?*
She says to the shadows dancing in her periphery. Silence. She
walks the path of letting go and an overwhelming sense of hope-
lessness hits—the sort of desperation that feels like falling into
a black, endless pit. She walks, looking on at eyes around her,
watching these strangers breath air in and then exhale, just to
continue onto their very next breath. It's the despair that she felt
after realizing she would never carry a child. The words *you'll
never be a mother,* and in the next moment wondering if it would
be easier not to exist. It hurt to search for the light in her darkness. It hurt to be happy.

She looks out to the lake for comfort. Tears of uncertainty
and fear creep to the corners of her eyes. The footsteps approach
her from behind and she feels the energy of this person as he
nears. Fear paralyzes her. Unable to turn toward the entity, she
continues to look out onto the lake. A large mechanical beast,
the size of a VW bus, materializes. It is munching on any green-
ery near the water. The crunching of matter, like bones snap-
ping in metal jaws, can be heard from the shoreline. Recognition
registers and the sound conjures the memory of a story she
heard long ago. Feeling the presence descending upon her, she

summons the courage to turn around. There, staring back at her is a shell of a man. His hollow eye sockets devoid of light, his skin peeling away from his bones, the stench of decaying flesh like week-old fish left out on the counter. The clothes he once wore, nothing but a disintegrating film. A scream is caught in her throat, willing its way out as this person, this thing, this water-logged, bloated body stands in front of her grinning through an empty orifice. He circles around Callie as she stands frozen in place. He hums to the melodic tune of the wind chime as he scatters what's in his hand around her. Callie's breath is shallow as she follows the objects falling to the ground with her eyes. The familiar oblong shapes of blue, white and pink surround her in a ring as the carcass continues to circle her. The smell of the rotting flesh makes it difficult for her to breath. It stops in front of her with a laugh as it throws the remaining objects to the ground and vanishes before her eyes. Once it is out of sight, she's able to move again. She takes a step forward and takes in a full, slow breath. Callie crouches to her knees and collects a handful of the items to inspect. *My pills.*

"Did you tell Wyatt about it?" Natasha asks Callie the next morning at the art table.

"No. It's just a weird, silly dream. I probably ate something that didn't agree with me."

"Who was the creepy guy in the dream?"

"The only person I can think of is the guy that my Aunt Marilyn was supposed to marry when she was young."

"Supposed to?"

"She turned him down and then he took his own life."

"Oh, geez. That's tragic."

"You know those cookie cutter machines that take the weeds out of the lake?" Natasha shakes her head. "Yeah, well that machine pulled up his body. That's how they discovered he was dead."

"Oh, man."

"I'm not quite sure why he was throwing my pills on the ground. That part is really weird. I can usually figure out my dreams." *You didn't take your pills last night.* The thought crosses her mind, but that part she's keeping to herself.

"Huh. Weird. I'm sure it'll come to you," Natasha says as the next group of art patients walks through the door.

"I'm gonna watch TV in bed, I'm pooped." Callie walks over and plants a kiss on Wyatt.

"Okay, I'll be in in a minute."

Callie walks to the bathroom to brush her teeth, wash her face, and take her medication—her nightly regime—but on her way she first stops in the laundry room to move over the wash to the dryer, irons a shirt for work in the morning, and waters the house plants. Fifteen minutes later, Wyatt is already in bed as Callie walks to the bathroom.

"I thought you said you were going to bed?"

"I am. I just wanted to get a few things done first."

Callie closes the bathroom door behind her. She takes out her pills and lines them up on the bathroom sink. Before taking the pills, she turns the sink on and fills up a cup of water to give the lone orchid a drink. As she reaches for the cup, one of the pills slips off the counter into the sink and down the drain. It's a slippery slope, and the pill is gone in an instant. Callie just stands there staring as it disappears. She's thoughtful for a moment. *I'm fine without these. I don't need this shit anymore.* She locks eyes with her reflection. In essence the image is Callie, yet something is off. She stares back, unflinching, looking into eyes devoid of life, the shell of a human. The light is nearly extinguished far beyond the recesses of her orbital bones. *Look what you have become: merely a prisoner of modern medicine.* Sensing the feeling of despair swallowing her whole, she's losing sight of the light beyond the onyx center. She slowly, methodically flicks the first of five oblong shapes down the drain in no particular order. She begins with the pink one. Watching with interest, she imagines the pink pill tumbling through the drain, around s-curves past the trap to its fateful end, whisked away into an abyss. Callie waits a tick before casually inching her fingers over to the blue tubular shape. She hears a voice in her head again. *One at a time. Nice and slow.* She imagines each pill dissolving steadily, eventually disappearing completely down the drain. She turns to water around the base of the orchid, brushes her teeth, washes her face, and without another thought, turns out the light.

CHAPTER 41
Maddie

Jason and Ryan prepare for Alice's fifth birthday. She's excited, dressed in her party dress and ready for her guests to arrive. Ryan is giddy with excitement for his daughter to celebrate another birthday. As every year, there is a theme, and this year the theme is dressing as your favorite kids' TV character. Ryan is dressed as Tinky Winky from the Tellytubbies, no longer a running series. He manages to get Jason to dress as Po, much to his chagrin. Alice loves the costumes. She's found a love for the show and can't get enough of the strange alien creatures in red and purple, yellow and green. Alice is dressed as Dipsy in green, her new favorite color.

Ryan answers the door in his purple costume carrying a big red handbag.

"Eh-oh," Ryan says in his best Tinky Winky impersonation, opening the door.

Wyatt rolls his eyes, standing at the door with his red sport coat on.

"Who are you supposed to be?"

"I'm Captain Kangaroo. Can't you tell?"

"I was kinda hoping you'd dress as something Alice would recognize, but this'll do." A disappointed Ryan steps back to let Callie and Wyatt walk through the door.

"I tried to tell him that," Callie says. She is wearing a backpack, shorts, and a t-shirt.

"Let me guess. You're Dora?"

"Yep," she smiles.

The party gets under way with characters from all eras of television. Callie is surprised at how many people dressed up, though Ryan really didn't give anyone an option. *You either dress up or don't come to the party.* There are relatives from both sides of the family, and work friends. One rather large family member is sitting at Callie's side as the cake is being cut and passed out to all. Ryan hands cake to Callie and the woman.

"Boy, is that woman a fatty," Callie says to Wyatt, sitting on the other side of her.

Leaning in to the woman eating the cake, Callie says, "Hey, sweetheart, lay off the cake."

Mortified, the woman takes her cake and walks away from Callie.

"*What* are you doing?" Wyatt says, setting his cake down, his eyes bulging. "That was so rude" he hisses, appalled at Callie's behavior.

Ryan marches in the room and pulls Callie by the arm to the front hall, furious.

"What was that? Can you explain to me what you meant by calling my aunt a fatty?"

Blinking, Callie looks at Ryan as if he's speaking another language.

"I … I … I'm sorry. I didn't mean anything by it," she stammers, clearly confused.

"You didn't *mean* anything by it? Are you kidding me? I think you and Wyatt should leave. My aunt is distraught because of what *you didn't really mean.*"

Jason rushes in and stands next to Ryan. "Hey, they don't have to leave. It was a mistake. She obviously didn't mean to make your aunt feel bad." Turning to Wyatt and Callie, "Just take a seat and we'll get the birthday girl to open her gifts.

Ryan walks away, fuming, "Fine," giving one final glance toward Callie as if she were just some filthy creature in Callie's skin.

They all walk back into the room where the party continues. Alice is none the wiser as she opens her gifts with glee. The next gift is from Jason and Ryan, but everyone really knows Ryan is the shopper. Alice squeals as she throws the wrapping paper aside and runs into Ryan's arms.

"Thank you, Papa! A new Dipsy doll. How did you know that's what I wanted?"

"I had a hunch," he says, beaming with pride. He continues to watch his daughter open her gifts between peels of laughter, hugging each person as she goes. Coming over to hug Callie and Wyatt, she thanks them each for their gift.

Wyatt stands and tugs on Callie's elbow, "We're leaving."

He walks to the hosts and says, "I'm really sorry, Ryan." He takes Callie by the elbow through the front door to the car, feeling the stares on their backs as they leave.

"What the hell was that?"

"I'm sorry. I'm so sorry," is all Callie can manage.

The drive home is silent. Wyatt feels disconnected from Callie, and it scares him.

"I think I need to lay down," Callie says as she walks through the door to her bedroom.

Wyatt's phone buzzes an hour into Callie's nap.

Jason: *Is Cal okay?*

Wyatt: *I'm not sure what's going on. All I know is that Callie would never humiliate someone like that. I don't know where it came from. Please tell Ryan I'm so sorry. I hope we didn't ruin the party.*

Jason: *You didn't ruin the party. For the record, his aunt really does need to lay off the cake.*

Ryan holds a grudge for weeks and then eventually gets over the embarrassing display. Callie apologizes multiple times, wearing him down. Finally putting the incident behind them, they move on, soon forgetting it even happened.

Months roll on without incident until Callie walks into the kitchen and Wyatt laughs at her choice of outfit. She has a blouse on with a camisole over the top.

"Cal, I think you made a slight mistake."

"What?"

"I think you meant to put that cami on first," he smiles.

"Oh, great," she says, looking down. She walks back to her room and Wyatt finishes his coffee and waits to say goodbye before he leaves for work. The minutes tick by and Wyatt continues to wait, finally walking back to the bedroom to check on Callie.

"You almost ready to go?" He stops in the doorway and looks in to see Callie sitting on the bed staring off into space in only her underwear.

Panic rises up. "Cal?"

She slowly turns to look at him.

"You okay, beautiful? Why don't you lie back and I'll get you a drink of water."

I'm calling the doctor.

He walks to the hall and pulls his cell phone out of his pocket.

"I'd like to make an appointment for Callie Wilson. It's kind of an emergency. Yes, we can come in today. Okay. Thanks." His next call is to Natasha.

"Hi, Tash, it's Wyatt Wilson. Callie isn't well today and won't be in to work. Nope, she'll be fine." *I hope. Please, God, let her be okay.*

"Is this something new that you're seeing?"

"This is the second really weird thing she's done in the past six months. The first time she told our friend's aunt she was too fat to eat cake and now this, but the woman really was heavy. It just seemed weird hearing her say something mean. She doesn't have a mean bone in her body. She's had some other things, but I just chalked it up to middle age. I forget things a lot, too."

"Tell me more about the forgetfulness."

"Sometimes she'll forget where she put her car keys. One time she put the TV remote in the fridge, but I've done stupid stuff like that before."

"Is she still able to cook meals and clean around the house?"

"We both do. There was this one time ..."

"What happened?"

"She couldn't remember how to make lasagna. We just laughed it off and I finished the recipe."

"Is she following the protocol?"

"She's been following it religiously for the past several years "

"Interesting. Let's get to the bottom of this then, shall we?"

The doctor calls Callie into the doctor's office from the reception area where she sits waiting.

Callie and the doctor talk as Wyatt sits and listens.

"Callie, can you try something for me?" The doctor places a blank sheet of paper in front of her and places a pen next to it.

"Can you draw a clock face and put the numbers on it for me?"

Callie picks up the pen and draws a circle, but is unable to continue.

"Cal, draw the numbers," Wyatt urges her on.

Callie stares at the paper, unsure what to do next.

"That's fine. Let's try something else. Can you count backwards from 100 by twos?"

"One hundred, ninety-eight, sixty-three, seventy-two, eighty-four."

"Okay thank you, that's enough. How about we try another drawing exercise. Can you draw some shapes for me? How about a circle and square and a triangle."

Callie starts to draw squiggly lines on the paper, nothing remotely like the shapes. The doctor places a hand on Callie's hand and stops her moving pen.

"That'll be all. Thank you, Callie."

"Am I going to be all right?"

"You're going to be just fine. Get some rest. Let me get your medication and a glass of water."

"NO!"

"Cal?"

"No more pills. I'm not taking them. You can't make me take them."

"They're going to make you better."

"I said no. Nonononono!" she screams, belligerent now.

"Okay, okay. No pills. Let me just get you a cup of water."

Callie watches as he walks to the bathroom. A ripple of laughter escapes her lips. It comes out in bursts, fast and loud, sounding maniacal. The hair on the back of Wyatt's neck stands on end and his hands perspire.

Wyatt walks to the bathroom, grabs at the plastic drinking cup, but it slips out of his hand. He watches as it tumbles in the air, and lands with a thud against the orchid planter, causing it to topple. Dirt falls to the tile floor, along with the orchid plant. He quickly lifts the plant in order to place it back in its home, but notices it no longer fits. Removing the plant once more reveals dozens of pills rolling around the bottom of the planter. He dumps out the pills into the cup, replaces the orchid, sets it back on the side of the tub. Hands shaking, he walks to the sink, places both hands under running water and splashes his face. Wyatt grips the sides of the sink and lowers his head. *Jesus.*

CHAPTER 42
Callie

2027

The seasons change and time marches on. A new normal emerges for Callie and Wyatt and all that love them. After years of trying to keep Callie on the road to wellness, she continues to refuse to take the medication that will keep her on the right track. She's belligerent each and every time she is given pills to take. Wyatt is no longer able to fight her on this and resigns to the fact that he is losing his beloved wife. He sees her slipping away little by little each day. It started slowly, but over the years, her ability to remember things is becoming more and more difficult. Wyatt is trying everything in his power to save her from herself. He brings up situations from the past, discussing family and friends, using pictures to help jog her memory. There are glimmers of recognition, but only momentarily. Even her sanctuary, after decades of dedication and hard work, is no longer. Unable to work for years now, she has had to close that chapter of her life. Father Time has crept in and wrinkled her skin. Her hair, once a beautiful chestnut, is now snow white as she drifts well into her sixties, unaware of her change. This new normal brings on adjustments. Wyatt, used to having just Callie and himself in the house, has found it difficult to have another in their space, but Betsy is a lifesaver in Wyatt's eyes. Well worth the discomfort of dancing around each other. She comes to the house to watch Callie while he's at work, and for that, he is eternally grateful.

"Morning, beautiful," Wyatt says with a smile on his face. "Time to get up. Betsy will be here shortly to spend some time with you." Wyatt opens the blinds on their bedroom window, allowing the bright spring sunshine to lighten up the room. He places her shoes at the side of the bed along with her clothes and leaves the room. When he returns, he can see that she's put the shoes on the wrong feet, but has the clothes on correctly.

"Sweetheart, let me help you with your shoes."

Callie smiles at Wyatt.

"Where are you going?"

"It's time for me to go to work. I'll be home soon." The doorbell rings. "Oop, there's Betsy. Come on, let's get the door."

Together they walk to the front door and let the pretty, forty-year-old brunette into the house.

"Good morning, Callie."

"Wyatt, I don't need her here."

Each morning they have this same discussion.

"Honey, I have to go to work. Betsy's going to hang out with you until I get home."

"I want to hang out with *you*," Callie says softly with tears in her eyes. This emotional outburst breaks Wyatt's heart.

"I know. I want to hang out with you, too, but someone has to pay the bills," he jokes.

Betsy looks on in sympathy.

Wyatt gives Callie a kiss on the lips and leaves the house.

"How about I make you some breakfast?" Betsy suggests.

"I'm not hungry."

"I'm going to make something anyway." Betsy knows this game all too well. Callie will claim she's not hungry, but the minute food is placed in front of her, she'll clean her plate. Betsy carries on a one-sided conversation, trying to engage Callie.

"It's starting to warm up outside. I think we should strap on our running shoes and go for a jog. Maybe stop by and see if Maddie is home today. I think today is her day off," she says, peeking at Callie as she continues to cook.

Betsy has been very good at keeping Callie busy throughout the day by exercising, yard work, running errands, walking to see Maddie for a visit, anything to keep her mind sharp. She always has a jigsaw puzzle at the ready for any downtime they may have. She's been a blessing to Wyatt. Setting a plate of scrambled eggs in front of Callie, Betsy sits and continues conversing while Callie mindlessly finishes her breakfast.

"Now see? You were hungry after all."

"Why are you still here?" Callie asks abruptly. Betsy has grown used to these outbursts. They no longer ruffle her feathers.

"Silly. I'm here to keep you company whether you like it or not. You know you like when I'm here. You know you do," Betsy says, elbowing Callie softly. Callie lets a giggle escape her lips.

"Let's get those shoes on and go find Maddie, shall we?"

The two women get Callie's running shoes on. Callie is in great shape for a woman in her sixties. She's in great shape for a woman half her age, for that matter, thanks to Betsy.

"You're not going to let me beat you today, are you?" Betsy teases.

"That's doubtful," Callie says, picking up the pace. It's a good day. Callie is full of energy, talkative and present. Not all days are this way. This is a blessing, and Betsy is thankful on this sunny, bluebird day.

Callie reaches Maddie's door and stops to catch her breath. Betsy knocks softly.

"Should I wait out here for you?" Callie asks Betsy.

"No, Callista, we're going to go in and have a visit with your friend, Maddie."

"Oh, okay. Right. I forgot."

The door opens and Maddie's smiling face comes into view.

"Holy shit, Cal. You look great!" This exclamation puts a smile on Callie's face. Maddie opens the door to allow both women in. Betsy stands next to Maddie and whispers, "She's having a good day. I'm going to leave you two alone for a bit. I have some errands to run. If you need anything at all, call me on my cell. I don't think you'll have any problems, though. Enjoy your time." Maddie closes the door behind Callie's caregiver.

"Want some coffee?"

"Sure," Callie says from her seat at the kitchen table. "Where's Sprout? Sprout! Here boy!" Callie calls out. Maddie tries to conceal her disappointment.

"Cal, Sprout's been gone for years."

"Oh. Sorry," she responds softly.

"It's okay. Sometimes I forget, too." Maddie carries two cups of coffee to the table, fixed the way Callie likes it. "Sometimes when I'm walking around the house in the morning, I think I hear him barking. It's really weird what your mind will do. Other times, I think I see him curled up under the end table in the family room. I miss him."

"That's the story of my life," Callie says.

"How so?"

"I miss everyone."

As Callie sits at the table, unable to hold her train of thought, she takes a paper napkin and folds it up into a small square, then places it in her pocket.

"How *are* you doing?"

"Most days are pretty good, some are bad. What can I tell you?"

Callie begins to fold a second paper napkin and places it with the first one, in her pocket.

"I'm glad you're here. Have you seen Natasha in a while?"

"I haven't been there ..." Maddie waits patiently for Callie to finish her sentence, but Callie just lets it die off.

"Zach should be home soon with the kids. He sent them to my parents for a visit. When Betsy called to tell me you were coming over, I thought it would be nice for the two of us to have some time to chat. Alone." Maddie sets two pictures on the table. "This one is Dylan and this one is-"

"Zoe. Oh, wow. Look how big they are," Callie looks on, surprised.

"Yeah, Dylan drove Zoe over to see their grandparents. He's 26 and Zoe is 23. I just wish they would find their own places. Marone! He should be having babies and making a life for himself—enough of living with Mom and Dad. He has a wonderful girlfriend. She's Italian," Maddie says with a smile.

"That's what I would think," one of Callie's favorite expressions as of late.

"Right? Let's hope Zoe finds a nice Italian man."

The two women talk about family and Maddie's children until Zach walks through the garage door.

"Hey there, Cal," he says, kissing her on the cheek.

"Hi, Zach."

"Remember Dylan and Zoe?"

"Pickle."

"Ha ha ha. Not many people call me that anymore," Dylan says with a laugh.

"Sorry. Sometimes it's hard for me to remember things."

"Oh, no, it's okay. I don't mind if you call me that. I like it. Especially coming from you."

"Knock, knock," Betsy says in a singsong voice as she enters Maddie's house. "How's everyone doing? Did we have a nice visit?"

"Hi, Betsy. It was good. Thanks for bringing Callie by."

"All right. You ready?" she says, looking at Callie.

"Sure."

They walk out the front door and begin a slow jog back to Callie's house.

CHAPTER 43
Wyatt

"I know, Pop. I'm trying really hard to keep it together. It's just awful watching her disappear before my eyes."

"Hang in there, son. Why don't you bring her up for a visit. You know how much she loves the lake. All the family she has up here might be good for her. You could stay with us, or I can check and see if her grandfather's place is available for rent."

"Can you check availability? I'd love to spend some time in that camp with her. Maybe that will jog her memory some."

"If it's not available, just plan on staying with us. You mother would love a visit."

"Thanks, Pop."

"Are you going someplace?" Callie says, hearing the tail end of his phone conversation.

"I thought it'd be fun to go to Vermont and visit this summer. What do you think?"

"That's what I would think."

Unable to respond to her repetitive phrase, he walks to the bathroom where he keeps the dirty clothes hamper and collects the clothes to do some laundry. Carrying it past Callie to the laundry room, he watches her sit on the couch looking through a magazine. For someone who used to be an avid reader, the fact that magazines are all that attract her attention ignites a low burn in the pit of his stomach.

Wyatt pulls the clothes, one article at a time, to check pockets. Callie has developed a paper napkin fetish, and he made the mistake of not checking pockets last time. He almost had to buy a new washer. Wyatt extends his hand deep into the first pocket and pulls out a fist full of napkins. That low burn is now a medium flame. He throws the wad into the trashcan before moving on to the second pocket. His hand hovers over the fabric, willing his shaking hand to find nothing. Slowly, he extends his hand to the depths of the pocket and closes his eyes. He drags his hand out and removes the contents, placing them on the counter. Looking down, he counts four more napkins. Wyatt clamps down on the pile and crumples them into his fist so tightly his knuckles turn white. He can feel his nails piercing his palm. He throws the remaining contents into the trash, then proceeds to kick the trashcan over. The flame inside him now an inferno. The anger consumes him as he pummels the washing machine until there is a mist of red fleck against the stark white of the appliance. His frustration slowly subsides into silent, angry tears. He drops to the floor of the laundry room, in a crumpled heap, red faced, out of breath, and bloodied

As Wyatt and Callie step off the plane from their last leg, Wyatt can see a change come over Callie. She's looking around and smiling. She recognizes her surroundings and seems clearer than she has been in years. Unsure why this transformation is coming over her, he just goes with it, and they enjoy their drive up to Vermont, to the Wilsons' home. Driving through Franklin, stopped at the light in front of Aunt Marilyn's house, Wyatt's heart skips a beat.

"Let's stop in and see my aunt."

"Now's not a good time. We'll come back," he says nervously.

"Okay, maybe after dinner."

"Maybe."

The two drive up the driveway to the saltbox home at the end of the gravel road. The red pickup truck is parked closest to the garage.

"Is Tyler home?"

"Oh, no, he's with his wife. They may stop by later."

"I'm so happy to hear he made it home safe and sound."

"Safe and sound? Oh, no, Cal. He never made it back. He died in Lebanon decades ago. Remember? We had a funeral for him. It was a terrible time for the family," Wyatt says gently.

"Right. Yes, of course. I saw the truck and thought of him."

"I drove that truck for years after he died. Pop wanted me to have it."

"That I remember," she smiles. Wyatt smiles back.

"Let's go in and see my folks, k?"

"Sure."

They bring their luggage in and set the bags down in Wyatt's old room. "There's a family in Gramp's Camp today. They're finishing up their week vacation and leave tomorrow morning. We'll be able to stay there starting tomorrow night, once the cleaning people change the sheets and get it all tidied up for us."

"That's wonderful."

The Wilsons, now in their 80s, still active yet slowing with age, are thrilled with their guests.

"How would you two like to go for a ride in the boat while we get the grill going?"

Wyatt looks to Callie and asks, "Whaddya say, beautiful?"

"Let's do it."

The boat ride is like going back in time. The two travel around the lake, passing the old rope swing, still intact—albeit with a newer rope. They travel pass Jimmy's old place, and past Aunt Marilyn's family's place when Callie says, "Oooh, look at that!

I can see the lightning tree from here. Funny I've never noticed that tree before. I guess I really never looked for it before."

This lightens Wyatt's heart.

"Yep, it's a great tree"

"We'll have to get a closer look tomorrow."

"You got it."

They continue around the lake, past the state park beach, rows of camps on the opposing shoreline, past Stewart's, the Black Forest, and back to the dock.

"I love this lake," she says wistfully.

"Me, too. We can take as many rides in this boat as you want while we're here."

"Can we visit the island?"

"Probably not right now, but at some point, I don't see why not."

Callie sits staring at the island from her seat in the boat.

"That first night on the island was so special. You made it so special for me."

"It wasn't that special. The bugs were awful, if you recall."

"It didn't matter to me. The way that night ended is what mattered."

"That part was very special," he says, squeezing her knee. She turns to him with a longing in her eyes he hasn't seen in a very long time. A foreign emotion bubbles up to the surface. Excitement wells up along with hope, but knowing how she can react and then retract a moment later, he's careful. Not wanting to overstep the boundary, he tamps down his amorous feelings. Disappointment registers as he says, "It's time to get inside for dinner. I'm sure Pop has it all grilled and ready to go." With that statement, the moment is whisked away like a dandelion seed torn from its base and cast upon a cool breeze.

The following afternoon, as the two are about to go for a jog to the lightning tree, Wyatt's father pulls him aside. "Son, have you told her yet?"

"No. I don't think she's going to handle it very well. Her memory is spotty most days, but up here … she's different. I feel like I'm getting her back. I'm not going to say anything until she asks."

"Is that a good idea? She's going to ask sooner or later."

"Enough, Pop. I'll tell her when I tell her."

"Tell who what?" Callie asks as she walks past the two men.

"Uh, that Gramp's Camp won't be ready until four this afternoon."

"No problem. Let's get going. I'm so excited to see the tree again. Bye, Mr. Wilson."

"Have a nice jog, sweet girl," Callie hears as she closes the front door behind her.

"Your dad is so sweet. It's a shame he's getting so old."

"It is. If you haven't noticed, so are we."

Getting closer to the tree, Wyatt starts to feel anxious and unconsciously slows the pace.

"What's going on? Is your hamstring bothering you again?"

"No, not really. Just feel slow today."

They continue on at a snail's pace, which frustrates Callie. "I'll meet you there," she says, taking off in a trot.

She marvels at the magnificent tree as she steps into the labyrinth. She circles slowly, following the path until she reaches the center. At this point, Wyatt has joined her, but has not entered. He stands watching her as she slides her hand across the textured bark. She looks on, wide-eyed, like a child full of wonder.

"So that's Tyler's wind chime?"

"My mom's, but Tyler gave it to her."

"And this is Aunt Marilyn's baby girl, Lilian. I remember that photo," she says pointing at the low hanging black and white photo.

"It is."

"That is your nephew Tyler's glass globe, right? Aunt Marilyn told me about that one. I remember seeing a glass blower work on those with kids at Art From the Heart each year I went. It's a pretty special globe."

"Yep, it really is. I'm happy Samantha got Tyler to make that for her."

"Is Aunt Marilyn coming over tonight?"

"Nope. Not tonight."

"Can we drive over to see her then?"

"We'll go by tomorrow, okay?"

"Should I call and let her know we won't be by until then?"

"Nah, I'll let her know," he lies.

CHAPTER 44
Callie

Callie can tell something is going on. Wyatt has always been a terrible liar. It must be important or Wyatt would be spilling the beans. She drops the subject and by the next morning has long forgotten being suspicious.

"Morning, beautiful," Wyatt says to Callie as she pulls on her running shoes.

"Where are you going?" he asks cautiously.

"I'd like to go for a run by myself today. Not far. Just around here, maybe as far as Stewart's and back."

"We just ran last night. Aren't your legs tired?"

"That was a short run. You know how I like to do longer ones than that."

"You're not as young as you used to be. You don't want to hurt your knees."

"Wyatt, you've never been worried about my knees before. What's going on?"

Walking up to her, he rests his hands on her waist. "I worry about you getting lost."

He went and mentioned the elephant in the room.

"I'm forgetful, yes. I get lost sometimes, yes. But I've been pretty good lately. I feel great right now, and I want to get some exercise. Didn't the doctor say to keep exercising to keep my mind as sharp as possible?"

"Yeah, but do you think it's a good idea?"

"Yes, I do."

Callie stands in front of Wyatt with hands on her hips, not backing down.

"Okay, fine. Just don't be gone too long."

Before he can say *be careful,* she is out the door.

This place makes her feel so alive. Something about the fresh air and farmland gives her a spring in her step. She rounds the corner, passing the pump, up the hill toward town. Pressing on, she can see the Vermont window come into view. Running up the drive, something feels different. Callie slows to a walk and knocks on the door.

"Hey there, Callie, good to see you."

"Steve? Is Aunt Marilyn here? Are you here for a visit?" she asks her cousin.

Steve realizes Callie has forgotten one very important detail.

"Uh, why don't you come in and sit a spell."

Callie enters the home, looking around at all the boxes on the floor.

"Is Aunt Marilyn moving?"

Steve is now on his phone texting. "Hang on a sec, Callie. I have to take this call." He walks outside and talks very animatedly, keeping an eye on Callie through the window. Callie busies herself by walking around the boxes and reading the labels. *Kitchen - keep. Linens - donate. Pictures - keep. Clothes - donate.*

Steve puts his phone back in his pocket and comes in as Callie rummages through an open box and comes up holding Lilian.

"What's going on?" Callie asks, agitated.

"We'll talk about it in a minute. Can I get you a drink of water? I'm gonna get a drink of water. I have some booze here, too, if you'd like something other than water. Maybe a snack? I think I may still have some food in here. I haven't been to the grocery in a few days." Steve is rambling with nervous energy.

As Steve hands Callie a drink, the old familiar red pickup truck pulls into the drive. Wyatt quickly puts the truck in park and hops out of the front. He opens the door without knocking and eyes Steve, then Callie.

Steve walks past Wyatt and whispers, "I haven't said anything yet." Turning to Callie, he says, "Well it was great to see you two, but I've got a thing I need to get to." He leaves hastily.

"Cal, why don't you sit down."

"I don't want to sit down. I want you to tell me what's going on." She feels her nerves fraying.

"I think you should sit," he says, as he places a hand gently on her back and guides her to the couch. "I need to tell you something. Something I thought you would remember, but it's obvious now, you don't." He clears his throat and takes a deep breath. "Aunt Marilyn died a few years ago."

Callie, still holding onto Lilian, leans back against the cushion.

"We came to the funeral. You said goodbye to her at your family's gravesite. You placed snapdragons on her burial ground at the cemetery. I'm so sorry you don't remember this. It was really difficult for you when it happened. I hate to think you are reliving that pain all over again."

"I want to see her."

"She … she's gone, Cal."

"I mean, I want to go to her gravesite. Where is she buried in the family plot?"

"Right next to her daughter and her parents."

"I wanna go right now."

Wyatt watches for a breakdown, but it doesn't come.

"Okay, I'll take you there. Why don't you leave the doll here and we'll go."

"No, I'm bringing her with me."

"All right."

The drive over to the cemetery is quiet. They park the car and Callie is the first to exit. She walks calmly over to the metal welcome pad. She lifts the lid and reads through the names. She searches and finds her own handwriting from years ago, just below her parents' names and her brother's name. *I don't remember.* She takes the pen and writes her name and the date and moves on to find the headstone. Looking at the names carved in stone, she finds it.

Marilyn Ann Riley

Daughter, Sister and beloved Aunt

The dates of her life are etched beneath the brief, but accurate description. Without a word, Callie places Lilian on the mound in front of the stone and turns to leave.

"Are you sure you want to leave that doll here?"

"Aunt Marilyn would want to be with Lilian," she says as she climbs back into the car. She sheds no tears, says no angry words. She is just silent.

Reaching the Wilsons' house, Wyatt puts the truck into park and turns to Callie. "Are you okay?"

"Fine."

"Is there anything I can do for you?"

"I need to be alone," she says as she leaves the car and starts walking. She walks to the end of the gravel road and steps into the labyrinth with a heavy heart. As she slowly walks the path, the tears spill from her lids. Once at the base of the lightning tree, Callie crumbles to a seated position, leaning against the massive trunk. The rough bark scratches her back as she slides down to the earth beneath her feet. She looks up through the branches and gazes upon each item precariously hanging from the low branches. Sobbing now with no sign of stopping, she lets the tears flow for the loss of her aunt, the loss of her confidant, the only one that really understood her.

"Why? *Why* can't I remember?"

The breeze picks up and whips around the tree causing the items to sway. Callie feels as though she has missed a big chunk of a great movie and there's no rewinding to see the missing parts.

She beats the back of her head against the tree. "This is so stupid! STUPID!"

Callie positions herself prone, beneath the tree, facing the darkening sky. She lays thinking of the good times she had with her aunt, all the fishing, dinners, happy hours, and laughter. The first raindrop falls upon her nose. Soon the ground just beyond the tree is saturated, but being safely under the tree, she is not drenched. Time passes as she lies there. The rain that has now found her, soaks her to the bone. Headlights cast an eerie shadow around her. Wyatt, in a panic, runs to her aid.

"Callie!"

From her position on the ground, it looks as if she is asleep, or worse. She lifts her head to peer over her toes at Wyatt.

"What are you doing?" he asks her as she scrambles to a seated position. She looks at him blankly.

"Let's get you back to the house." He helps her to the car and drives her back to the house. He turns on a hot shower for her to warm her soaked body. She stands in the shower, letting the water beat on her skin, feeling the pain of the bump she developed from hitting the tree with her head. She stands wrapped in a towel looking at herself in the mirror when she hears a soft knock on the door. Wyatt opens it a crack. "You all done?"

"Yep."

"Do you need anything?"

She walks past him to the bedroom.

"Yes."

"What is it? What can I get you?"

Callie walks to Wyatt and takes his arms and wraps them around her waist, then places her arms around him and rests her head against his chest.

"I don't want to forget you."

These words create a chasm, a deep fissure within his soul. He wants to tell her it will be all right, that everything will work out in the end. He nestles his face into her hair and breathes her in.

"We're going to do our best to not let that happen," he says softly.

"But I'm already forgetting important people in my life. How do we know that I won't wake up and not know who you are?"

"We don't."

She lifts her head and kisses him passionately. He returns the kiss and pulls her closer to his aching heart. She removes her towel and he mutters, *beautiful* sweetly in her ear. They reach the bed, and for the remainder of the evening into the wee hours, cherish each other like it's the last time, not sure what tomorrow will bring, the uncertainty tangible.

CHAPTER 45
Wyatt

Dawn breaks the horizon, and Wyatt marvels at its beauty. He quietly leaves the bed, unable to sleep. The feeling that Callie is slipping away from him has his mind in overdrive.

He walks out of the room pulling his t-shirt over his head, down his toned 60-something body. As he walks up the stairs, the aroma of coffee reaches his senses.

"Pop, what are you doing up?"

"I'm old. This is what old people do. We take naps in the afternoon, we eat dinner at 4:30, then we go to bed at eight," he jokes. "Why are you up so early?"

"I'm worried about Callie," he says, taking a mug from the cabinet. His dad pours the coffee to the rim.

"I know you are, son. Not sure what to tell you. It's awful that you both are going through this. I have to admit, for a few days I forgot about your predicament. She's doing so well up here."

"I guess it's because she has so many memories here. That's the only thing I can think of. I worry that when I get her home she'll revert to what she was like: not very pleasant to be around, angry, unhappy. It's so not in her nature to be ugly like that. I wish we could stay here forever." Wyatt takes a sip of his coffee, contemplative.

"Why don't you?"

"Why don't I what?"

"Move up here. You don't really know how much time you have with her. Don't you want the remainder of the time you *do* have to be memorable?"

"Yes, but she won't go for that. She won't leave her family back home."

"Son, her family is *here*. Her folks will understand. Plus, it's not like they won't want to come up to visit."

"I'll think about it."

They sit at the kitchen table talking as Callie sleeps.

In Callie's slumber, she dreams deeply. In this dream, she feels an urgency to close all the doors and windows. It's dark. There's a storm brewing outside. She climbs out of bed and walks to the kitchen to check all the locks on the doors. She walks past the answering machine and see's she has missed a call. This doesn't seem important, so she continues with the task at hand. Crossing the dark kitchen a second time, the missed call light flashes brightly. She walks to the machine and presses the play button.

"One missed call," the machine utters, followed by a loud beep. She can hear the wind chimes tinkling in the breeze, but nothing more. The phone's display reads *Marilyn Riley.*

Wyatt walks back downstairs a few hours later with a fresh cup of coffee for Callie. He opens the door and sets the cup on the nightstand next to his beloved. He sits on the bed next to the waking Callie, who opens her eyes and looks at him blankly.

"Morning, beautiful."

Callie pulls up the bedspread to the base of her throat with wide eyes.

"Cal?"

"Get out. GET OUT!"

Every nerve ending in Wyatt screams. He jumps off the bed quickly reaching the other side of the room.

"Callie, it's me, Wyatt," he says, as his face blanches.

"Where's Charlie? You're not Charlie."

"I'm your husband. We met when you were 15. Come on, Cal, please remember," he pleads, but no recognition crosses her face. Resigned to the fact that she's not going to spontaneously remember, he leaves the room. Wyatt's mother comes down the stairs to find out what the commotion is all about and comes face to face with Wyatt. His face is sheet white and his hands are shaking.

"This has never happened before. I'm not sure what to do."

"Let me go in and check on her. I'll be right back."

Wyatt's mom goes in and calms the agitated Callie.

"All right, sweetheart. It's going to be all right. Let's just take a breath in and blow it out. That's it. Nice and slow," Mrs. Wilson speaks softly and slowly as she approaches Callie. She sits on the bed and takes Callie's hand into her own. Callie's eyes dart around the room.

"I know you're confused. I know this is hard to take in. We'll get through this together," she says, as Callie relaxes and rests her head against the backboard.

"Okay. That's what I would think."

"Let's snuggle up under these covers," Mrs. Wilson murmurs, helping Callie lie down, fluffing the pillows as she goes. Callie falls back asleep as Wyatt's mom smooth's Callie's hair and tucks it behind her ear. This seems to sooth Callie, reminding her of how her own mother used to do this to her as a child. Mrs. Wilson leaves the room and closes the door.

"Why don't you check on her later. Perhaps a little more rest is what she needs." They walk back upstairs together.

"Wyatt, you wanna come with me to the store? I need to get a few things. It might help take your mind off things for a bit." Mr. Wilson throws the keys to Wyatt.

In the pickup truck, Wyatt says, "Where to, Pop?"

"Stewart's."

The ring of the bell being struck by the opening door brings Wyatt back decades. A wave of nostalgia hits him, nearly toppling him over.

"Hi, Wyatt, hi, Mr. Wilson," the cashier calls out. Wyatt turns to the familiar voice.

"Megan. Holy cow. How are you?" Wyatt says, as Mr. Wilson waves and moves on down the aisle.

"Oh, you know. Same old, same old."

"I didn't know you still worked here."

"Actually, I'm just helping my daughter out. I'm retired. Been retired for a while now. When my grandmother died, and then Riley, it was up to me to take care of the business. My daughter moved home to help me out and eventually took over, thank goodness."

"I'm glad it's still in the family."

"How's Callie?"

Feeling uncomfortable, he tries, "She's doing fine, thanks." He turns his head, searching the store. "I'm gonna go check on my Pop."

Mr. Wilson pays for his items and meets Wyatt in the truck.

"Sorry about that," Wyatt says, nodding to the store. "I just don't know what to say to people anymore about Callie. It's just easier for me to avoid the whole conversation all together."

"Mmmhmm. I get that."

Wyatt drives them home and helps his father with the items purchased. When they walk into the kitchen they're greeted by Callie sitting at the table drinking coffee with Mrs. Wilson.

"Hi, fellas. How was the store?" Mrs. Wilson asks while looking at Wyatt, then back at Callie for recognition.

"Good. I saw Megan. It's been a really long time since I've seen her. I think the last time I saw her was at the funeral."

Mrs. Wilson cringes.

"I remember that," Callie says, stirring her coffee.

"How're you feeling?" Wyatt asks.

"Good," as if nothing odd happened a few hours earlier.

He sits down across from her at the table and reaches for her hand. She extends it.

Mr. and Mrs. Wilson look on with worry.

"Cal, you like it up here, don't you?" Wyatt says this more like a statement than a question.

"I do, yes. It feels like home."

"What if we looked into getting a place on the lake? Maybe Aunt Marilyn's old camp?"

The mention of Aunt Marilyn causes Callie's face to grimace.

"What about my family?"

"They love it up here, too. I'm sure they'd be happy for you to move to a place that keeps you with us," tiptoeing on eggshells. "You know they'll visit often."

Callie mulls this over. "I don't know. I can't make a decision right now." Wyatt thinks, *it's probably best she talks it over with her mom and dad before saying yes or no.*

"Is Aunt Marilyn really gone? I didn't just dream that, right?"

"I'm afraid so," Mr. Wilson offers. "She was a lovely woman and we all miss her."

"Is our tree still here?" she switches gears on the fly.

"You mean the one with our initials in? It was cut down years ago, but as luck would have it, my sister and your brother tracked it down and made a bench out of it for our anniversary. Do you remember that?"

Callie nods her head with a smile, and slowly that smile slides down into a frown and she shakes her head.

"Don't worry about that. I'll show it to you and maybe you'll remember then, hmm?" he asks gently, stroking her thumb with his own.

"That's what I would think," she simply states.

CHAPTER 46
Jimmy

Jimmy rolls along in life with Prue and Jennifer as a happy family unit. Life seems to be a breeze. He's in love, Jennifer accepts his proposal and Prue is super *stoked* for the wedding.

"That's a good thing, right?"

Prue and Jennifer laugh.

"Come on, Dad, don't act so old."

"Yeah, old man," Jennifer chides.

The plan is to have a destination wedding with only close family on both sides. As of now, only Prue has seen the wedding dress, which is the last piece of the puzzle.

"Did you figure out what you're wearing yet?"

"Sorta. I just can't figure out what'll match my jorts."

"Hey, you do you," Jennifer giggles.

"Oh, gawd. Please say you're kidding."

"What? They're in fashion again. I just saw them in a magazine."

"Yeah, on what not to wear," Prue rolls her eyes, playing along.

"Yes, I figured out what I'm going to wear. I'm not telling you until you tell me what you're wearing."

"I'll be the one in white, but I'm not giving you any more details than that."

"Fine."

"I can't wait!" Prue says, clapping her hands.

"You're going to make a beautiful maid of honor," Jennifer says, winking at Prue.

"Do you have a best man yet?"

"Yep. I asked him last week, and he's super *stoked.*"

"Remind me never to use that word again," Prue says to Jennifer.

"Who'd you ask?"

"Tom Brubeck, you know, Tommy from work. We started working at the company at the same time. Been friends for many years."

"That's great. Is he bringing anyone with him?"

"His wife, Trina. You'll like her. She's very sweet."

"I'm sure I will. I'll send them the flight information. I hope they have their passports ready."

"I'm sure they've checked, but I'll remind them just in case."

"Good idea."

The day of the wedding comes and goes with a beautiful bride, gorgeous Mexican weather, and many happy tears. The newlyweds celebrate with revelers well into the night at the reception on the beach.

"So you're Jimmy's sister?" Trina asks Callie as they sway to the music on the side of the dance floor. Full glasses of wine spill from their hands. Wyatt stands with a protective arm around Callie's waist.

"I am," Callie says, taking a sip.

"He and Jen seem so happy together. I'm so happy that he's so happy," Trina says enthusiastically. Watching the masses leave the dance floor, as instructed by the MC, the party-goers each collect a Japanese lantern and, after watching the bride and groom light and release their wedding wish lanterns, they each do the same. In mere minutes, the night sky is illuminated with a magnificent display of dots of light peppering the sky. It looks like a migration of fireflies, and the scene is breathtaking. As Wyatt releases his lantern, Callie lights hers. Just as she's about to release hers, she looks over at Tommy lighting his lantern with Trina. Gasping, Callie drops her lantern and it begins to burn the paper enveloping the lantern into flames.

"Cal, your lantern," Wyatt says, as he stamps on the burning paper to extinguish the flame.

"Charlie?"

Wyatt, frantically putting out the fire, looks to Callie as she continues calling out to her deceased friend. She walks over to Tommy, who doesn't realize she's referring to him. She asks again, "Charlie? Oh, my God. Charlie. You're here. What are you doing here? I can't believe this!"

Tommy, in utter confusion, looks to Wyatt for help. Quickly snuffing the remainder of the smoldering lantern out with sand, Wyatt comes to Tommy's aid.

"Callie, that's not Charlie," he says gently.

"Yes, it is. Look at him."

"I realize they look a lot alike, but trust me, it's not Charlie."

Callie's voice rises above the din of conversation on the beach.

"That's Charlie, you idiot, I'd know him anywhere. He's my boyfriend." Callie is beginning to make a scene, and Wyatt tries his best to guide her back to the pool deck. She continues to push and kick at him as he guides her.

"Don't touch me. Let me go! Charlie!" Callie says as she extends her arms in the direction of Tommy, who looks on in horror. Wyatt manages to get her back to the pool deck and has her sit on a lounge chair.

"Cal, Charlie is gone."

"He's not. He's right on the beach. I need to go see him," she stands, and Wyatt grabs her hand to have her sit again.

"What are you doing? I need to see him." She sits facing Wyatt with her hands in his.

"Callie, Charlie's not here. He died years ago. Honey, please remember," Wyatt says, suddenly feeling exhausted.

Callie looks on in pain as the memory slowly creeps back in. She crumbles in front of Wyatt, slowly piecing it together.

"He was in New York,"

"That's right."

"Oh, God. He's dead."

"Yes, Callie. I'm afraid he is. I'm so sorry."

Wyatt, feeling the weight of the world on his shoulders, helps her from her seat and they walk back to their hotel room. Closing the door muffles the sound of life moving on without them, and with it all his hopes and dreams. It feels like the beginning of the end.

After putting her to bed, Wyatt stays in the room and watches her chest rise and fall in rhythmic movements until he's confident that she's sound asleep. He quietly walks back to the beach where there are only a smattering of guests left enjoying the beautiful night. In the distance, he watches as the last lantern light dies out. He takes a deep breath and releases it with a, "*hmmph.*"

"Hey, buddy."

Wyatt looks up to see Tommy walking toward him with a bottle of beer. He hands it to Wyatt and sits next to him on the sand.

"I suppose you want to know what all that was about?"

"Only if you want to tell me."

"Where to begin," Wyatt says, more to himself. Tommy sits patiently waiting. Wyatt begins at the beginning, when Callie fell and hit her head. He tells Tommy about the child they lost, and before he can contain his feelings, he breaks down.

"The one thing I really wanted us to have was a family, and we can't even do that right. What am I going to do? I've lost her," he says as the tears roll down his cheek. Tommy continues to listen quietly as Wyatt continues explaining the situation.

"She refuses to take her meds. And when she does feel well enough to take them, it's very infrequently so it's not helping her at all. I never know what I'm going to wake up next to. Some days she doesn't even know who I am," he says, raking his face open palmed. "*Fuck.*"

"I wish there was something I could do for you, man," Tommy pats Wyatt's back.

"Me, too. My parents think I should move her to Vermont. I just don't know if that's the right move. I wish I could have someone tell me what to do. Give me a sign or something."

They continue to sit quietly when Wyatt scratches an itch on his arm. Something continues to tickle his skin. When he looks down, he sees silver wings of a dragonfly sparkling in the moonlight, resting above his wrist.

CHAPTER 47
Wyatt

After having a conversation with his father, Wyatt decides to look into camps around the lake—a place to keep Callie with him in the present as long as possible. He meets Samantha at the Wilsons' home and drives to the State Park. They drive on looking for open house signs. After looking through several, Wyatt decides that this side of the lake doesn't feel quite right.

"I want Callie to be able to look through the window and see the lake, the island, and the trees."

"And the dock, the boats, and the rope swing? You're trying to recreate Callie's youth." Samantha says as gently as possible, "it's not going to be the same. The past is the past. You have to look for a new tomorrow with her. I know you don't want to hear this, Erp, but I think you've lost the Callie we all know and love."

"No, I can't let that happen, Sam. I can't. I won't give up on her. I know she's in there most days. I see her bright eyes and zest for life come out when I least expect it. She's still in there."

"I know, but is that really how you want to continue what time you have left with her? Waiting for the good days?"

"The good days *are* what I live for."

"Oh, Wyatt," Samantha says with a shake of her head.

"Don't. Don't do that. Don't shake your head at me. I know what I'm doing. If you're not going to help me look for the perfect camp, then just get back in your car and go home."

"Come on, Wyatt. I'm here to help."

"I don't know if you've noticed, but this isn't helping."

"Okay. I'm sorry. I'll keep my negative thoughts to myself," she says as she loops her arm through his. "Come on. Let's find you and Callie the perfect cabin."

Dusk is approaching and they decide to end their search for the day. Wyatt is anxious to get back to Callie.

"Pop, we're back."

"How'd it go? Find anything?"

"Where's Callie?"

"She's in watching TV with your mother. So did you find anything?"

"No. I'm not done searching, though."

"We'll get back to it tomorrow," Samantha says to their father. "Hungry?"

"Famished."

Wyatt walks to the TV room.

"Hi, beautiful," he says, walking to Callie and kissing her head.

"Hi," she smiles.

"Let's go to the kitchen for some dinner. You hungry?"

"Not really."

"We had a late snack," Wyatt's mom says.

"At least come sit with me. I wanna tell you about my day. I'm looking at some places up here for us to move into."

"Why? We can stay with Aunt Marilyn. She has plenty of room for us."

"Right," he says slowly.

Changing the subject, he asks about her day.

"Tell me what you did with Mom all afternoon."

"We went for a walk to the lightning tree. It's so beautiful there. I love walking around the maze. I want to add something to the tree."

"That's a great idea. We'll have to think of something, maybe a picture or something?"

Sitting at the table, enjoying a homecooked meal, Mr. Wilson's phone jingles in his pocket.

"Sam, I told you I don't like those at the table. Turn that thing off."

Looking sheepishly to his wife, then down at his phone, he says, "Sorry, honey, I have to take this call."

Mrs. Wilson lets out a sigh as he leaves the table.

"You let him off easy," Wyatt chides.

Mr. Wilson reenters in the kitchen placing his phone on vibrate and slips it back into his pocket.

"Someone is looking down on you. As luck would have it, the Schultzs are willing to discuss price on their place. Now that their kids have grown, they're interested in moving back home."

"Who are the Shultzs?" Wyatt asks.

"The couple that live in the Lamplys' old camp."

Quiet for a moment, Wyatt thinks about this new development.

"Isn't that something," he says, lost in thought.

"Welp, that about does her," Bob Schultz says.

"Thanks for the walk through, Bob."

"I'll have the papers drawn up if you'd like. They can be faxed directly to your realtor." He looks to Wyatt and Callie for a response when he sees that Callie has gone to the old red leather glider to sit down. "Unless you want to think about it a while longer."

"No need to think. I'm pretty sure we need this place," Wyatt says more to himself.

"I'm sorry?"

"We'll take it." He walks to Callie to pull her from her daydream. "Cal, we need to leave."

"Just a little longer, they're just about to come out."

"Who are?"

"Chip and Dale."

Bob Schultz looks on with sadness. "Take all the time you need. I'll be in the garage getting some things boxed up."

"Thanks, Bob." He watches as Callie rises up off the red chair and opens the screen door. She takes a seat on the front stoop.

"Do you have any peanuts?"

"I don't, sorry."

"That's okay. I'm sure they know I'm here."

"Chip and Dale were here decades ago. I'm pretty sure they're gone by now." As if understanding what Callie is saying, Wyatt takes a sharp intake of air as one chipmunk tentatively darts his head out from under the stoop. In a flash he is in plain sight in front of Callie, up on his hind legs twitching his nose.

"See? There he is," Callie says in delight.

"Well, I'll be." Once the chipmunk realizes there is no reward for coming out of hiding, he retreats back under the camp.

"Next time I need to bring out some peanuts."

"I'll be sure to buy some at the store next time I go," he promises, still surprised by the visitor.

"Okay, Cal. We should head back to Mom and Dad's."

She stands and begins walking back to the Wilsons'.

"Maybe we can go fishing tomorrow?"

"I'd like that."

"We can pick up Aunt Marilyn. She'd love that."

Not again. "We'll see."

CHAPTER 48
Maddie

"Okay, thanks for letting me know. Yep, I will. We'll talk soon," Maddie says into the phone.

"Who was that?"

"Wyatt. He was giving me an update on Callie. He just bought Cal's grandfather's camp. They'll be home soon to pack up and move. For good." She busies herself with stacking the magazines on the coffee table in the family room, obviously full of nervous energy.

"Mad, you okay?"

"Sure," she says as she fluffs, then folds, and refolds the afghan on the back of the couch.

"You want to talk about it?" She continues to tidy up. Now in the kitchen, she empties the dishwasher gently at first, then more loudly. She slams the cupboard shut, rattling the glasses inside.

"Oh, *fangul*! He's taking her away from me. She's not going to remember me anymore. This isn't fair to *me*. Doesn't he realize she's the only family I have left?" She turns, leaning against the sink, white knuckles on the countertop.

Zach walks to her and gently takes her hand. He pries her hands one at a time from the counter and wraps her arm around his waist. He hums a tune and sways with her resistant body. Eventually, her body gives in, and she rests her head on his chest as they move around the kitchen floor.

"You still have me," he says sweetly.

"Thank God for that," she says into his shirt. Looking up into his eyes, she continues, "but she's like a sister to me."

"I know. This has to be hard. We'll have to make the most of the time we have with her."

"Don't talk like that. You make it sound like she's dying," her eyes narrow.

"I mean until she moves. Make the most of the time we have until she moves. I didn't mean anything more by that." Resting her head back down, they continue swaying.

"Mad, you have to come to terms with the fact that she's moving and … Alzheimer's is an awful disease. I hate to say it, but she probably won't outlive you," Zach says, trying to choose his words carefully. Maddie drops her hands.

"Zachary, I don't want to hear that. I know my friend is a little hazy on things going on around her, but she's my friend, and as long as she's here, I will do everything I can to help her remember me."

"When she gets back, we'll have Jason, Ryan, Wyatt and Callie over, okay? We'll have a little party. We'll have everyone bring pictures to refresh her memory. I think this'll be good for everyone. A little reminder of our friendship."

"I like that idea. Callie always liked a good party."

The following week sneaks up on Maddie and Zach quickly, and with it comes a party that is not quite organized.

"Are you ready?" Zach hollers to Maddie as he frantically gets the paper goods out on the table.

"Quit screaming at me!" Maddie barks, ripping the flowers from the paper and plunking them in a vase with water. No time for trimming the stems or arranging the colorful display. Guests are outside parking their cars.

"I'm not screaming at you. If I were screaming at you I'D BE TALKING LIKE THIS!" he hollers, frustration getting the best of him.

The doorbell rings.

"Ah, shit!" Maddie mutters.

Jason and Ryan enter without waiting to be welcomed.

"Are we early?" Jason asks, as he watches Zach and Maddie scurry around their home.

"Nope. Not at all," she fakes calm.

"Here, we brought you some wine. It's from our wine club. If you don't like it, give it back and we'll bring something next month that you might like better."

"Thanks, guys." Maddie gives each a kiss on the cheek and takes the bottle to the fridge.

"Anything we can do to help? You know how great Ryan is at throwing parties. I think he majored in that in college," Jason teases his husband.

"When is the guest of honor supposed to arrive?"

Maddie looks down at her Apple watch, which informs her that she's reached 12,000 steps already today. Tapping it to switch screens, she says, "In about a half hour."

Then she looks out the front window and she sees Callie and Wyatt walking to the front door.

"*Marone a mia!*" Maddie exclaims, throwing her hands in the air.

"It's fine. It'll be fine. Not to worry," Zach says, passing her with a love tap on her behind.

"There she is!" Zach says, opening the door to allow Callie and Wyatt to enter. He hugs Callie, evaluating her behavior. He notices that she taps his shoulders with a quick tap, uncharacteristically.

"Hey, Wyatt. How are you?"

"We're here," he says, exhaling. The demand of his daily responsibility as caregiver for Callie is evident in his body language, as his shoulders slightly slump forward and the blond hair from his youth is now overtaken by the gray.

"And we're so happy you're here! It's so great to get everyone together before your big move up north," he says, trying to sound much more chipper than he's feeling internally. They all sit and catch up, talk about kids, where they've been traveling, and mostly ask Wyatt questions about going to live in Vermont. Callie sits listening, but not participating. She seems preoccupied with what's going on outside the window.

"Cal, you want to tell people about seeing your relatives in Vermont? And how great it'll be to be in your Gramps Camp again?"

"I'll be right back." She stands and walks to the back yard. Once there, she stands, talking animatedly to an oak tree.

Wyatt watches from the window for a few minutes, then worry sets in. *Is this normal behavior for Alzheimer's patients?*

"Callie, whaddya doing out here?"

"Talking with Aunt Marilyn."

Wyatt feels a shiver run down his spine. "Oh?"

Callie turns from him and silence lingers as Callie nods her head in agreement to the wind. Wyatt sits watching.

"She agrees with you. She'll see us up in Vermont. Someone has to take care of the lightning tree," and with that, she returns to the party. The partygoers are all standing at the back window watching the two (or three) talk. Once they realize that Callie is walking back inside, they all rush away from the window, resuming party mode.

CHAPTER 49
Maddie

Weeks pass and the boxes get packed. Wyatt decides to rent the house he shares with Callie, rather than sell it, to a nice young couple that is interested in bringing up their family in the Rockwood School District. Their budget is tight, so renting is a win-win for all parties.

Maddie, still upset about Callie moving away, comes to say goodbye to her friend, unsure of the reception she will encounter.

"Hey, Mad, can you give me a hand for a sec?" Wyatt asks as he tries to open the door to the house with two boxes in hand.

"Sure. Is Callie up?"

"She is. She's out back, go on in."

Maddie walks into the home and can see Callie through the back window, sitting on the porch, looking up and gesturing with her hands. Maddie stops and stands, watching from the middle of the room. Wyatt walks back into the house to gather more boxes.

"It's okay. She does this a lot. It freaked me out the first few times. She says she's talking to Aunt Marilyn or Tyler. You know, the usual stuff. Talking to dead people. That's normal, right?" he says sarcastically.

"*Fangul* … How are you handling all this? If Zach was telling me that he was talking to my dead relatives, I would think it's time to send him to a home." As soon as the words come out of her mouth, she regrets it. Wyatt's face crumbles. Tears linger on his lids. He drops his head and sniffs loudly, busying himself with another box to avoid eye contact with Maddie.

"Shit. Wyatt, I'm sorry. I'm so stupid. I'm a terrible person. Callie always says I don't have a filter."

"It's fine. The thought has crossed my mind. I think it's time to start looking into nursing homes up in Vermont. Eventually that's what I'm going to have to do, as much as it's going to break my heart. I can manage her behavior right now, but I'm not sure how much longer I'll be able to take care of her properly."

Callie walks into the room and stands staring at Wyatt. It makes Wyatt jump, not expecting to see her standing there. He nearly drops the box he has picked up.

"Hey, beautiful, look who came to say hello."

"Goodbye, actually," she says under her breath, looking at Wyatt, then to Callie.

"Hey, friend." Maddie walks over to Callie and hugs her. Callie does the tap, tap, tap on the shoulder she does when she is unfamiliar with a person. It's obvious she doesn't know who Maddie is today.

"Why don't you two sit down, and I'll get something cold for you to drink while you visit. First let me put this box in the car. I'll be right back."

Maddie and Callie sit across from each other at the kitchen table. Emotions well up, and Maddie finds it hard to sit across from the best friend she has had since college—this friend who can hardly make eye contact with her now. She looks around this house that holds so many memories of their friendship.

"Callie, do you remember when I lived here with you?"

"What can I tell you? Is Charlie coming over?" Callie asks with a flicker of excitement.

"No, Cal, he's not, but that's right. We all lived here together, you, me and Charlie."

"That's the story of my life. Where's Sprout? I'm sure he's thirsty after our run."

The mention of the long lost dog makes her heart hammer in her chest. The dog named Sprout, a gift given to her after she lost her baby girl. This visit is proving to be too painful to handle.

"I love you, Cal. Take care of yourself." Maddie stands, walks over to her seated friend, and kisses the top of her head.

"Bye for now," Callie says to Maddie as she opens the door, allowing Wyatt to enter the house as she exits. Sobbing now, she's unable to say a word to Wyatt. They just share a heartfelt hug.

"If ever you find yourself in Vermont, don't be a stranger. Callie and I would love to have company." Still holding her firmly, he says, "I know it doesn't seem like it now, but she's still your best friend. She still loves you. Thank you for being such a good friend to her over the years." He releases Maddie, and they stand facing one another. Maddie tries to wipe the tears that have erupted from her lids once more. She can't formulate her thoughts into words, the thought that she will never have a friend like Callie again. How there really was no other friend in her life that would put up with her shenanigans. No other friend has helped her through her life's ups and downs. How she loves Callie like a sister. How she's going to miss her friend and feels like this is the last time she will see her. Nothing comes out. The thoughts flood her mind, yet all she can do is nod her head.

"Take care, Maddie," Wyatt offers as she practically runs to her car.

She rushes out of the driveway nearly hitting Jason's car as he comes to say goodbye. The squeak of the brakes is loud, and Maddie waves to Jason as she flees. Jason pulls into the driveway and exits the car.

"That didn't go so well, did it?"

Wyatt wipes his eyes. "Not so much. This is so hard. Can I see her?"

"She's inside. I have to warn you, she's not really here today. That's why Maddie left in such a rush."

"Got it. Thanks. I won't be long." Jason walks into the house carrying a card in his hand. He places it on the kitchen table where Callie is still sitting.

"Hey, Cal," he says, sitting across from her in the seat Maddie was just in.

Callie looks up blankly. "Hi."

"Just wanted to come over to say hey before you take off."

"What can I tell you?" Callie speaks using one of her standby phrases.

Jason smiles and slides the card across the table to her. "I wanted to give this to you from the kids at the hospital. I know many of the kids you worked with over the years have come and gone. The new group I've been working with drew some pictures on here. I explained that you used to work there and had to stop … you had to retire early." He continues explaining as Callie opens the card. It is a beautiful card with bright, colorful drawings on the inside. There is a drawing of a flower, a heart, words that say good luck, among others. She closes the card and turns it over. On the back is a dragonfly.

"Did Pheonix draw this for me? She's such a good artist."

Unsure what to say, Jason says, "Yes. She helped," he lies, knowing full well that Pheonix died decades ago. *What's the harm?* Jason thinks to himself.

"You keep that safe up in Vermont, okay? Hopefully when you look at it, it'll remind you of us."

"That's what I would think."

"All right then," Jason says, standing up. "Love you, Cal," he says and walks over to give her an awkward hug.

Jason walks outside and gives Wyatt a hug. "Good luck up in Vermont."

"Thanks. Where's Ryan?"

"He's with Alice, listening to her sing at a gig she's at. Honestly, I think he's just avoiding the whole goodbye thing."

"Tell them we say goodbye," Wyatt says as the men shake hands.

"Will do," Jason says as he opens the driver side door and sits down. He rolls the passenger side window down. "Wyatt, I'm so sorry about all this. We all love her so much. I can't imagine what you're going through. It has to be really hard. If you ever need anything, we're just a phone call away." The two men just smile sadly at each other as Jason rolls out of the driveway.

Thankfully, Callie's parents already said their goodbyes. That went better than expected, as Callie remembered who they were, albeit thinking they still lived in Connecticut.

The last item he has to take care of is leaving the keys to the house for the couple coming to move in. He puts the keys in an envelope and places the envelope in the mailbox. Thankfully, he rented the place as is, furniture and all. The camp is also fully furnished, so that is a blessing.

Wyatt walks back into the house and stands next to Callie. Everything feels so final. He helps Callie to the car and stands in the middle of the lawn, looking at the house that held their lives with all the twists and turns, the good the bad, and the ugly. *It's time for a new chapter in our lives.* "Bye for now," he says softly as he walks to the car to begin their journey up north.

CHAPTER 50
Wyatt

"Home again, home again, jiggidy jog," Wyatt says to Callie, using her family's phrase. Callie just looks on quietly as Wyatt drives down the serpentine camp road overlooking the lake dotted by the colorful cabins and fall foliage.

"Are you ready to move into Gramp's Camp?"

"Are Nanny and Gramp home?"

"Not now, no," Wyatt says uncomfortably.

Wyatt pulls his car into the gravel driveway opposite the camp, where Gramp used to keep his beloved Cadillac. There's a crispness in the air, as winter is but a season away.

Callie steps out of the car and looks over to the Wilsons' house. "I should go see if Wyatt's home."

"Callie, I'm Wyatt."

She looks at him confused, "Yes, of course you are."

"Let's go inside and get comfortable, then I'll come back for the boxes."

They walk together across the gravel road, down the slope in the grass to the old wooden steps. Wyatt reaches for the camp keys in his pocket and opens the heavy wooden door. It smells stale from being closed down for a few weeks.

"Let me open the windows and doors to get some fresh air in here." Wyatt goes to the back rooms and the memory of their first intimate encounter enters his thoughts. *The first time we made love was in this room.* He releases a sigh and kneels on the bed to place the wooden sticks in the sill to keep the window open.

He does the same in the other bedroom, which once belonged to Jimmy. He walks to the front of the camp, opens the door, and immediately he's hit with a blast of cool fresh air.

"There. That's better," he says, turning to find Callie still standing where he left her. "Come on in and stay a while."

"I should really get going." Callie pulls her sweater around herself tightly and heads for the door. Alarms ring inside Wyatt's head.

"Wait. No, Cal. You're staying here with me," he says, holding her shoulders gently.

"No. Aunt Marilyn is waiting up for me. She'll be worried."

"She'll understand," playing along with her dementia moment.

"Are you sure?"

"Very."

"Okay then."

The two walk out lakeside and sit on two lounge chairs. They sit like this for some time, quietly in their thoughts. Wyatt looks out toward the island, thinking of the failed attempt to woo Callie that day many moons ago. Callie looks on, wondering when Dad is going to take them on the lake, unaware of her situation.

Mr. Wilson clears his throat as he rounds the corner. Startled, Wyatt nearly loses his balance in his chair.

"Didn't mean to startle you. No one answered the side door, so I thought I would come around to see where you were. How's everything going?"

"Hi, Pop. We've been here for a bit. Just settling in and getting used to our surroundings again."

"Mom put some ribs on the grill if you're interested in coming over for dinner."

"Sounds great, thank you. We'll be over in a bit."

"Hi, Callie," Mr. Wilson says, trying to engage her in conversation. In return, she gives him a smile.

"Okay then. See you in a bit."

"Thanks, Pop."

"Oh, hey, since I'm here, why don't I help you bring in those boxes that I saw in the back of your car. Many hands make lighter work."

"That'd be great, thanks."

The two men walk to the garage, remove the boxes, and place them on the gravel, each bringing one box in at a time.

"Just set them on the dining room table in the back, Pop."

Several trips back and forth and the dining room table is covered in boxes.

"One last trip should do it," Wyatt's dad says. As they walk to the car, Sam Wilson says to Wyatt, "Son, if this gets to be too much a burden-"

"Pop, please. Not now."

"I know, I know. Just know that she'd want to do right by you if the shoe were on the other foot. Have you at least looked around for a facility when that time comes?"

"I can't talk about this right now. We're not there yet." Wyatt stops walking and shifts the box to settle under his arm and against his hip. "Let me ask you something. Is it wrong that I'm trying to do everything in my power to jog her memory? To try and bring back my Callie? My best friend, my first love, my wife?" Wyatt's voice breaks as he completes the last sentence. Sam's heart breaks, seeing his son in turmoil.

"No, son, it's not wrong. I would do the same for your mother."

"Okay, then. No more talk about a facility. We'll cross that bridge when we come to it."

Walking down the slope of a yard, Sam slips and catches himself on the tree that used to hold an old swing. During the slip, the box falls from his arm and out flow the contents: letters bound by yarn, some with rubber bands, and yellowing envelopes. Wyatt hustles over to retrieve the letters and places them back in the box without a word.

"You okay, Pop?"

"Yep. Right as rain." Wyatt hands the box back to his father, and the two place the last of the boxes on the floor of the dining room.

"See you in a few," Mr. Wilson says as he closes the screen door.

After having dinner with Mr. and Mrs. Wilson, Callie and Wyatt take a walk down the road past the water pump and turn into the lot next to Riley's grandmother's place. There, still attached to the tree, is the well-loved rope swing.

"Ah, there it is. The times we had here with Tyler and Riley sitting around the fire, reminiscing about our youth. Do you remember any of that?"

Callie walks over to the rope to touch its rough texture. She walks around the tree until she finds it. Reaching into the knot in the bark, she retrieves a book of matches. "I can't believe they're still here," she marvels. Wyatt continues speaking of the past since Callie seems to be present.

"That's amazing," he says, walking to her side. "Remember when Tyler-"

"Tyler's dead," Callie says matter of factly.

"Yes."

"I remember that. It was awful. I couldn't do anything for you. You were so sad."

"You were there for me. That's all I could have asked for."

Laughing now, Callie says, "I remember your sister Sarah and your brother Tommy seeing me half naked, climbing out of the lake. That was so humiliating."

"Yeah, that was pretty bad. They forgot about it within a day or two. You survived."

"Am I going to survive this?" Callie asks, placing the matches back in the knot. A deathly silence befalls them.

"We're going to do the best we can to keep you with us as long as possible."

"That's not what I asked," Callie says directly. "Eventually I'm not going to know who you are," she explains, walking to Wyatt.

"I want you to know I love you. I always have and I always will, even if it doesn't seem that way. Tell me you know that I love you. Just say that you know."

"Of course I know," he says, gathering her in his arms. "We had a great life, the two of us. We've grown old together. We were just kids when we met. Literally. I've loved you my whole life, Callie-flower." Wyatt runs his hand through her graying hair and kisses her forehead, her cheek, and her warm lips.

"It shouldn't end this way for us."

"It's not over yet. I'll take it day by day. I can live with that," he says, kissing her once more.

A shiver brings goose bumps to her arms.

"We should head back. I'm thinking tomorrow we should go for a boat ride. Whaddya say? Just like old times."

Walking back as dusk turns to darkness, Wyatt places an arm around Callie's shoulders. "I'd like that very much."

CHAPTER 51
Mr. Wilson

Waking up this morning, it is evident it's going to be a bad day. Callie is confused and calling out for Stubby, her childhood pet. It takes the better part of the morning for her to settle down in the clothes that she wore the previous day. Wyatt gets Callie to sit at the dining room table and places a grilled cheese sandwich in front of her. Rather than pick it up by her hands, she cuts up the sandwich with a fork and knife. Wyatt worries but forges on, remembering the promise he made to her not 24 hours ago.

"Cal, let's go for a walk when you're done eating lunch, okay? Would you like that?"

"What can I tell you?"

Wyatt takes that as a yes and gets her a lightweight sweater to wear, as there is a fall chill in the air.

"Here you go, beautiful," he says, handing her the sweater. She looks on blankly. It's obvious she doesn't know what to do with the sweater so Wyatt takes one arm and gently feeds it through the sleeve of the sweater, then does the other. He leaves her in the dining room as he cleans up the lunch dishes, then collects some items he wants to bring on the walk.

"How would you like to walk through the maze today?" he asks as he closes the heavy door behind them.

"Okay," she says, devoid of emotion.

He puts his hands in his pockets and delicately traces an item he placed there. They walk to the maze in silence. Stepping into the maze brings on tears from Callie.

"It's okay to cry, Cal. That's what makes this place so special. Just let it go." And let it go she does. She is soon wailing and uncontrollable. Wyatt looks on concerned as they continue to the middle of the labyrinth. She places her hands on the tree and looks over at Wyatt, then up to the objects swaying in the breeze.

As he always does, he gladly goes through each item.

"That's the wind chime that Tyler gave to my parents when he was a little boy. That's the picture of Aunt Marilyn's baby girl who passed away as an infant, and today I'm going to hang something on here for you."

Callie looks on in anticipation, then in surprise as Wyatt begins to climb the tree the best he can to get to the second rung of branches. When his grunting and groaning has quieted he straddles the branch he has climbed up to and dangles one golden ring with its ruby red heart centered in the middle. It hangs delicately from a string that Wyatt has tied to it as he attaches it to the lightning tree. The light catches the ruby and casts a glow of amber to the ground below. Callie looks to the glow on the ground and places her hand in the line of trajectory. The glow on her hand causes her to smile.

Wyatt calls down to her, "Do you like that, Callie?" Without looking up to him in the tree, she nods her head.

"Good," he says, as he ambles down the tree trunk. Reaching the first rung of branches, he slips and comes crashing down to Callie's feet.

"Ooph." A bit bruised but no worse for the wear, he collects photographs that have fallen from his pocket. He then takes Callie's hand and they walk out of the maze to a bench to watch the lake. Sitting next to Callie, he holds out one photo at a time and says, "This is your Aunt Marilyn. She's really a second or third cousin or something like that." He hands the photo to Callie who looks on blankly and puts it down next to her on the bench. "And here's one of your brother, Jimmy, and your niece, Prue." He places it on top of the first.

"Callie, do you know who you're married to?"

"Mr.- I can't remember his name, no. Who is it?"

He hands her a picture of the two of them on their wedding day. "It's me."

"I'm sorry," she says, taking the picture into her hand and setting it aside as Wyatt's heart slowly breaks into a million pieces.

They sit and watch the lake until dark, ominous storm clouds fill the sky. There's a disturbance in the atmosphere. He can feel physical disruptions to the usual conditions, the potential to harm lives. The opposing forces in the heavens are creating entropy.

"We should get back," he says, with the heaviness of the clouds.

The air grows thick and, like the clouds straining to withstand the burden and weight of the rain, soon Wyatt will give in. During the walk, he decides that it's time to start looking into a care facility nearby. *I'll do that tomorrow.* Fat raindrops fall on their shoulders as they round the water pump. Wyatt is paces ahead of Callie and reaches the door before her. He hears laughter and turns to see Callie jumping in a puddle next to the yard. Her laughter is contagious. He joins her, and soon they are both drenched and muddy. They walk back to the camp, and Wyatt helps her get out of her clothes and into the shower. It's an intimate scene, but nothing like the scene that runs through his head from their youth. He hadn't realized he could feel any lower and finds it difficult to breath. He regains his composure and helps with the shower, soaping up her aging skin and tenderly washing her coarse hair. He rinses her off and wraps a towel around her glowing skin. *She's just as beautiful today as she was the day we first met.*

"Callie-flower," he whispers to himself.

He sets clothes out on her bed to change into. "You put this on and I'll start getting dinner ready." He leaves the room and busies himself with dinner preparations. Ten, fifteen minutes go by and he walks back to the bedroom to check on her. She's put her pants on, her sweater with her t-shirt over the top and shoes on the wrong feet. Knowing something is off, but unable to process, she sits on the bed, baffled at her predicament.

"Here, let me help you. There, that's better," he says, as he puts each top on the right way. Bending over, he places the shoes on the correct feet.

The remainder of the evening is uneventful, and after watching a TV show, Callie goes to bed. Once Wyatt sees that she's calmly sleeping, he slips out of the camp and walks to his folks' house. He can see that his Pop is still up, which he anticipated. For years now, Wyatt has marveled at the fact that his father can run on little to no sleep.

His father is sitting in the living room reading by the soft glow of the light. Wyatt softly raps on the door, and watches as his pop pads to the door in his slippers.

"Wyatt, is everything okay?" he asks, alarmed.

"Yep, everything is fine. I would have called if anything were wrong."

His father opens the door to allow him entry. Sam notices Wyatt's slumped shoulders looking like a man much older than he.

"Would you like some hot cocoa? You used to love that as a kid when you couldn't sleep at night."

"That'd be great, thanks," he says, feeling melancholy.

"Let me get the pot on the stove."

"You know you can make that in the microwave, Pop."

"It just doesn't taste the same."

Wyatt sits at the kitchen table with a laugh. His father takes down two mugs from the cabinet and puts two scoops of powdered chocolate into each mug as he waits for the milk in the pot to boil.

"You couldn't sleep?" Wyatt asks his dad.

"Your mom is snoring so loudly that I thought the walls would cave in." He takes the pot off the stove as it begins to whistle. Pouring the warm milk into the waiting mug sends a chocolate aroma wafting through the room. Wyatt's dad sets the mugs on the thick slab of wood that they have used for their kitchen table as long as Wyatt can remember. Mr. Wilson takes a seat opposite Wyatt and waits. Mr. Wilson looks at his son and remembers that as a child he would never divulge information until he was good and ready. Wyatt takes a sip of his hot cocoa and looks at his dad.

"This was the hardest day of my life," he says, his voice breaking as he sets his mug on the table. Looking on with worry, Mr. Wilson holds his tongue.

Wyatt stirs his cocoa looking into it for strength. "My wife doesn't know who I am," he says, sniffing loudly. "It seems like it's time to start looking into a nursing home facility."

Mr. Wilson reaches out to his son, resting his hand on Wyatt's. "This must be weighing heavily on you. If it helps, I have done some research that I'd be happy to share with you. There's a great facility in town, not far. I'd be willing to go visit it with you tomorrow if you'd like. I can have Mom stay with Callie while we're gone."

Wyatt's red-rimmed eyes look at his Pop, and he nods his head. He takes one last sip from his mug and uses his sleeve as he wipes his nose and mouth.

"Thanks, Pop. Maybe around lunchtime?"

The men stand and walk to the door. Mr. Wilson stops at the door and hugs his son. Wyatt grabs the back of Mr. Wilson's robe and lets it all out. He sobs on his dad's shoulder until his stomach aches. All the while, Mr. Wilson rubs Wyatt's back and allows him to let go. Once a parent, always a parent, no matter how old your child is.

Once the tears have subsided, they clap each other's backs, and without another word, Wyatt leaves the house.

CHAPTER 52
Callie

Two months later

Callie wakes up in her new home. Unfamiliar with her surroundings, she calls out.

"Hello? Hello?"

A friendly nurse comes to the room to check on her.

"Good morning, Callie. My name is Wanda. Are you ready to get up and get breakfast? I hope you're ready to meet some new friends here at Franklin Carriage House. We're so happy to have you here."

"Franklin Carriage House?"

"Yes. This is your new home. Let's get up and get dressed. I believe you have a visitor coming in this afternoon," the attendant says in a singsong voice as she exits the room.

My new home?

Callie gets up and dressed and walks out to the hallway.

"Excuse me?"

People walk the halls without batting an eye at her.

"Hello?"

The helpful nurse returns. "Oh, good. You're ready to take on the day. Would you like me to walk you down to the cafeteria for breakfast?"

Looking confused, "Yes, please."

"Right this way." The nurse talks non-stop until they have walked through the cafeteria line and are seated at a table to dine.

"… And you'll meet many new friends here. Your husband is on his way to see you right now. He said he would be here before you are done eating."

"My husband?"

"Yes, Wyatt."

She is thoughtful for a moment, then "Okay."

She spends the remainder of her mealtime pushing food around her plate as the nurse continues to talk incessantly.

"Callie, this is where we put our dirty dishes. Very good."

Callie follows suit, putting the dishes away on the conveyor belt. She follows the nurse back down the corridor to her unit. She opens the door and follows her in.

"All right then. Make yourself comfortable, and if you need anything, just press this call button right here," she says, indicating the remote placed on the wall near her bed.

"Oh, looky here. I didn't see this before we left for breakfast." She hands Callie an envelope with her name on the front. Unsure what to do with it, Callie sets it on the table in the living space she has.

"Oh, no, dear, I think it's meant to be read." Reading the confusion on Callie's face, the nurse takes the envelope and opens it. She theatrically snaps the tri-fold letter open and clears her throat.

"Dear Callie." As the nurse begins to read, Callie takes a seat on the loveseat in the living space and listens. "I'm writing to you from one of your favorite places on earth. It's a beautiful day, and though the lake is working, it still sparkles in the sunshine." Callie can picture the place, and it produces a smile.

"I'm going to try to recreate for you the many wonderful memories we have here. The lightning tree, a place that your aunt made sacred, is waiting for you. Do you remember the tree?

I'm looking at the picture of her daughter, Lilian, hanging from the lowest branch. She reminds me of you. I can see the family resemblance ..." Callie listens with a far-off look in her eye. She feels that if she thinks hard enough, she can conjure up an image of the tree she's speaking of. Her thought process is interrupted by a knock at the door.

"Oops. We'll close this letter for now. I believe your visitor has arrived."

When the door opens, Callie sees a man that she doesn't recognize. He greets her with a smile and looks to the nurse for guidance.

"Good morning, Wyatt. Take a seat. We've been expecting you. I was just reading your letter aloud to Callie."

"Great, thank you. I can read the rest, if you'd like."

"Absolutely. I'll leave you two be. I'll be right down the hall if you need anything," she says. As she leaves to close the door, the phone in Callie's room rings once. Wanda picks it up only to find the line has gone dead. "Huh. That's strange." She closes the door behind her.

Something registers in Callie when hearing the phone ring. It brings a smile to her face. She continues watching this man cautiously. He, too, feels familiar, but she just can't place him. She allows him to read the remainder of the letter without interruption. Wyatt notices she listens with interest.

"Do you remember the lightning tree that I wrote to you about? It's your favorite place in Vermont right now."

She looks at him and slowly shakes her head, on the verge of tears. Wyatt walks to her side and kneels. He takes hold of her weathered hand.

"Oh, beautiful, don't cry. It's okay. It'll come to you," thinking to himself, *dear God, let it come to her.*

He gently wipes a lone tear as it escapes. She looks on now with admiration, feeling familiar kindness, then looks away.

Wyatt brings out photos, naming each person as he places them on the table at her side. "… And this is your mom and dad from the summer that your dad helped my brother, Tyler, out of the lake. Do you remember that incident?" Without getting a response, he continues. "He was drunk and was peeing over the side of our fishing boat. The numbskull leaned too far over and fell in the lake with his pants around his ankles. Your dad swam out and saved him." Chuckling to himself, "That was a day. My mom and dad were beside themselves. Tyler left for his assignment overseas the very next day."

"Tyler," Callie whispers to herself with vague recognition. Wyatt jumps on this with renewed energy.

"Yes. That's right, Tyler. He was my big brother, and he was distraught about going off to war.

"Was?" Callie questions quietly, looking directly at Wyatt.

"Yes. Unfortunately, there was a bombing, and he died in his barracks." He takes a moment to collect his thoughts. Wyatt stands and runs his hand through his gray hair, reminding Callie of a young man she met decades ago.

"How would you like to go outside and get some fresh air?"

Callie nods. She stands unsteadily. Wyatt notices how her athletic body is taking a toll from this ugly disease. The once muscular, toned, tomboyish young woman now wears an old woman's body. Yet he looks at her with adoration as she struggles to walk out the door. He reaches her arm, links his with hers, and together they walk down the hall. They reach the sliding glass door and exit to the garden in the back.

"These are the kind of days that are your favorite." He helps Callie to a bench and sees that she's smiling. The smile brings his beautiful young Callie back, and for a moment he forgets where they are. Her smile takes his breath away. She looks out at the trees just beyond the garden and takes a deep breath. The sun shines down on her skin and she closes her eyes, lifting her face like a flower unfolding in the spring. He sits beside her and takes her hand. She opens her eyes and looks at him as if searching his soul.

"Those eyes," she says, reaching up and gently placing a hand on his cheek. "I know those eyes."

Wyatt's eyes cloud. "Yes, you do. It's me, Wyatt."

CHAPTER 53
Wyatt

"But she remembered me," Wyatt moans to the physician.

"I understand. This will happen from time to time. Please don't get your hopes up, Wyatt," the doctor warns as gently as possible. "This situation will not turn around. You need to plan for the rapidly approaching late stage."

"How can you be so sure? She seemed so with it. She recognized me. She recognized things I talked about in the past."

"But everything else that you've described to me sounds like textbook Alzheimer patterns. The inability to communicate well, being unable to control her bladder consistently, I'm afraid the late stage is upon us. The Homestead is a wonderful facility, and they will make her remaining time here as comfortable as possible."

Ice water clenches his heart. It feels as if it is seizing up.

"Remaining time?" Panic sets in, causing his heart to race. Eyes dilated, he searches the doctor's face for some clarification.

"Wyatt, you need to make sure all your finances are in order. Does she have an advanced directive?"

Eyes wild, he can't wrap his head around what the doctor is discussing with him.

"Wyatt? Does Callie have an advanced directive?"

Mentioning Callie's name snaps him back to the present. "Yes."

"Good. This will be helpful for you and your family members. Does she have family in the area?"

"Yes. Well, no. Her parents are in Missouri along with her brother and his family."

"Do you have any children here?"

Mentioning children stabs a stake right through his heart. He remembers in a flash the lost pregnancy years ago and the heartbreak that went along with that—all hopes dashed for creating a family.

"No children. She has a niece that she's very close to back in Missouri."

"We have a hospice program here at this facility, and I would recommend, if you haven't already done so, to reach out to them. Hospice is here to support you and Callie and your family members. It's important to know that there are people here whose passion is helping families navigate these very trying waters."

"Thank you. I'll look into it. I guess I …" Wyatt steadies himself with a deep intake of air. "I guess I didn't know we had come to this point yet. I'll do whatever I need to help Callie."

As he has done every evening for many weeks now, he takes out a sheet of paper and begins to write to Callie. When he goes to visit her each day, he leaves a letter for the nurse to read to her each morning. Sometimes he also adds a letter from his stack of love letters that Callie has saved over the years. He, in return, saved all of her love letters. Taking a moment, he reads one from the time he was losing her. He had been young and stupid and let that incident at Samantha's wedding create a chasm between them. His heart hurts just thinking of the moronic situation he put himself and Callie in back in that fateful coatroom. *Thank God she took me back.* They've been happily married over 20 years, and though unable to have children of their own, they have been blessed with extended family and friends that they cherish.

None of that matters now. This disease is taking away the one thing I want more than life itself.

Folding his arms and resting them on the table in front of him, he rests his forehead on them and closes his eyes. One after another, different stages of Callie's life come into view. The vision of Callie's face lighting up in the dark with each explosion of fireworks floats through first. The beauty in her face as she lies next to him watching the northern lights for the first time is next. The look of surprise on her face when he placed the promise ring on her finger—one of his favorite memories—but the favorite one from their life together is most definitely the day she became his wife. She was radiant in white. The church was brimming with love.

Lifting his head, he rubs both hands up and down his face to remove any trace of tears that may have trickled out. He releases a deep sigh. He has a sense of urgency to leave Gramp's Camp and opens the heavy wooden door to exit. He slowly walks down memory lane as he enters the Black Forest behind his childhood home. Looking from tree to tree, he notices the sparseness of the forest due to all of the construction over the years. He leaves the forest and continues down the gravel road, past the pump, the rope swing, the camp that Riley's grandmother used to live in, the camp that Aunt Marilyn's family owned, all the way to the end of the road. Stepping over the stones leading him to the center of the labyrinth, he takes a pocketknife from his pocket and etches letters into the tree. Stepping back to inspect his handiwork, he smiles. The energy here at the tree helps to lift his spirits. He looks up at what dangles from the branches above. Smiling at his brother's wind chime, he's happy here. Feeling renewed, he retreats from the tree, leaving behind their initials deep within the bark.

Wyatt walks back to retrieve the boat keys and gets in for a twirl around the lake. *Callie would love this.* The lake is still. The breeze is soft. Darkness descends as the sun rests. The colors of the sky turn from rose and yellow to navy and black. Soon the stars look as though someone has poked holes through a shadow box, allowing dots of light. He continues his ride, making slow loops around the lake until he is certain he's going to run out of gas. He drives the boat to the end of the lake, docks it to fill the tank at Stewart's.

"Hey, stranger."

"Hey ,Megan."

"Why the long face? Everything all right with Callie?"

"Status quo."

"Mmmm. So nothing has improved?"

"No," not wanting to share with her the heartbreaking details that he just received. *She's slipping fast. She's having difficulty eating, swallowing and speaking.* He closes his eyes and rolls his neck as the memory of this conversation runs through his head. *She's sleeping more than she's awake during the day.*

"Can I help you find anything?"

"Toothpaste? It seems Callie is out." She points him in the right direction.

Wyatt places the toiletries on the counter and Megan bags them up. She hands the bag to Wyatt and smiles, "It's on the house."

"Thanks, Megan."

Hopping back into his boat, he drives back and docks at Gramp's Camp. He raises the boat onto the lift and walks back into the camp as his phone buzzes.

"Wyatt, this is Wanda, the nurse attending Callie. I think it would be in your best interest to see Callie immediately. She's acting peculiar and this may be the beginning of … well, the beginning." *Of the end.* "Jimmy and Prue just arrived."

"I'm on my way."

CHAPTER 54
Callie

Callie sits up on the loveseat in the living room of her assisted living apartment. Jimmy stands with his hands in his pockets looking uncomfortable as Prue sits at Callie's side, holding her hand.

"Hi, Aunt Callie."

Looking up at Jimmy, she can't place him. But the girl … she's different.

"I know those eyes," comes out garbled, and Prue has difficulty understanding what she's trying to say. After repeating it a second time, Prue says, "Yes, it's me, Prue. I'm your niece."

Callie nods her head and smiles. *You know so much. You've seen so much. Pay attention to signs.* Callie thinks to herself, but all that comes out is, "Signs."

Prue is lost with this word and unsure what her aunt is trying to say. Callie tries again, pointing at her head repeating, *signs.* Then in her final attempt, she points to her eyes and head and says *signs.*

"Watch for the signs? Is that what you're trying to say?"

Callie nods and smiles, knowing that it may take her a bit to fully understand what is being said. Jimmy is completely lost.

"What does that mean?" Jimmy asks out of the side of his mouth.

"I think I know, but we'll talk about it later," Prue says, dismissing her father.

"Aunt Callie, this is your brother, Jimmy."

Callie smiles, but doesn't recognize him.

"Who would like some refreshments? Perhaps this would be a good time for you both to join me in the cafeteria?" Wanda says as she watches Callie fighting to keep her eyes open. "You rest a few minutes, sweetheart. We'll be back soon."

Wanda leads the two to the cafeteria, talking as she walks. "She gets tired quickly. Usually thirty minutes is all she can handle at a time. We'll give her a few minutes to rest, then we'll return to the room. Please help yourself to a cup of coffee or a soda. These cookies over here were baked this morning, and dare I say, they are the most delicious chocolate chip cookies I've ever tasted." Wanda excuses herself to tend to another resident.

Back in the room, Callie feels exhausted after her short visit. She leans her head back on the cushions. Keeping her eyes closed feels wonderful. Surprisingly, she feels an overwhelming urge to keep them closed forever. There's a commotion in the room. She feels a hand slip into hers and whispering erupts. Tentatively, with one eye, she peeks out under hooded lid to see what's going on. Stillness. It takes a moment for her vision to clear from sleep. The warm hand gently squeezes her own and she turns from her position on the couch to see Charlie sitting next to her. In disbelief, she gasps.

"Hi, Cal, wanna toddle?" *Charlie. My Charlie.* He's sitting by her side, hand in hand. She looks across the room to Aunt Marilyn, who is reading a letter out loud.

Dear Callie,

I'm writing to you from one of your favorite places on earth. It's a beautiful day, and though the lake is working, it still sparkles in the sunshine. I'm going to try and recreate for you the many wonderful memories we have here. The lightning tree, a place that your aunt made sacred, is waiting for you. Do you remember the tree? I'm looking at the picture of her daughter, Lilian, hanging from the lowest branch. She reminds me of you. I can see the family resemblance ..."

"Now, that's a fine young man you got there, Callista. Not only does he recognize the significance of your magnificent aunt and the importance of the lightning tree, he recognizes the beauty in our gene pool. You're welcome," she says with a smile.

Callie is filled with such pure joy at seeing her loved ones that she doesn't figure in the fact that they are all deceased.

Someone clears their throat across the room. Callie turns to see Gramp sitting hand in hand with Nanny. "Marilyn, I do believe that you have Wilma and Doris to thank for that gene pool."

"Good point. Thank you, Aunt Wilma and Mom, wherever you are. "

"Sorry I'm late to the party," Doris says as she and Oscar walk in without using the door. Shirley and Fred follow closely behind with their black fur baby. "Justa had to take care of business. That Stubby just wouldn't let him be," she chuckles. Callie's heart flutters as the snorting, curly tailed pug scampers in, jumping up into her lap, bringing yet another round of tears—tears that are soon removed from her face by the licking dog. Callie gives a belly laugh.

Aunt Marilyn speaks up from her seat, still holding the letter that Wyatt left. "Callista, honey, you have quite a journey ahead of you. We're all so excited to be here to see you through."

Does it hurt?

"No, you won't feel a thing."

"She's resting for a little bit. I think Prue and I wore her out. I didn't realize how tired she was until Wanda mentioned it," Jimmy explains to Wyatt as he stands next to the table where Jimmy and Prue sit. "She says we should let her rest for a while before we go back in for a visit."

Wyatt isn't comfortable with this, but fixes himself a coffee and joins Jimmy and Prue.

"How was she when you saw her?"

"She didn't recognize me today, but she recognized Prue. Well, sort of."

"She said she knows my eyes," Prue says, wide eyed. "And then she kept saying sign."

Jimmy turns to Prue. "Yeah, tell me about that, because it seemed like you thought you knew what she meant."

"She wants me to watch for signs. Things have a way of representing themselves in our lives when we need them, but we have to be open and pay attention to the signs."

"Honey, I know you love your aunt, but I wouldn't hold much stock in what she has to say these days," Jimmy says gently.

"I need to go down there," Wyatt announces, feeling antsy.

"It hasn't been that long. Maybe we should wait?" Jimmy says cautiously.

"I'll be damned if I wait here and miss an opportunity to be with my wife. It may be the last time ..." Wyatt trails off, thick with emotion. He stands and tosses his cup in the trash.

Jimmy and Prue follow a few steps behind.

Pheonix comes forward from the shadows in the kitchen. Callie is taken aback, surprised to see the girl standing before her.

"Pheonix," she utters with outstretched arms. Pheonix walks to Callie and wraps her arms around her.

You look so healthy. Your hair is beautiful!

"And you're old." The room laughs.

I think of you every day. I have so many questions for you.

"We'll have time for that later." Pheonix steps back and releases Callie.

Thank you for coming.

"We're not leaving without you."

When Wyatt approaches the door, Jimmy and Prue stay back to give he and Callie some privacy for a few minutes.

Wyatt quietly opens the door and notices that Callie is awake and animated. She's looking in the opposite direction so she doesn't see him at the door. She's smiling and at one point laughing. It looks as though she's reaching for something.

Callie grabs hold of Charlie's hand again. *Was that you the day that it snowed. Did you throw that snowball at the window?*

"Of course it was."

Simultaneously, everyone in the room turns their heads to the door and vanishes before Callie's eyes. Callie feels panic rise in her chest as she, too, turns toward the door.

The door closes behind Wyatt. He stands in the room as he watches a paper float to the ground. He walks to it to see that it is his letter from earlier today. Not sure what to make of it, he sets it down.

"Hi, beautiful."

Callie is agitated and is trying to speak. Her eyes dart around the room still clinging to some imaginary object.

Alarmed, Wyatt rushes to her and kisses her forehead. He sits next to her and speaks softly.

"It's all right. Look at me. Look at me." They press forehead to forehead. Callie closes her eyes briefly, and in her mind's eye, she sees all her loved ones again, gathered around her. Charlie has his hand in hers giving a gentle squeeze, Aunt Marilyn smiles sweetly, Gramp and Nanny nod sympathetically, and Stubby stops snorting to listen to Pheonix say softly, *It's time.*

"It's all right. I'm here." Wyatt breaths slowly to have Callie sync her breathing, and it works. She slowly opens dilated eyes. "I'm here," he says softly.

She closes her eyes again and her body relaxes. He fears that she's left him.

"Callie?"

She partially opens her heavy lids, and just as quickly, they shut. Wyatt feels a lump in his throat form, making it difficult to swallow.

"I love you, Callie-flower." Taking a deep breath, a sob escapes his lips. "This isn't goodbye, this is just bye for now."

Callie's body goes limp as a last breath is expelled.

Wyatt cradles her now as he's wracked with waves of emotion.

Wanda rushes to his side, trying to check Callie's vitals.

"Back off," he hollers as his voice breaks. "Let me have a moment with my wife," Wyatt barks at Wanda, unashamed of the tears streaking his cheeks. Wanda retreats and ushers everyone out of the room to give him some space.

"Is she dead?" Jimmy asks.

"Yes, I'm afraid so," Wanda speaks softly, resting a hand on his shoulder.

"She just seemed so ... so peaceful in the end. It doesn't seem possible."

"Dad, she's been living with this disease for years. She's finally at rest. We should be thankful that she passed without pain. I bet Aunt Marilyn is waiting at the pearly gates for her right now."

"Welcome, my sweet Callista!" Aunt Marilyn screams to all awaiting her passage.

Stubby is chasing Freckles and Justa around the courtyard. He rushes her and nearly collides with her legs. She bends to scratch his velvety ears. "Hey there, Master Stubbing. I've missed you." Stubby clamors to give her sloppy kisses before he's off and running once more.

Charlie walks over to greet her with a hug, and soon, a long line of people are there waiting for their chance to say hello.

CHAPTER 55
Wyatt

The day of the funeral is a captivating day with a plentitude of sunshine. Callista's parents are there sitting graveside, waiting to say their final goodbye.

"Callie must be so pleased with this weather. And I'm so happy she's decided her final resting place is here with all of her relatives. These plots we bought years ago were well worth the money. See, Callista, I told you they would come in handy," she says, head lifted to the sky. The leaves rustle as a soft breeze picks up. Callie's mother smiles and closes her eyes. "I know she's here."

"Bobbi, please. You're not going to start with all that nonsense, are you? Talking to things that aren't there?" Callie's dad says to her mom.

"People."

"What people?"

"People that aren't here."

Wyatt rests a snapdragon atop Callie's grave and takes a seat next to Callie's parents.

"A parent, no matter how old, should never have to bury their child. I'm so sorry for your loss."

"It's all right, Wyatt. I'll see her soon, and when I do, I'll send her your love."

Jimmy and Prue sit beside Mr. and Mrs. Lamply listening to this exchange when something causes Prue to look off in the distance, behind the gravesite.

"What is it, Prue?" Jimmy asks his daughter.

"I'm not sure. I'm just looking for a sign."

Callie watches from a distance with Charlie and Aunt Marilyn by her side.

"He's hurting. Can't I go to him? Let him know that it'll be all right?"

"It's not time. You'll know when the time is right," Pheonix says to Callie, "just like I knew when it was time."

"The dragonfly, I remember that day like it was yesterday. I was so sad that day you passed."

"I know. I'm sorry I didn't get a chance to say goodbye, but you're here now."

Weeks pass and Wyatt continues living and breathing. Some days are harder than others. He's a constant at the lightning tree. Many tears flow as he walks the labyrinth and contemplates his life without his love. This day is a particularly difficult one. He walks to the center, stares up at the objects in the lightning tree and cries silently. He runs his hands over his face and through his hair, still facing the treetop. "I don't know if I can do this alone," he says to no one. He exits the path and sits on their bench beside the lake, watching it ripple as the remnants of a boat wake wash to shore. As the sky turns from blue to orange, pink to purple, he's oblivious to his surroundings. Deep in thought, there's a flicker in his periphery. He ignores the twinkle of incandescent light and continues to watch the ripple of the lake water. Wyatt looks down and runs his hand over the carved initials under the varnished surface. He can no longer ignore the dancing light. He turns to witness the silver wings of dragonflies dancing all around him. One lands silently on his outstretched hand. This wink from above proves more than he can bear. With a stuttering intake of air, Wyatt smiles with the realization that Callie has found her way home.

ACKNOWLEDGMENTS

First and foremost I'd like to thank Jen Nicoll for allowing me into the mind of her husband dealing with Alzheimer's. I gained valuable insight from the caregiver's perspective that truly helped guide this story to the very end. Sadly, Jen lost Bill to this terrible disease. He will be greatly missed.

Keltin Barney, thank you for guiding me gently through this whole process. I feel like I've come a long way! None of it would have been possible without your help.

Katie Mullaly … you're awesome! What you do to the inside of my books is remarkable. I thank you from the bottom of my heart. It's been a pleasure getting to know you as we worked together.

Sharisse Coulter, thank you for your continued support and encouragement. Without your gentle nudge on the playground years ago, this trilogy wouldn't have happened. So happy to have you in my corner.

Cindy Eckenrode, thank you for once again agreeing to proofread this book. I know you have little free time, so the time you are giving to edit is greatly appreciated.

John Lynch, thank you for being my cheerleader. Having your support is immeasurable.

Denise Cronin, thank you for listening to my crazy ideas and playing along. I'm excited for you to finally read this book. It seems like it has taken forever.

Laurie Contrera, thank you for giving Maddie a voice through the wonderful Italian expressions you use daily.

Jack, Ian and Michael, I can't wait for you to read this trilogy. I look forward to discussing the characters with you. Your mom actually finished what she set out to do. See what you can accomplish when you put your mind to something? I love you guys with all my heart.

I can't believe this is the final installment of the Bye for Now trilogy. It's been an amazing journey. I must admit, I'm extremely proud of what I've accomplished. The closure is bittersweet. I love this story that has been in my head since I was 14. I'll miss not being in their world anymore, but who knows? Perhaps I'll take one of these characters and build another world to live in. I'd love to see this story unfold on the big screen. Just believe, right? Who knows what the future holds. I'll just have to hurry up and wait.

ABOUT THE AUTHOR

Cindy Lynch lived in many states growing up, but still considers Newtown, Connecticut home. Living in Sandy Hook throughout her high school and college years brought her many great memories; many of which occurred up at "Gramp's Camp." She always wanted to write a fictionalized memoir of her time on the lake, but never found the time. The Sandy Hook shootings both devastated and resonated with Cindy in a way she couldn't ignore, and the time to bring forward the stored memories of her youth felt more important than ever. These images of her past were woven into a fictional story that became the fabric for the "Bye For Now" trilogy.

After meeting her husband, John, at Central Connecticut State University, they moved to Missouri to be closer to Cindy's family. They live in Chesterfield, Missouri with their three teenage sons, Jack, Ian and Michael. When she's not writing, editing or otherwise engaged in writing activities, she's coming up with plot line and character development while running, biking, swimming and spending time with her family.